Caviar Marriage

by **JULIA BYRD**

CAVIAR MARRIAGE
Copyrighted © 2025 by JULIA BYRD
SC ISBN: 9781645385813
CAVIAR MARRIAGE
by JULIA BYRD

Cover design by Dana Breunig
Interior design by Kelly Maddern

For information, please contact:

Ten16 Press, an imprint of Orange Hat Publishing
www.orangehatpublishing.com
Wauwatosa, WI

Dedication

In Memory of Elaine Immke

Chapter 1

DIVINATION AND A DINNER INVITATION

Chicago, February 2025.

The first buzzed forewarning from Stella Woodward's apartment door was twinkly, delicate, polite. She recognized the mood of it. It was only an electronic noise, but she inferred that someone at the exterior entrance three levels down had gently tapped the doorbell. A request that Stella easily ignored. It was soon followed, however, by a double buzz, each zap more forceful. A demand.

She glared at the speaker set into the wall. "Don't take that tone with me," she muttered.

Her home office—a.k.a the couch—was where she received customers she didn't respect for a job she had never meant to do. When they arrived, she liked to wait and see if they would simply go away.

The insistent alert came again. She sighed, tossed aside her book, and picked up her phone. The building's security camera and lock were linked to her device, and she opened the feed. Outside, two girls stood huddled together, faces smushed up close to the camera, brows furrowed. They were young. They were always so young and dumb.

Stella activated the microphone. The shoddy, water-damaged speaker downstairs made her voice faint and echoey, and she preferred it that way.

"This is Miss Woodward," she announced in a singsong tone. "I see your question; I see your intentions. I see everything, past and future. The answers are within you. You're welcome. Goodbye, have a nice day."

One of the girls leaned in so her nose almost filled the screen. "But please, miss, I made an online appointment—"

Stella cut off the feed. The young women downstairs would know by the abrupt jolt of static. It wasn't like she'd taken any credit card info. No refunds necessary.

For a minute, she thought they'd followed her command and departed. There was silence. She returned her attention to the paperback thriller she'd been reading. On the low table beside her battered gray sofa was a cooling cup of tea. The book's plot was excellent, enough to distract her from her beverage, although she had already guessed the heroine's uncle was not as selfless as he seemed.

Then came a thudding that rattled the door in its frame. Not the security door—*her* door, only a dozen feet away from her position on the couch. They had gained access to the building.

Stella sat up. "No one's here," she yelled.

"Miss Woodward," came a plaintive young woman's voice that belied the strength of the door-pounding. "Please, I have an appointment, and I need your insight. Tell me my fate, please, it's urgent."

Both girls were in the hallway, apparently, but there was one customer. Of any pair, there was always one who insisted on visiting to learn of her future, and one who followed nervously. Stella never divined the futures of the nervous ones. It was unkind.

"Ugh," she said on a groan.

"I can pay," implored the unseen woman, only slightly muffled by the impeding door. "Cash."

"I know you can." Stella rose and drained her teacup to the dregs in two gulps. The lukewarm brew had left a damp ring on her table and a bitter taste on her tongue. "That doesn't mean you should. It's important that I try to dissuade all my customers from pursuing my services."

A hesitation. "Isn't that bad for business?"

"Not as much as you'd think. And you should not have come up uninvited."

"I know, but someone let us in."

Stella pursed her lips. She knew exactly who'd admitted them: Philip, her nosy, chatty, yucky building manager who lurked all day in the first-floor office. Philip occasionally carried packages upstairs for her, and if the box was labeled, he always read the brand name aloud. As if she couldn't see it. *Sephora*, he'd announce, rattling the carton. *Williams-Sonoma. Isn't that a bit pricey for you?* Worst, once, *Look, ze Agent Provocateur has arrived*, he'd said with a waggle of his eyebrows and an atrocious French accent.

Into Stella's wavering silence, as though sensing her weakness, the woman added, "I need you."

No one seemed to have any use for Stella elsewhere. Those who knew her agreed she was insouciant, heedless of serious matters. Some, not all, found her loosely attentive attitude charming. Maybe she was not terribly responsible or ambitious, but she could boast an intuitive mind, a fantastic figure, and an expensive education. Those gifts were all put to no good use whatsoever.

"I will lie to you," said Stella truthfully. "I'll tell you what I choose to say, not what you want to hear. I'll invent useless nonsense."

"Oh, yes," said the woman. "Yes, please."

"There is no supernatural power in me. There's nothing in the cards. You might as well receive a free divination from an especially streetwise cat."

"No, no," cried the woman. "Miss Woodward, please."

Stella sighed and went to the door, as she'd known she eventually would. Her protestations were sincere yet part of the act. The customers loved to feel as if they'd finagled their way inside. She maintained no social media and paid for no advertising. They had to know how to find her bare-bones website. She turned back the bolt and twisted the knob.

The young woman in front, clearly the ringleader, looked to be short of her twentieth birthday and wore a baggy sorority sweatshirt. She had lovely arching eyebrows and small blemishes on her chin and forehead. Her meeker friend hovered behind her shoulder, a girl with dark doe eyes and a charming curl to her hair.

Stella said nothing, merely left the door standing open and drifted away. They entered and shed their jackets onto the hooks in the narrow entryway.

"Thank you, Miss Woodward," said the bold one. "I am—"

Stella raised a hand. "Don't tell me your name. Sit down right there. And stop calling me Miss Woodward. You make me sound like a rheumatic Victorian spinster."

Her eyes widened, and she sat with a whoosh on the floor. "But you gave your name at the door as—sorry. Stella. You can divine my true name from the spirits?"

"No, of course not. I simply don't need to know it." And, of course, the girl had filled out a release form online. Stella resumed her seat on the couch and sat spread-legged, with her elbows braced on her knees. If most fortune-tellers wore strings of beads and flowing skirts, no one had ever complained about her stretchy leggings and sweaters. "Open that drawer in the table. You see the lacquered box? Yes. Put your money in the box. Then remove the cards and set them before you."

She never touched the cards. She never urged anyone to come inside. She wouldn't divine anything for anyone who did not insist upon it. She would not foretell for those who could not—or should not—make the payment. But a certain number of customers per week were necessary to cover her expenses without resorting to asking her mother for money. For more money.

These were the measures by which she assuaged her guilty conscience over collecting payments for her false divinations.

Plus, the cards had been handled by hundreds of people over the years, leaving them furred at the edges and undeniably grimy. Best not to touch them.

The young woman eagerly stuffed crumpled bills into the box. Stella watched, summing them silently. Then the girl picked up the thick deck of illustrated cards as instructed.

"Should I spread them?" she asked. "Or flip them over one by one? Or set them in a box arrangement? No, a pyramid shape! That's what I heard from my cousin in—"

"It doesn't matter." Stella shrugged.

The girl hesitated, then fanned the cards face up.

Stella did not look at them. She knew their suits, the daggers, kites, wine bottles, and sheep, and the nearly two dozen that had no suit at all. She also knew that it did not matter. There was no meaning to any of it. The deck had belonged to her French grandmother, who had it from her own mother, who used it to play triomphe and take endless tricks and pennies from her unwary friends and lovers. The cards themselves were nothing.

She looked instead at the girl, with her pretty eyebrows and blotchy complexion. She considered the way she'd sneaked into the building and pounded upon the door. And she had spread the deck eagerly with the cards' faces showing. That was unusual. Many of Stella's customers acted as if the detailed illustrations might scorch their fingertips. This was not a girl who left her desserts uneaten, her text messages unread, or her opinion unspoken. This girl was a horns-grabber.

"Him?" Stella asked without context. It was a gamble, but low risk. There was almost always a relevant *him* for young women such as the one before her.

"Yes," said the woman. "Yes, yes. Is it him?"

Stella nodded. She covertly examined the girl's fingernails, which were nibbled, and her legs, which were crossed tightly at the ankles and jouncing. "It is him. But consider: Is it *you*?"

The girl shrieked and pressed her hands across her chest. "I think so!"

"Mm-hm," said Stella. The girl didn't like the boy as much as she wanted to. Otherwise, she would have given a more forceful affirmation. "But it is not today, that much I assure you."

"No," breathed the girl. "It's not. The social is Friday. Tomorrow."

"Of course." Stella nodded as if that explained everything. She pitched her voice to an authoritative drone. "Remember to wear blue and white."

The girl's eyes were huge and shone with naive, youthful zeal. "Those are the colors of his soccer team," she whispered with awe. "How did you know that?"

Those were the school colors of the nearest university.

"Wear blue and white," Stella repeated, "and you will understand. He will not, but then again, men so rarely do. Watch how he watches you, not what he says to you. The wordless question arrives on Friday. Florals? No, a plaid. By the way, your mother is wrong about you. She always has been. Nevertheless. Wear blue. Seek to understand while asking him nothing, and make sure it is *you*."

The woman nodded so fast her high bun slipped loose. "Thank you, thank you. I will, I promise. Now, will you read the cards for Kerilyn?" She gestured toward the other girl, who was lurking by the window.

"No," said Stella firmly. "That would be a mistake."

The customer gasped and leaned backward like the words were a dire prediction, and Kerilyn paled.

"A mistake for me, I meant to say," Stella added. She did not intend to cause alarm. "Because I want to go make myself fresh tea. Return the cards to the drawer, please.

7

"Thank you again, Stella. And please, don't tell my mother about this. I suspected she was wrong all along. I have my intuition, too."

"That I gladly promise, for I am not acquainted with you or your mother," Stella said, rising. "In return, do not mention my name or my service anywhere online. Goodbye, ladies."

The girls went to the entryway and fetched their coats. "So smart, not to learn my name. For ensuring secrecy," murmured one. "And she knew about Marcus and the social!" whispered the other.

They opened the door, and the customer walked through first. Kerilyn turned back. To Stella's surprise, the quieter girl looked her straight in the eye for the first time.

"You said you would lie to us. You think all this is nonsense," said Kerilyn, gesturing back toward the table with the cards hidden in its drawer. "It's really not. You're not useless. It's only too bad you don't do any of this for real."

She slipped away behind her friend before Stella could argue.

Stella bolted the door once they were gone, then took the folded bills from the lacquered box. She needed the money in her pocket. She needed it almost as much as she had needed the looks of awe and gratitude on the girls' faces.

What she didn't need was people showing up at her doorstep. She picked up her phone and texted her building's superintendent, Philip.

Please don't admit visitors

He began typing a reply immediately, because all he did was sit in his chair and wait for trouble. Not to solve it, but to insert himself into it.

They're your customers u should be working for them

Stella rolled her eyes and typed out a pithy response before muting his thread.

N E V E R T H E L E S S P H I L

In the kitchen of her cramped apartment, Stella gathered corn chips, salsa, black bean dip, and warm white wine for dinner. At the table she pushed aside unopened mail and a skirt whose zipper she intended to repair. It freed up space for her tidy mountain of processed carbohydrates.

When her phone vibrated, Stella flipped it over, hoping to see her best friend Michaela's smiling image pop up. Instead, it was her Aunt Elizabeth, who was about the only other person Stella would have answered for. Her stomach lurched. She and her aunt spoke regularly, but always on weekends. For Elizabeth Novak to call unexpectedly, it had to be something important. *Is it Mom?* Her mother was Elizabeth's youngest sister, although they had very different priorities and weren't particularly close. But no, her mother was fine. They had texted only yesterday. But why else would Aunt Elizabeth call out of the blue? It had to be horrible family news. Her finger quivered as she swiped to accept.

"Auntie Liz," Stella said through the knot in her throat. "What is it? Are you all right?"

"Hello, Stella," came her aunt's kind, elderly voice in a rich merlot timbre. "What was that? Yes, didn't I tell you I got the parakeet-shaped platter you sent me for Valentine's Day? I mailed you a note. How are you, sweetie? How did you know it was me calling?"

It wasn't the tone of someone who was delivering bad news. Stella's guts unfurled in a way that made her regret the corn chips. If she really could see the future, perhaps she wouldn't leap to such terrible conclusions. "My mom is all right? And Uncle Leon?"

"Well, I'd assume so; I haven't chatted with her today. Leon is fine, dear. Yesterday your mom said she was going out to buy those awful sandals that are supposed to burn calories while you—But I said to wait until spring. Nobody's walking anywhere in sandals in February. Anyway, did you *sense* me?"

"Got it." Stella closed her eyes and pinched the bridge of her nose. She'd personally burned through a thousand calories of anxiety in thirty seconds. And Elizabeth had grandiose ideas about Stella's supposed abilities. Stella wouldn't tell her she'd only sensed impending doom. "Ok. No, I have the number programmed so your name pops up. You know that, right? Your phone does that, too. What's up? How are you?"

"Fine, fine. Just calling to invite you to dinner tomorrow at the house. Seven o'clock."

"Um," said Stella. She preferred not to make the long drive up to her aunt's remote mansion on short notice, especially in the winter, but she didn't have a good excuse at the ready. The roads were clear. The season had been unusually dry, with temperatures hovering around freezing and no snow accumulation. She had no customers in the evening, and her aunt would not have believed her if she said she had a date.

The truth was that Stella would have gone to almost any lengths if her wonderful, smart, warm-hearted aunt summoned her. There was no way she would have declined dinner. Aunt Elizabeth was a childless woman who would have dearly loved a daughter and surely would have done a fantastic job of raising one. Stella's mother had a daughter she did not particularly want and whom she had not done a great job of shepherding into adulthood, if Stella's lackluster career and romantic prospects were any evidence. Stella had often wondered how nicely she might've turned out if she'd grown up under Elizabeth's tutelage. She might have been the sort of person who jogged five kilometers for charities and hosted chic bridal showers for her friends. Instead, she conned people and filed her taxes with her fingers crossed.

"All right, I'd love to. Thanks," she said.

"Excellent. Do you want Leon to pick you up from the Racine train station?"

Stella was distracted by the pleasant recollection that her aunt's husband, Uncle Leon, always slipped her a crisp hundred-dollar bill. "What? Oh, no, thank you. I'll drive."

"All right, drive safely. See you tomorrow. Pack an overnight bag and wear a dress. Nothing fancy. It's just family, of course."

Stella smiled and said, "Yes, ma'am." Elizabeth, elegant and nouveau bohemian, did not approve of stretchy pants as evening wear, even for a family dinner. Stella recalled another person who did not approve of her—neither her fashion nor her general existence. "Will, uh, will Leon's nephew be there?"

"Everett? I haven't spoken to him." Elizabeth's voice was airy, nonchalant. "Why do you ask? Is he a problem?"

Stella had not seen Everett for a long time, and she wasn't sure if they would ever cross paths again. That was probably for the best.

"No problem," she said. "See you tomorrow."

Maybe it would do her good to be away from the city, away from the cards and the customers, for a weekend. Elizabeth's uncomplicated love was good for her soul and a boost to her self-confidence. And there was always caviar at Name Estate.

Chapter 2

NAME ESTATE

Elizabeth and Leon lived an hour and a half north of Chicago, over the state line into Wisconsin, on a windswept portion of the endless coastline of Lake Michigan. They'd bought the house and adjoining land decades prior for some unfathomable amount. Stella could not begin to estimate how much the place would be worth in the modern market— millions, easily. Leon had made a fortune investing his family's money, and Elizabeth retired from working as a school music teacher. With no children of their own, they had ample time and resources to spend on a unique property.

Stella didn't look at her gas needle as she crept along the last quarter mile. The traffic outbound from the city had been brutal, but she'd decided long ago that one cannot manufacture fuel by checking the gauge. It hardly mattered once she safely arrived at her aunt's stone-fenced property. The two-hundred acres of forested land was mostly flat, although the residence wasn't visible from the road. A grove of old trees shielded its perch on a rugged part of the coastline that sloped abruptly into the lake.

The private turnoff from the state route would have been easy to miss, even though Stella had made the drive often over the years, except Uncle Leon was standing at the entrance, waving heartily. She broke into a smile. How long had he been waiting? Stella was only a few minutes late. He carried a hefty flashlight and wore an all-weather jacket against the damp evening air, and his reddened face endeared him to her. He pulled open the double wrought-iron gates to admit Stella. Affixed to the metal bars was a plaque bearing Name Estate in curlicue lettering. Stella assumed it was a tongue-in-cheek twist on No-Name Estate, although she didn't really get the joke. She eased her red hatchback through slowly, then halted on the other side and rolled down her window. Outside air flooded in with a bit of a fishy, coastal odor, minus the salt.

"Permission to come aboard," she said. "I do have the gate code. Somewhere. No, I remember, it's on a sticky note stuck to my kitchen window, where it functions as a red herring for robbers who think it's for my ATM card."

"Ahoy, Stella. Very clever of you. I've been meaning to reset the box anyway, since you've been bat-signaling my secrets to all the window-peepers of Chicago."

She shoved a pile of junk from the passenger seat. "You want a ride up the lane? Hop in."

He waved her off. "No, go ahead. I'm going to check the mail and lock up. Got to get my steps in or my damned watch scolds me. Be right behind you."

Stella drove on. Watery moonlight filtered through a thin covering of fog. Although she glimpsed neighboring lights in the distance, entering felt like changing from one world to another. A mulched footpath led from the lane down to a large, stream-fed pond where she'd learned to skip rocks. It was the pond where the colony of sturgeon returned year after year to spawn in the spring.

At the end of the lane, the horseshoe-shaped gravel drive was occupied by a gleaming black electric SUV that somehow highlighted the galaxy of dead bugs smeared on Stella's windshield when she parked beside it. It wasn't a vehicle she recognized. She grabbed her purse and climbed out, smoothing her deep orange dress down over her hips. With it she wore leather heels and matching orange baubles in her ears. The dress was good enough, and it complimented the faint tinge of auburn in her dark hair. But the pause gave her an extra moment to admire the house, as she always did upon arriving.

The structure was...strange. The previous owner had it custom-built in the 1960s, and its style was unlike the other grand lakefront estates, which all seemed to strive for European opulence via white pillars and rigorous symmetry. The Novak house was instead a stack of three squat concrete rectangles, cantilevered, rotated askew from one another, and partially sunk into the rocky hillside. Each level had odd corners and eastern terraces that overlooked the spectacular view.

Stella had loved visiting over the years despite its oddness—or maybe because of it. There were no traditional shingled peaks, no flowerboxes on the windowsills. The weathered gray concrete provided camouflage on overcast days, but the brutal lines of the place rose in defiant angles from the hill's natural slope. It was somehow both a part of the coastline and a blatant, awkward interloper, and Stella sympathized. The overall effect from outside was forbidding, even bleak. The warmth and love were all on the inside.

She rapped on the front door, let herself in, and stepped out of her shoes. The polished concrete floors were warm all year round thanks to radiant heat. Walking on toasty stone in bare feet was another of the house's odd delights.

"Hello?" she shouted.

"Kitchen," Elizabeth yelled back cheerfully.

Stella passed through the narrow foyer and glanced into the formal dining room on her way by. Elizabeth complained that she and Leon rarely used it, but Stella remembered plenty of holidays and family dinners she had eaten at Elizabeth's long table. It was set with candles, old-fashioned high-backed chairs, and the sort of matched porcelain plates and silver cutlery that people used to add to their wedding registries. Stella expected she would never own a set of a dozen good plates. If she did, she'd probably use them for grilled cheese sandwiches and chip them in the dishwasher.

And presently there were four places set, one on each side. *Hmm.* Apparently, whoever had arrived in the black SUV was staying for dinner.

After another short passageway, she turned a corner into the open kitchen. The maple cabinets and marble counters were sleek and minimalist. One wall was entirely glass and faced the lake. In the distance, the dark water was ruffled into white-tipped waves. Pinpoint up-lights silhouetted a few of the taller trees.

"Ah," Stella said. "Beautiful as always."

"Thank you, sweetie," said Elizabeth, with the usual sparkle in her eye. "You're not so bad yourself. Come here."

Stella stooped and hugged her petite aunt. Elizabeth was the eldest of five siblings in her family, twelve years older than Stella's mother, and she had always treated Stella with a maternal indulgence. She wore her graying hair in a short crop and preferred jangly accessories and floaty scarves. She smelled of fresh bread and a smoky French perfume, and Stella breathed in the scent of love, acceptance, and family.

"You worried me yesterday," Stella said quietly.

"Don't," said Elizabeth with a final squeeze. "Not about me."

"Here, before I forget." Stella pulled two hostess gifts from her bag and set them on the counter.

Elizabeth maintained a neutral expression. "You brought me a bottle of pink wine and—" she inspected the garish purple bag's logo—"Takis Fuego."

"Yes. You're welcome."

"And did you also bring my grandmother's oracle cards?"

"What? Like bring them here with my *hands*? No. You know I try not to touch them." Reading fortunes wasn't the sort of thing Stella did openly around anybody else, like plucking the two weird hairs on her chin or putting thousands of dollars' worth of purchases into an online shopping cart she would never revisit. Elizabeth was the one who dabbled in a mystical mélange of Catholicism and personal superstitions. "If you asked me to bring them, I must have forgotten. Did you need to borrow them? I know they should be yours by rights."

Elizabeth shook her head, and her expression revealed nothing. "No, I gave them to you, what, eight years ago? They're yours. It only occurred to me that I could use some clarity myself this evening. But we'll discuss that later. Will you please add your contribution to the charcuterie plate?"

"Sure." Stella wouldn't spar with Elizabeth, but surely her aunt understood the cards did not bring clarity. Instead, she inspected the tray of finger foods, which was lovely and organized, then popped a tiny pickle into her mouth. There was plenty of room for the addition of spicy, salty, artificially colored crunch. She tugged on both sides of the party-sized package to open it. "I met Uncle Leon out by the road; he was guarding the gate like a squishy gargoyle. And there was another car. Who else is here?"

"Hm? Oh, he was out on the terrace with—look, here they both are."

Stella turned to see her uncle stepping over the threshold of the sliding-glass door. And behind him was his nephew, Everett Novak.

Her hands clenched involuntarily. Everett was standing right there. The Takis bag tore open with a sudden pop, and reddish sticks exploded into the air and scattered over the counter and floor.

"Well, shit," said Stella.

"Stella," said Everett. "Hello."

There was red dust everywhere. It must have been the inhalation of chili powder that made Stella's cheeks burn. She stepped backward, away from Everett, and grimaced at the smush of processed snack foods under her bare heel.

Elizabeth, ever calm, wordlessly handed her a broom. Stella began sweeping.

"Allow me to help," said Everett, reaching out. "It's my fault. I startled you."

"I've got it." Stella pivoted away.

"For the best," boomed Leon, dodging the broomstick to grab Stella in a sideways squeeze. "You shouldn't eat that crap anyway."

Leon was totally bald and thick around the middle, and he'd recently adopted a fitness lifestyle at the urging of his cardiologist after a diagnosis of heart disease.

"Oh, hush," said Elizabeth. "You had sixty-odd years of beer, bourbon, and bratwurst before switching to veggies and mineral water, so let the young people enjoy themselves."

Everett said nothing. He probably consumed only vegetables and mineral water, anyway, and sent thank-you notes and never received parking tickets and wore sweaters and blazers. He was always perfectly polite in a starchy way. Elizabeth had mentioned once that he worked in the accounting department of a private manufacturing company in Milwaukee, and Stella had silently absorbed the information, like she'd absorbed everything about him she'd ever learned. She snuck another glance. Tall and trim, with pale skin, brown eyes, and dark hair that brushed the tops of his ears. The creased brackets on either side of his mouth were new, though.

Stella retrieved a single Taki from the pale marble countertop and chomped it, then directed a feral smile at Elizabeth, thinking of her deflection on the phone the previous day. *I haven't spoken to him*, indeed. Her aunt should have warned her about Everett.

But no, that was unfair. She didn't require forewarning. Because Stella didn't hate him. She spun away and exchanged the broom for a dustpan, then crouched. He didn't hate her, either, because Everett was too civilized, too restrained, for any emotion as heated as hatred. Some antiquated code of personal honor to which he held himself prevented him from criticizing her openly. But she'd occasionally felt the weight of his gaze on her, all dark-brown intensity and twitching eyebrows. Like Stella was a family pet he didn't entirely trust not to chew on the furniture.

They'd only encountered each other a few times over the years— three times, all at the Novak house. Not enough for any cousinly vibes, especially from across separate family trees. One Christmas when Stella was about nine or ten, Elizabeth and Leon had hosted everyone from both their families, and Everett had built an igloo beside an elaborate snowman and pronounced it a gift to Stella, who gleefully draped the snow structure in Elizabeth's colorful scarves and hats. Those few days became one of the happiest holidays of her memory.

Then one spring when she was sixteen, her parents had booked a vacation in the Bahamas without consulting her, which she'd considered an unforgiveable betrayal, plus it was during the phase before their divorce when they had sniped at each other nonstop. She had demanded to be allowed to stay home in Chicago by herself. They didn't really want her tagging along anyway. Their compromise was to leave her with Aunt Elizabeth for proper supervision.

And Everett was there. He was twenty-three-ish at the time, on spring break from college, and he'd been handsome and aloof. Stella was lonely and bored. Her aunt and uncle had hosted their annual vecherinka, the caviar harvest soiree, while Stella was there. Everett had avoided her assiduously, and Stella didn't like to be ignored. Her mind veered from recalling how she'd embarrassed herself, but she'd certainly made herself obnoxious. For all her time at Name Estate since then, she'd never been invited back for another vecherinka.

And then the third time, five minutes prior, when she'd tossed a bag of snacks in the air like confetti at the sight of him.

She dumped a dustpan full of salty, crunchy dust into the trash bin.

"How are you, Stella?" he asked. "And your family? I trust your mother is well."

"It's been a minute, hasn't it," she said, although that wasn't really an answer.

Everett nodded. "About ten years, I believe."

It was a couple of months short of ten years. She angled her head to catch his profile from the edge of her vision. She wished he looked a little more like a stranger and a lot less like someone whose face she could have sketched from memory.

He was austere and coolly formal, and Stella knew that people found him rigid. Polite yet distant. But sometimes, back then and again now, when Everett looked at her, she glimpsed a side of him that was far from robotic. She saw something wistful and fervent in him that he didn't openly reveal. Perhaps that idea was merely her own fanciful invention, but she had always been terribly curious to know if she was right about him.

"Wine?" asked Elizabeth.

"Yes," they both said.

Chapter 3

IN SEARCH OF HEIRS

Elizabeth poured two glasses of a chilled, pale white. Stella's bottle of cheap pink had somehow disappeared. She drained her glass in two big gulps and slid the stemware back toward her aunt for a refill. Everett looked away.

He disapproved. Of the wine, of the mess she'd made, of her existence. She shivered at the silent critique flowing off him in waves. As if he'd never spilled food or felt thirsty. The Novaks had been wealthy for at least three generations, and his SUV outside and his well-tailored sport coat led her to understand that Everett was no different. He'd been friendly when she was nine, dismissive when she was sixteen, and now that she was twenty-six, he disapproved of her.

Clearly, she'd sunk in his estimation over the years, and he didn't know half of her worst decisions. He didn't know about her false divinations, her ongoing con job of a useless career. Her friend Michaela, for example, knew her well and often had valid reasons for being irritated with Stella. Michaela loved her anyway. Everett could go jump in the enormous lake outside.

It made Stella reckless. He was no one to judge her.

"Uncle Leon," she asked, "do you have a spare jerrycan of gasoline in the shed? My car is gasping on fumes."

Leon shook his head. "I drain the lines of the riding mower for the season. That stuff has a short shelf-life. But there's a gas station no more than twenty minutes away in town. In fact, you would have driven past it."

"Oh, whoops," said Stella airily. Let Everett think she couldn't properly manage a hundred-mile drive. It was unlikely to lower his already poor opinion of her. "Darn."

"Don't worry about it, sweetie." Elizabeth glanced at Stella's wine glass, which was empty again. "We'll go out in the morning and put gas in your car. You must have been too busy. Were you out and about last weekend?"

"Oh, uh," Stella stumbled. Her aunt had an inflated idea of the excitement on Stella's calendar. "Yes, quite busy. Quite." She'd spent all Saturday watching two seasons of a complicated small-town romantical streaming series, complete with a secret baby and a handsome mechanic, before sloppily folding laundry and ordering a fantastic crispy tavern-style pizza on Sunday. "Mickey asked me to go to Aspen because her boss wanted her to attend a gallery show opening."

Stella hadn't gone to Aspen, although Michaela had invited her. She wished she were a person who jetted off on a whim, a person who had the resources to be out of town.

"You've recently returned from Aspen? I enjoy the fresh air there," said Everett.

"So fresh," said Stella. She looked him straight in the eye for the first time, held his dark gaze. Some self-destructive part of her wished he would ask *what airline? Which hotel did you stay in?* Thus uncovering her pointless deception, and his abysmal opinion of her would be confirmed.

Making a bad impression was better than striving for his good opinion.

"Aspen is wonderful for the mind, body, and spirit," said Elizabeth, like a glossy spa brochure.

"Aren't the mountains beautiful?" Stella agreed with a bright smile. "And, you know, the skiing, of course."

Everett nodded once and glanced away.

"Everett, honey, you look so tense," Elizabeth scolded. "You'll put a kink in your neck if you march around like that all the time. There are very healthful mushrooms on the north side of that pin oak past the hill where the—you know where I'm talking about? We buried a cat nearby; there's a stone marker. Or was it a St. Joseph statue we buried? Anyway, I once sat in deep conversation with that oak and came home feeling two years younger. The mushrooms relieve tension. You want me to find some for you? It's more efficacious if you pick them yourself, you know, but I could walk out there with you sometime."

Silence. Stella narrowed her eyes at Everett. If he scoffed at her sweet aunt's irrational beliefs, as harmless as they were kooky, she would have to haul him outside for a lecture on the oak limb apparently lodged up his own ass. He had no reason to make fun of Elizabeth when she'd been so kind over all the—

"Thank you," he said with a grave nod.

"Now, Everett, if you would take the salad from the fridge," said Elizabeth, turning to the wall oven. "The cod brandade should be finished soon, so we'll move ourselves into the dining room."

The idea of that small room, with its straight chairs and white tablecloth, was oppressive. They would all be on their best behavior in there, but Stella's best behavior was sliding out of reach. She didn't deserve a fancy dinner.

"Let's not," she said. "Why don't we stay here, in the kitchen?" She gestured at the stools tucked under the overhanging counter. "Saves you the work of carrying things around. And it's awfully formal in there."

There was a flash of hurt in Elizabeth's eyes. Stella swallowed hard but did not relent.

"All right," said Elizabeth. "If that's what you prefer. Leon, go blow out the pillar candles in the dining room. Stella, get the regular-old white plates from that cupboard."

"Sure," said Stella. "Cozy, casual dinner. That's all we need for the occasion—what *is* the occasion, by the way? Why did you invite us here?"

Elizabeth paused, opened her mouth, and closed it again before her expression cleared to a strained neutrality. Stella hadn't intended to ask a tricky question. She looked at Everett, who was adding crumbles of feta to a bowl of spinach and slivered almonds, but he either didn't notice or didn't care. Did he already know the occasion?

"We'll talk about it over dinner," Elizabeth said. "But first, caviar."

She pulled a tray from a shelf in the refrigerator, then removed a small jar. It was glass with a metal top, like a squat mason jar etched with diamond shapes, and filled with glistening black beads. The lid twisted off with a satisfying *pock*. Elizabeth spooned out portions of the dark pearls.

With a bit of a flourish, she placed at the center of the island a heavy black slate platter. On it were coin-sized rounds of a dark, dense bread, sliced thin and smeared with cream cheese. Then a silky, almost transparent piece of pink gravlax. Finally, atop the salmon, a delicate scoop of Name Estate's own caviar, made from the eggs of the freshwater sturgeon that spawned on the property.

"Schmancy," said Stella.

"Thank you." Elizabeth laid out four dainty mother-of-pearl spoons for retrieving any dropped bits. "It's only the pasteurized stuff. Nothing as good as fresh, but the only option at this time of year."

Despite her aunt's demurral, the small amount of caviar on the tray would have been ridiculously expensive. But the Novaks didn't have to buy it. A good thing, too, because top-grade fresh caviar was one of the most sought-after delicacies in the world. Stella had looked it up. Name Estate sold no product, but if they had, it might have fetched a thousand dollars a pound.

Stella chose a piece from the board and carefully bit into the bread, piercing the gravlax with her teeth. She paused for a moment with the fragile caviar against the roof of her mouth and felt the salted roe pop. She closed her eyes. The flavor was subtle, complex, distinct but almost unplaceable, with a hint of dill and the creaminess of butter. It was as fleeting as a dream and she wanted more immediately, but the flavor was so earthy and rich she needed only a taste. She swallowed and put the other half of the bread into her mouth. It was intoxicating, disorienting, luxurious.

When she opened her lids, she caught Everett watching her. His dark eyes were heavy and assessing. He probably thought she was a hedonist. So be it. He glanced away and said nothing. Stella swallowed a mouthful of wine and allowed herself a moment to feel utterly indulgent.

Leon returned, rubbing his hands together, and pulled out a stool at the counter. He was not of the generation or inclination to assist with cooking. "How's business?" he said to Stella. "You see any visions of the Packers score this weekend?"

Leon teased her mercilessly over her dumb job, and Stella mostly played along in the same spirit. It was too much to hope he wouldn't bring it up in front of Everett. She pushed aside the dizzying experience of the caviar and tossed her uncle a grin. "If only," she said with a laugh. "If I did, I would fast-forward through the football games straight to the lottery numbers."

"Smart girl," said Leon, laying a finger aside his nose. "Thinking big. After that, zip right ahead to next quarter's stock market returns." He popped a gravlax-caviar bite into his mouth like it was nothing, then turned to speak to Everett. "Stella reads the future from spirits as revealed in magic cards. She turns a card, and the little picture on it means something. Zapped straight into the skull. Boom. It's a feminine skill from Grandmother Barbeau's side of the family, so don't piss off either of these ladies. They'll foretell the date when your manliest parts will turn to pudding."

"Leon," Elizabeth admonished. "For goodness' sake."

Stella busied herself with napkins and silverware. She couldn't consider Everett's manly parts. Listening to Leon describe her in that way was like rubbing at a hangnail with a salted lemon wedge. It was silly and wrong, but then, her actual occupation *was silly* and wrong. She deserved the needling and didn't bother to protest.

"Hmm," said Everett. He pondered his own appetizer held between two fingertips, then ate it in one bite. "Tarot?"

Stella looked away. She didn't want to see his face relaxed into physical pleasure. "No, not tarot, which many Roma cite as a closed cultural practice. My oracle deck is of French origin from a few generations back. We don't know who made it, and my interpretations are my own."

She invented her own bullshit, in other words. Everett frowned. He was smart enough to grasp the underlying truth.

"But you don't really believe in what you sell?" he asked.

"I mean, I believe that I sell it," she said. "I sell it effectively even after waving all sorts of red flags about my own inherent phony-baloney."

He considered for a moment. "The thicket of contradictions you contain," he said, "must be difficult."

"No need to be redundant," she said. "We all know you think I'm a mess."

"That is not what I said."

"All right, all right, take your seats," said Elizabeth. "She's effective whether she thinks so or not. No assigned places, obviously."

Stella picked the one furthest from Everett, and her aunt sat beside her. She scooped a heap of salad onto her plate. She was beginning to feel the alcohol at the edges of her vision—somebody had filled her glass again. If only it would make the evening pass quickly. As Elizabeth served steaming fish and potatoes, Leon planted his elbows on the counter and leaned forward.

"So, your aunt and I have been thinking," he began.

He pronounced "aunt" like "haunt" and wore a very serious expression. Stella hid a smile behind her wineglass.

"You may find this hard to believe, but we're not getting any younger," he said. "We have increasingly found that living up here—"

"Oh, honey bear, give them a minute to eat their dinner in peace," said Elizabeth.

Stella sat up straight to peek over the tops of the intervening heads and caught Everett's eye.

Honey bear, she mouthed. Everett raised his eyebrows. She had finished her wine again.

"—Found that living up here," said Leon, ignoring his wife, "is no longer the most conducive to our health and happiness. However, this property, including the house, and especially the land and the lakefront, are meaningful to us. This place is our legacy. You know how much work we've poured in over the years. Lately, Everett, you've done so much to help, both with the damned computer stuff and sweat equity in the land. That brush pile last fall, and the section of retaining wall that collapsed. I do appreciate it."

"My pleasure," Everett murmured.

"Even with the extra help, the work seems to pile up. We're already behind in some areas. We'd hate to see the house torn down or the land damaged. There are waterways here that drain into the lake. Unusual, um, resources that we have cultivated over the decades. There have been some external pressures—nothing that bothers me, of course, but your aunt doesn't like the—anyway, never mind. So, it's time for us to move on and to begin a new chapter for this heirloom. But without direct heirs of our own, we find ourselves assessing our extended relations."

Leon beamed, first to Stella on his far left, then to Everett beside him, as if he had clarified something important.

"Ah, that explains it," said Everett.

"It certainly does not," said Stella. "What unusual resources?"

"He means the fish," said Elizabeth. "He cares about the sturgeon more than most humans, and they are such a hassle."

"I do not," said Leon. "But they're a protected species, Lizzie. This is a unique habitat."

"Stella and Everett don't need to know about those details right now. Continue."

Leon continued. "We want to move to Florida. To our condo in Vero Beach."

Everett nodded.

Thus, Stella nodded, too. "Sounds great. You have my permission." She made a benevolent, faintly sacrilegious gesture with her right hand. "Go in peace."

"Stella," said Everett, "I believe your aunt and my uncle intend to inquire if either of us is interested in taking on responsibility for this estate."

"Ohhh," said Stella. That didn't seem like much of a concern. "Why didn't you say so? I'm happy to drive up and check on this place every month while you're away. Shoo out any raccoons who find a way inside the garage. You don't feed the sturgeon, do you? How much of a hassle could they really be? There's nothing to do there. Leave me a key and a list of instructions. But maybe hire a groundskeeper. I've never been great with power tools. Apart from the chainsaw, I'm happy to take on some, you know, household duties. Gather the mail, change the batteries in the smoke alarms. It's the least I owe you for all the birthday sweaters over the years. This dinner is delicious, Auntie Liz."

"Thank you, sweetie. We're not looking for a house sitter."

"This would be permanent," said Leon. "Everett, you've also been thinking about your earthly legacy ever since you found out about the—"

"Leon." Everett shook his head once, and Leon stopped with a zipping motion across his mouth.

"It would be a gift," said Elizabeth. "And we'd like to go before the weather changes."

Everett stood and strode to the other end of the kitchen, his eyes assessing the beams in the ceiling and the elegant rise of the wide staircase in the next room. Stella swiveled to watch him as she considered what was on offer.

A gift. An earthly legacy, as Leon had put it. Stella had a vague idea of what he might have been referring to before Everett cut off his sentence, based on a half-overheard conversation between her mother and Elizabeth many years prior. What interested her most wasn't that but rather the idea of a house as a gift. Elizabeth had been profligate with presents over the years. Stella had a vintage necklace of lavender-gray freshwater pearls and topaz that Elizabeth had given her casually one autumn afternoon, not even for a birthday or holiday. She wasn't as shocked as she might have been if Elizabeth were finicky about material possessions, but still, giving away an entire residence was another stratosphere of generosity.

"This is all quite sudden. It would be a shame to see this place leave the family. It's really special, isn't it?" Everett said.

Everything about him exuded poise, surety, in stark contrast to the muddiness Stella felt.

"Yes," she said, although he hadn't been speaking to her. Their reflections wavered in the glass panels that shielded the blackness of the lake beyond.

"If I took this on," he said, "it would be a huge commitment. A lifetime commitment. My employer in Milwaukee offers flexible working arrangements, but I would still need to travel there for staff meetings twice a month. And board meetings. A few other things."

"No problem," said Leon. "You wouldn't be chained here."

"My job also has very flexible working arrangements." Stella enunciated her syllables carefully. "I am my own boss."

Elizabeth turned sharply toward her with wide eyes. "What are you saying? That you might want the property, too? I hardly dared to hope— are you sure? Stella, you should understand, it's quite a lot of..." Elizabeth looked pained. "It's a lot of responsibility. If you don't want to be involved with the house, my jewelry and other things will go to you someday."

Stella froze her smile in place. She didn't want to think ahead to Elizabeth's death. Her kindhearted, generous aunt, the person who'd loved her seamlessly her entire life. And yet she was gently implying a house was *too much* obligation for a person as ridiculous as Stella. For a person who did not have her shit together.

She was probably right. It still stung. Stella turned her head to hide the sudden welling of tears, then gulped the last swallow of her wine. Elizabeth and Leon had both thought she wouldn't—or *couldn't*—step up to maintain their legacy. Her willingness surprised them; they had invited her simply because they wanted to be fair. Everett was the clear choice; from what Leon had said, he had already taken up a lot of responsibility. He could do it without her.

She, however, could not do it without him.

Everett stood rigidly upright. His impeccable posture implied that real-estate deals were no excuse for a slouch. "If I made an offer," he said, "Hypothetically. If you're serious about all this. Are you looking for market price? Have you had it appraised? I would need a few months to sell my place and sign a mortgage. Insurance, structural inspection. Not that I doubt the diligence of your upkeep, of course."

"Well, hold on," said Leon. "We are serious, but nobody said anything about buying. Elizabeth said gift, and she's right. We want to gift the property while we're still living. I looked all this up myself, so we'll need to verify the details with our lawyer. Then, when one of us kicks the big ol' bucket—" He reached over and squeezed his wife's hand, and Elizabeth's lips faded as she pressed them together. "—If one of us were to pass, the property is already handled. Tax-exempt up to twelve-point-whatever million. Which I think we squeak right under."

"*Twelve*," Stella gasped. The idea of twelve million left her dazed. Only a week before, she'd spent half an hour arguing on the phone with a city employee over a thirty-five-dollar speeding infraction caught on a camera trap. And she'd lost, despite a vociferous rationale invoking a tree branch overhanging the speed-limit sign and her Fourth Amendment rights against unreasonable search and seizure.

Everett looked a little pale, too. "It's too much, Uncle Leon. I couldn't. This isn't why I've been helping on weekends. I hope you don't think that."

"Nonsense, of course not. As I said, this place is our legacy. I no longer have the energy to keep resisting the...certain pressures. Our main concern has been that we worked hard on this *together*, and we're not trying to favor either the Novak or the Barbeau side of our two families,"

Leon said. "And I suspect the current lifetime gift tax exemption levels won't stay so high for much longer. My strategy is to transfer ownership of the estate while the laws are favorable."

"But you could sell it and retire to a yacht," said Stella. "Or to Rio de Janeiro. Tuscany. All the above."

Elizabeth shook her head and sniffled. "Then it would be in the hands of strangers. Leon's parents gave us a very generous gift when we were first married, and we always appreciated how it got us off to a fast start in life. We would feel pride in doing that for... for one of you, I suppose. But I don't want to decide between you. If you both want it, you both deserve it. And it was always intended to be the perfect home for two. But that's not possible. I'm not pulling a King Solomon with a strip of duct tape down the center of the house and a fence splitting the land."

"Well, I don't recall all my British monarchs," Stella muttered, "but I saw the Jennifer Aniston movie."

"I really cannot imagine clutching at such an extraordinary offer," said Everett. "I won't snatch it away from Stella, and to be quite honest, I don't know if I could do the place justice on my own."

Elizabeth pressed both hands over her face. "Oh, honey bear, this is what I was afraid of. Maybe we'll have to sell it, after all."

Stella patted her aunt's arm to reassure her. If Leon and Elizabeth could make extravagant, outlandish gestures, then she could fit right in with their reckless mindset. And she could prove her willingness to assume mature obligations. Everett could accept the generosity he clearly deserved. She could leave behind her yucky landlord's lackey and her embarrassing job. The whole situation seemed so fantastical anyway that, as usual, she gave her words no heavy consideration.

"Then I'll marry him," she said, turning a thumb in Everett's direction. "Whatever. Problem solved. The whole domain is inherited by both sides of your family."

Chapter 4

AN EXCELLENT SUGGESTION

Stella laughed. Nobody else did.

"You aren't serious," said Elizabeth.

She wasn't, entirely, it was true. It was dangerous to be serious about such things. She avoided looking at Everett.

"No," said Everett. "She is not."

"Sure, I am," Stella said. "Absolutely. Why not? It's the oldest land-inheritance trick in the book for rich white people."

"We don't prefer that word," Elizabeth chided. "It's so gauche."

"Sorry, *wealthy* white people," said Stella. "Keeps the estate intact across generations. It's basically a form of business contract." She affected a nasal, Eastern accent. "'Jeeves, draw me up the usual K-six-niner-dot-alpha for the old gal.'"

"You don't love him," said Elizabeth. "Marriage is only tolerable in the case of love. Wait—Stella! Did you *sense* something? A future awareness? What did you feel? Is this the true way forward?"

"To hell with that," said Leon, and Stella was glad, because she hadn't sensed anything more supernatural than a bottle of wine and twelve million dollars. Anyway, her parents had been madly in love when they were married, and it had done them no good.

"You don't know him," Leon continued. "If you both agree you want the estate, we could make this into a regular business obligation. A limited-liability partnership, or something along those lines. Keep it strictly professional. Contractual. Not the K-six-niner but a real deal."

Stella struggled not to wince. Leon was making sense, and yet she couldn't articulate why the idea of a professional contract felt so... *wrong*. But wasn't the type of marriage she was suggesting really the same thing, in the end? "Sure," she said, grasping for some rational explanation. She'd been the one to mention contracts, anyway. "But, um. Calling this residence a place of business might be contrary to zoning laws. We could check with the county."

"No," said Everett slowly. "She's right, Leon. Not about the zoning laws—forgive me for contradicting you, Stella. But consider the tax repercussions of making the place a business venture instead of the primary residence of legal relations."

"Hmm," said Leon in a slow rumble. "It is true that if a marriage dissolves, assets transfer without incurring further taxes. So, you'd be no worse off, anyway."

"Yes," said Everett. "You're right. It should be us."

Stella finally looked at him. He was gazing back steadily. There was no humor in his impassive face. His perfect, flawless face. She glimpsed no sign of the pensive, ardent nature she suspected was deep within him. But that stark plane from his cheekbone to his jaw wasn't why she'd made her impulsive marital suggestion. It couldn't be that. It was because Everett had always been good at everything. He would take excellent care of their inheritance. He would behave with cool politeness toward her, and maybe some of his competence would rub off on his contractual partner. His wife.

Oh, God. What had she done?

"Wha—um." For somebody who read people frequently and professionally, she had misread him. *Yes* was the last thing she expected. "Yes?" she repeated.

"Yes."

One word, as if it were simple. She wondered again about the faint lines bracketing his mouth. What did a man who never made mistakes have to worry about? Maybe he got his wrinkles by chastising other, less perfect human beings. What would she have done if he had responded to her proposal by impaling her with his icy disdain? Or worse, *laughed*?

She would have fled into the night. Without her shoes.

But he hadn't laughed. He had said yes.

"It's impetuous," said Elizabeth.

Stella shrugged, still watching Everett's reactions. "I have three tattoos. Only two of which I can recall getting. A quick decision has never bothered me."

Small underlying muscles shifted in his face. One corner of his mouth quirked up, and his eyelids drooped a bit lower.

"Business," he said, "can be quick. Other things can't happen so quickly. We can agree to remain—um. It's a big house. We'll each have our own private space."

Leon rumbled again. "You said this would happen, Lizzie."

Stella stared at her aunt. *What* would happen? Leon continued before she could pursue that odd remark.

"They're practically cousins." Leon glowered at his wife.

"Nooo," said Stella. "Nope. Nuh-uh. Definitely not that. Different family trees, with only your marriage connecting us."

"Agreed," said Everett. "Ten years ago, she was a child. Today, she's a little more than an acquaintance. And she was never a cousin."

"What will you tell your sister?" Leon asked Elizabeth. "What will Stella say to her mother?"

"We needn't lie. We'll say the young people have come to a happy agreement. We don't need to explain any financial details. And neither of you—" Elizabeth pointed a finger at Stella and Everett in turn in a way that reminded Stella of her past career as a teacher. "Neither of you is trapped into anything. I'm not buying the misery of my favorite niece and Leon's only nephew for twelve million dollars. Understood? If this doesn't work, then it doesn't work. We'll sell the house, you'll inherit the proceeds, and I won't hold it against you."

"*I'll* hold it against you," said Leon. "The coastline is fragile, and I've been protecting the spawning pond for decades from—"

"Hush," said Elizabeth. "No. You won't hold a grudge."

As Elizabeth iterated plans, the idea shifted from whimsical nonsense to something tangible. Something they were considering like rational adults. Stella didn't want to poke at her emotions too hard lest something explode—was it fear, bubbling in her stomach? Or anticipation? She kept quiet and nodded sagely as Leon and Everett discussed property taxes and maintenance funds.

"I formally request," said Leon, "after many years of experience, that you promise to discontinue the annual dinners. The gala. The vecherinka. It's a damned nuisance, and it needs to end."

"We can't insist on that," said Elizabeth. "We talked about this, Leon. If this becomes their house, it's truly their house. We can't be making judgmental comments about new paint colors or dust on the bookshelves or whatever parties they have or don't have."

"Hmph," Leon said.

"I tend toward Leon's view on that point, anyway," said Everett. "Hosting large events is not one of my skills."

"I, however, throw sensational shindigs," said Stella. "I don't know anything about the vecherinka, but we could invite your friends for a going-away party. Send you off in style."

"Stella," said Elizabeth abruptly. "May I speak to you alone for a moment?"

Stella rose from her stool. Her first stop was at the kitchen sink, where she filled an enormous glass with cold water from the tap. She perhaps should not have suggested major life-altering plans after wine with little food. Then she followed her aunt into the living room, which was situated around a fireplace almost as tall as Stella. It was laid with logs but unlit. One corner of windows looked out into dark trees, and the other gave a veiled glimpse of the lake. The ceiling was double-height, open to the mezzanine level above, which the elderly residents had not used much since Elizabeth's hip replacement several years prior. Elizabeth sat on one of two matching floral couches. The same pair had been in the spot for a decade at least.

Stella sat opposite her. "You won't mind if I change the furniture, will you?" she asked.

Elizabeth snorted delicately. "No."

"And get rid of that colonial-era floor lamp?"

"I'll be glad to have fewer possessions to look after, to be honest."

"And paint the kitchen cabinets a really deep, moody evergreen with brass knobs and—"

"All right, sweetie, I'm dodging that line of questioning." Elizabeth sketched an arc through the air with her glassware. "As I said, it must truly be your house. Although don't paint the maple cupboards. It's his heart, you know."

"Everett's?"

"No, Leon's. He's been having cardiac episodes. I want to leave before spring so he can have the ablation surgery. He has a well-regarded cardiologist in Florida. The stress he creates for himself here, with worrying over the land and the water and the fish. I know it seems rugged, but this place can be rather fragile. Leon performs bird counts every season and has been battling erosion and...and questions about the sturgeon." She plucked at the armrest cover, smoothing invisible creases. "He thinks I don't know. I wish he'd quit, but he can't make himself. Not while we're here. So, I'm getting him out."

"What sort of questions about the sturgeon?"

Elizabeth laughed and waved her off. "Oh, there's nothing out there to worry about. He grumbles. Leon, the dear old fool, got a reputation for being an easy target, so the rudest people seem to find him. Everett is no easy target, and you don't tolerate fools."

There was so much her aunt clearly wasn't saying, but one point was easy to read through the murk. "You're very good to be so thoughtful of Leon," Stella said.

"Child, I *am* him. Forty-five years later. Forty-six. And he is me, so we're going together. Like we've always done. I know Everett is a good man, but... Watch out for him. He's also a little softer than he looks on the outside. You're tough. I don't worry about you."

"I am not tough. I'm a bone-china teacup who used to be brittle but now is already in shards on the floor."

"Nonsense," Elizabeth said tartly. "Silly. You're a take-charge girl, a bounce-back woman. You have skills and discernment. I admire you, Stella. And I envy the years you still have ahead of you. I had fun when I was your age. I hope you can, too."

Stella shifted her shoulders. *Fun* wasn't her problem. Fun she could always be trusted to manufacture or find or buy. It was responsibility and respectability that seemed to elude her.

"Will do," she said.

"But you know... not *too* much fun. There are parts of managing this place that you know nothing about. Leon will leave instructions. I don't want it to become overwhelming and get out of hand."

Stella studied her aunt's face. Was Elizabeth trying to talk her out of it? "Did you expect me to decline? Or rather—do you *prefer* that I decline? Because Everett would be better for the job, clearly."

The pause before Elizabeth replied was long enough that Stella wished she hadn't asked.

"No, of course not," Elizabeth said. "I'm glad you're willing to take on the work because it's important to me that my side of the vision here is represented, too. And Everett was right that a single man alone isn't ideal. I know you won't go around mounting deer heads on the walls or jackhammering the floors in favor of gray carpeting. We won't speak again of green cabinets. And you'll help Everett with the pond and the shoreline, won't you?"

Stella forced a smile. "Yeah."

"This will be worthwhile, I promise you. I feel so much better knowing you're interested in a life here. It means everything we worked for won't be lost to time. But really, don't bother with the vecherinka unless you want to. You'll do things your own way, and I'm glad of that."

Stella had no intention of bothering the fish. She would have the time and money for any number of new pastimes, like lounging on the terrace and admiring the view. Being so far away from her usual clientele, and with no rent to pay, she wouldn't need to sell her false divinations. Maybe she'd find an easy, respectable job she could do online, even part-time.

But what was she doing, really? Marrying a man to get away from a bad job she should have quit years ago? She wouldn't be the first woman to make that choice, nor the most optimistic. Some of those surely jumped from a frying pan into a blazing inferno. But Everett wasn't an inferno so much as an icicle. She'd freeze her fingertips trying to poke him to life. There was too much to consider for one evening. Suddenly Stella was aching for bed although it wasn't much past nine o'clock. She planted her hands on her knees and levered herself to her feet.

"Right. I'm like Cinderella with an earlier bedtime and worse shoes. Can I take the guest room on the lake side?"

There were two bedrooms on the lower level at opposite ends of the house, both with their own ensuite bathrooms. She wouldn't encounter

Everett wrapped only in his towel, nor would she hear him snoring or padding around barefoot. Which was good. It was essential.

Elizabeth eyed her. "Are you sure?"

"Oh yeah. You know me. I may look like fun, but the name of my favorite nightclub is Leave Early," Stella said, tracing out a neon marquee sign with her hand, "where my DJ song request is In Fact Let's Not And Say We Did."

"Yes, sweetie, I know. I meant are you alright?"

"I'm... Yes, I'm fine. And if I haven't said it already, thank you. Truly." Stella bent and hugged her aunt, and she heard a faint sniffle from Elizabeth. "Thank you for this chance. Let's talk more tomorrow. Goodnight."

Back in the dimly lit kitchen, a cool draft slipped around her feet. The sliding door had been left open an inch. Everett and Leon must have stepped out onto the terrace. She reached for the handle, ready to push it closed with a newfound sensibility for the heating bills the place must rack up. But she heard the men's quiet voices and paused.

She shouldn't listen. Of course, she did anyway. She flattened herself against the wall and peeked around the edge of the doorframe. Leon leaned with both elbows on the concrete barrier, gazing out toward the water, and Everett stood with his hands in his trouser pockets. Stella pulled away lest they catch sight of her pale face in the window.

"...Binders on the shelf behind my desk," Leon was saying. "And in the desk drawers. And folders in the closet. Maybe more in the garage. At least one in the john. I'll get you a list of the utility accounts. That's one thing I won't miss. Probably lower my blood pressure five points by getting my name off the gas bill."

"Understood," said Everett. "Now, will you please say whatever it is you're not saying? What you and Elizabeth haven't been saying all evening."

"Oh, it won't be anything for you, anyway. I think. I think it must be a ways off. And Elizabeth doesn't know as much as she thinks."

"What are you protecting me from?"

"You? Nothing. You can handle it. There are a few things I regret, and most of them I screwed up years ago. That's my old-man advice to you, my boy. Don't mismanage things now that will make your life difficult in a few decades. The trick, of course," Leon said with a dry chuckle, "is knowing what the hell those things are. I think if it had been only you, I would have...well, it doesn't matter. Elizabeth said—and I agreed—that if Stella was involved, we would keep things as simple as possible. Keep Stella out of the muck and the...the bloody mess. I hope you'll look out for her."

From her hiding place in the shadows, Stella quirked a wry smile. Minutes ago, Elizabeth had pleaded with her to watch out for fragile Everett, while Leon was now advocating that Everett look after herself. The older generation cared for each of them.

Everett replied, "Stella." His voice was a coil of cold steel in the night. "I don't want to get close enough to Stella to look after her."

"Now, my boy," Leon admonished.

"If it weren't for the enticement of owning the estate," Everett said, "I would have no reason to speak to her at all."

Leon grunted. "Keep that to yourself, I'd say."

"It's the truth."

Stella pressed her hands over her mouth to stifle a gasp. Quickly, she turned and shuffled away into the hall like a wounded animal.

That casual cruelty was what she deserved for eavesdropping. Wasn't it what she expected from him? She had already known he didn't approve of her, yet his words still pierced her lungs like an arrow. *No reason to speak to her at all.* And to think she'd manufactured a hidden attraction that did not exist between them. He was just awful. An old memory arose—not of Everett, but of her mother. Of Christine Barbeau Woodward talking with a friend on the patio one evening, wineglasses in hand, while Stella was still young enough to want to be included. The friend had made a glib remark about how they should zip away for a girls' weekend, a spa trip to California. Christine had darted her eyes at Stella. *If only,* she had said. *If only I had no reason to be stuck here.*

It had been clear to Stella, even aged ten or so, that she was the reason her mother felt trapped in a bad situation. Everett could not have found a better way to slice her if he had wielded a scalpel.

The sliding door moved on its oiled track, then Everett was in the doorway, with his crisp collar and a question on his lips. "Stella, there you are. May I speak to you privately for a moment out on the—"

Stella had no energy to give him and no defense against him. If she spoke to him now, while hurt and still buzzing with a strange anticipation that roiled like nausea, she might say something regrettable. Something like *I wish this could have been real.*

But clearly, he didn't think the same. At least she knew.

"Nope," she said. "You may not."

He shifted aside as she passed by him. She carefully allowed nothing of herself to touch anything of him. *I don't want to get close enough to Stella.*

He smelled faintly herbal, either a cologne or whatever balm kept each strand of his hair in place. It was sage and rosemary and black pepper, Stella decided, the scent of an expensive cocktail she would never forget from a bar she couldn't afford.

At least she knew.

Chapter 5

LURKING ON THE BEACH

The following morning, Stella awoke with a headache throbbing to a rhythm of regret. Not that she'd accepted the offer of the estate, or that she had essentially proposed marriage to a man who didn't like her. Those still seemed like the best options, given her circumstances. Her regret, as she stared at the ceiling, was that she'd done it all so gracelessly. Like a walrus on a rocky beach, or a kitten in a bathtub. Her usual fashion. Everett had surely felt cornered into agreeing. She had to find a way to offer him a more elegant escape. The desire to have it done with drove her from bed.

The guest room was spartan in its minimalism, the only furniture a queen bed on a frame under a wall-mounted headboard, two nightstands bearing lamps, and a cushioned chair in the corner. But the warmth emanating from the heated floor and the tree-hemmed view to the lake created a luxurious effect. The adjoining bathroom had hexagon tiles in the shower and sleek faucets. Her orange dress tossed over the chair, with its faint streak of reddish Takis dust along one hip, provided the only spot of bold color.

She brushed her teeth, then donned leggings and a waffle-knit long-sleeved shirt from her never-been-to-Aspen overnight bag, along with her bauble earrings. She crept from her room into the quiet hallway. Beyond the glass doors in the open downstairs lounge, the water looked restive and moody in the morning fog. The stretch of Lake Michigan was not a family-friendly, picnics-and-tubing kind of playground. It was immense and dangerous, and it beckoned her. One side of the lounge had a small secondary kitchen, so she paused to make a pot of coffee. The machine's gurgles and sputters seemed unnecessarily rude. She poured a mugful and added an incautious dose of sugar and cream. Then she let herself out onto the lower-level patio. There was a nearby path that descended to the beach.

The steep trail was overhung with branches and festooned by cobwebs that glinted with dew. Stella raised her forearm before her face to intercept spiders and only once had to pause for a hopping, coffee-sloshing dance of flicking away sticky webbing. She was again struck by a fishy aroma, not foul but certainly nothing like the lake smelled in Chicago.

The beach was narrow, no more than twenty yards from the vegetation to the water, and made up of a grayish, pebbly sand and fist-sized rocks. Stella stepped up onto a friendly boulder and soaked in the view. Michigan was over there somewhere, a hundred or so miles distant, invisible. She might have been staring across an ocean. The wind teased her hair and tickled its way into the crevices of her lungs, and her headache eased as she swallowed another mouthful of coffee.

Sunrise was still a few minutes distant, and the horizon had lightened to translucence. The sky showed no signs of flaunting any spectacular pinks or oranges. It would turn light gray, then light blue. Stella was pleased—spectacular sunrises always made her morose. Nothing so beautiful should be so fleeting.

She turned to catch sight of someone at the edge of her peripheral vision—Everett was nearby, walking along the beach where the sand was damp. He wore athletic shorts, a baseball hat, and a sleeveless gray tank darkened at the neckline by sweat. As she had guessed, he was the exact sort of distastefully efficient person who would arise before dawn on a Saturday and immediately begin exercising.

Stella studied him without acknowledgment. He hesitated for a step, a minor falter in his stride, and she wondered for a moment if he might take the path up to the house.

But he continued toward her, and she watched him as she sipped her brew. In the bracing morning, away from the murk of the previous evening, she could be polite. She *had* to be polite. It wasn't his fault she'd overheard his private conversation, and she could use her professional skills to guide him toward an acceptable withdrawal that allowed him to uphold his honor.

Anyway, his comment about her had been rude but basically correct. Aside from the allure of an inheritance, she didn't have much to offer a potential husband. Only a prickly personality and a terrible, weird job that made little money. She knew she was smart, but Everett didn't know that. Many people found her attractive, but Everett was perfect. He would have countless beautiful women at his feet.

He was one of those men who looked better at thirty-three—was he thirty-four, now? She didn't know his birthday. Anyway, he looked more settled in himself than he had in his twenties. Everett always had a strong, stubborn chin and a sharp peak to the outer wing of his eyebrows. In any deck of illustrated cards, his face would have made him an authority figure. Sternness, rationality, ambition. But if a client had turned him over, Stella would have ignored the card. That strain of dominance in him elicited rebellion and defiance in her.

Regardless, he was much too sensible to ever find himself woven into an oracle deck.

"Good morning," he said from a few paces away. "I'm surprised you're up so early."

The lake hadn't seemed especially noisy until it muffled his voice. Stella stayed atop her rock and raised her volume to reach him. Last night he'd said he wanted to talk to her. Well, now she wanted to talk, too.

"Are you one of the preponderance of people who conflate early risers with moral rectitude?" she asked. "And night owls with hedonism? If so, I'm proof of the contrary. If I could stay up until three and sleep until eleven each day, I would. Alas, I'm not wired for it. Six o'clock mornings must be the cosmic penance for my many sins."

"Preponderance," he said.

"I could be doing molly or ecstasy on this beach as easily as I could in a club after midnight," she said. Perhaps the directive to remain polite had not yet traveled from her brain to her mouth.

"You're not." He lifted his chin in the direction of her mug.

"No," she said, "but the point stands. Caffeine and alcohol are my favorite vices. Tardiness is my least favorite vice. The one I'd like to break."

"And your favorite virtues?"

She considered. "I like people with a sense of humor, those who don't take themselves too seriously. I like good tippers. I like anybody who can bake a cake based on whatever ingredients are in the pantry."

He smiled, nothing more than a faint curve to his mouth. "Very enlightening," he said, "but I meant a favorite of your own virtues."

"Oh." Stella swallowed more of her rapidly cooling beverage. His arms and most of his shoulders were bare and sweaty, and he'd be chilled quickly. She forced her eyes away from the smooth contour of deltoid to biceps. "I don't talk shit about people behind their backs, and I acknowledge my own weaknesses. You don't have a sweatshirt. We should go inside."

"I'm not cold."

"Because you were running," she said.

He nodded. "Clears my head. Did you also come out to... exercise?"

"Ha! No." She gestured with one hand to draw an exaggerated hourglass figure from her breasts to her hips. "Do I look like a kale smoothie sort of girl to you?"

"No." He kept his eyes on hers without tracing the path along her body. "You look like a milkshake woman. But no standard flavor, not chocolate or strawberry."

Stella had to laugh at that, despite his overall awfulness. "All right, Ev, then what flavor of milkshake am I?"

It was hard to tell if he blushed or was simply flushed from his workout.

"Something odd that shouldn't work but does," he said. "I don't know. Like a blackberry-gingerbread-bourbon milkshake."

"Hang on." She blinked. "Blackberry—do you get those in Milwaukee? Is it a real milkshake? Because I need one immediately."

That faint smile returned to his rigid features. "If I find a place selling blackberry-gingerbread-bourbon milkshakes, I'll let you know. But if you have another moment," he said, the usual seriousness resettling over his face, "I wanted to speak to you privately about the... about the situation."

"Yes," she said. *Despite your desire not to speak to me at all,* she did not say.

"Doesn't it seem oddly sudden that Elizabeth and Leon are in such a rush to go now?"

"He didn't tell you about his heart?"

"Leon? What about it?" he asked quickly.

"It's the reason for their rush, according to Auntie Liz. Something about fibrillation and an ablation surgery with his cardiologist in Florida."

Everett exhaled and turned to face away. He pulled off his hat and pushed his hand into his damp hair, and Stella watched in fascination. The gesture was about as much discomposure as she'd ever seen from him. His hair stuck out. He shoved his hat back on and tugged the brim low.

"Well," Everett said after a moment. "Thank you for telling me. It's not the sort of thing Leon brings up. I suppose I'm glad it's not the fish. I did worry for a moment he'd engaged in some sort of local feud, and they were being run out of town."

"Right. So, Everett," said Stella, "are we truly going to marry?"

Everett's shoulders jerked. A moment passed, and he did not turn around.

"I was considering the idea of a trust," Stella said casually. "We could ask Leon and Elizabeth to place the property into a revocable trust.

After their deaths, it becomes irrevocable, and we become the trustees. Instead of, like, a faux married couple. If you would rather pursue a trust, I would agree."

He did pivot then, his eyebrows raised in question. Was he surprised she contributed anything useful?

"Don't look at me like that," she said. "I can Google like anybody else. I spent half an hour researching online last night before dozing off with my phone in my hand. My knowledge is both shallow and shaky, but I did manage to read a few paragraphs."

"I see," he said. "There are downsides to the tax structure of a trust, as well. You sound as if you're changing your mind on the marriage suggestion. Is this what you would prefer?"

"The trust would skip probate. It probably makes more sense."

"But would you prefer it?"

"Would you?" she countered.

"Are you seeing anyone?" he asked. "Romantically."

As if he cared. Stella gave a flutter of her eyelashes. "Why, Everett, you cheeky bastard. No, I'm not." Then, with a hitch in her next inhalation, she remembered what he'd said about a need to *resolve several practical matters* back home. Would he call another woman a practical matter? Were there *several* of them? Jesus. It shouldn't have mattered to her. "Um. Are you?"

"No. No one."

She released the smallest of pent-up breaths. "Now tell me," she said firmly, "aloud, in words, the smartest, most practical way to proceed. Trust, marriage, or otherwise."

They eyed each other in silence for a space that stretched into seconds.

"Elizabeth and Leon are both alive and well," he said eventually. "We needn't make drastic decisions right now."

"Got it. We simply wait until a medical emergency arises for one or both of our beloved relatives, then attempt to convert adrenaline into good, solid, life-altering decisions. And harass them with paperwork."

Everett frowned. "You're about as delicate as a bulldozer, Stella."

"Only when I want to be. And I *don't* want to become the reason you're stuck here."

She waited, watching him wrestle with himself. She was accustomed to watching her clients carefully, listening between the words to what they didn't say, so she could parry with the most leading question and make them think she had some drop of magical knowledge. But Everett was different because it was so hard to look at him. The masculine beauty of his sculpted face was undermined by the knowledge he didn't like her and wouldn't choose her. Gazing at him felt like whispering the blade of a knife over her lips. Kiss and bleed.

But she watched him anyway because she needed to wait him out. She wanted to hear it from his own mouth. And she had to practice looking at him without wincing at the agony of his appeal.

For a moment, it seemed as if he would not oblige. That he would not walk the pathway out she'd created for him. That he would say *yes,*

Stella, of course we should marry for the most practical of reasons. He raised his face to the sky, then dropped his chin to contemplate his running shoes.

"You're wise to think twice," he said. "Let's take the time to reconsider. Neither of us has fully examined the consequences of such a decision. Leon and Elizabeth wouldn't require us to rush anything we're not comfortable with, but I don't see a need to confuse them with the details of this personal conversation."

Stella nodded once sharply, and the motion sank down through her neck and landed painfully in her stomach. She had achieved what she intended, but the win pinched inside her more like a loss.

"Of course," she said. "Very wise."

Chapter 6

A CLOSER LOOK AT THE POND

Stella had her bag repacked and her purse over her shoulder before she'd even glimpsed Elizabeth. She scribbled a few words of thanks and goodbye on a magnetic grocery pad on the refrigerator door. If she lingered, Elizabeth would insist on cooking a big breakfast. And if Everett wanted to explain anything to their family, he could do it alone. Stella poured more coffee into a travel mug and left quietly out the back door.

A yellow note stuck to her steering wheel had four digits written on it in black marker. *The gate code.* Stella smiled. It was zero-five-zero-eight, and her birthday was the eighth of May. Good old Uncle Leon. After she turned the key in the ignition, the gas dial spun all the way up to full. Had he filled it last night or some bleary hour of the early morning? She didn't deserve such favors. He hadn't even mentioned it.

But halfway to the gate, Stella rolled her red hatchback to a slow stop. Talking with Everett had left her senses tingly. Movement snagged her attention. There had been a disturbance, a person, off in the scrubby growth beside the lane.

There. She glimpsed motion through her windshield—which was spotless, unobscured by any smudges of dead insects. Some outsider was on Novak property. Stella exited the car, then walked to the path that led down to the pond. The damp mulch underfoot made her steps silent.

No one in the house knew where she was, though. Pursuing a trespasser was only smart if she longed to be the star of a true-crime documentary. The fish would certainly upstage her, although Everett would look fantastic on camera.

"Hello?" she called anyway. "Who's there?"

There was no response. Even the birds fell silent at her intrusion. She should have returned to her car and driven away. Instead, she followed a half-remembered trail into two hundred acres of forest that was thick enough to get lost in. But with the enormous, indifferent presence of the lake anchoring the east, unseen yet heard and felt, she could turn around and find her vehicle. She traipsed along and told herself the interloper was almost certainly a weekend deer hunter or an awkward neighbor. She'd meet them and smooth out relations.

Maybe even clarify the estate's boundaries. Although one might assume the locked gate and stone wall made the borders clear.

Stella focused on the path ahead. The spiders had all decided to build their webs at precisely the height of her face. Combined smells of wet wood, decaying leaves, and a strong fishy funk made her scrunch her nose. It wasn't *bad*, she told herself. *City girl.* It was nature. But it was a strong odor, nevertheless. She missed the crisp, ozone scent of the snow that had not fallen that season.

She walked in long strides and stepped over fallen branches. The trail sloped gently down toward the sturgeons' pond in a natural, shallow indentation. It was two ponds, in truth, a relative puddle not much bigger than the stormwater that collected under Chicago's overpasses during a rainstorm, and a bean-shaped body the size of an Olympic pool. It was nearly a small lake. Folks in Wisconsin probably had a cultural cutoff point for such vocabulary niceties. The ponds were separated by a closed sluice gate and a narrow channel choked with rotting weeds. All of it should have been frozen solid until April, but ice laced only the margins.

Stella put her hands on her hips and stepped up as close as she could get before the reedy muck at the edge. It was no swimming hole, even in midsummer. In February, it was downright unappealing. *Unless you're a sturgeon.*

"Hello?" she called again.

She stood still, listening, then behind her came a faint crunch.

"You there!" came a man's voice.

Stella jerked in startlement. A strong, subconscious part of her wanted *away*. But *away* was down the gloopy slope. Suddenly, she was flailing. Her balance was gone, all her weight shifted forward. She took a huge step, arms windmilling, trying to regain her footing, but under her shoes was untrustworthy mud. The angle of the bank was enough to send her toppling.

"Shit," was all she had time to say before she splashed through the rime and into the murky water.

She ended up half-sideways in the small pond and fully submerged for a second, then two. Stella's first thought, absurdly, was relief that her expensive smartphone, which held the mundane details of her entire life and was not yet paid off, was safely in her purse on the passenger seat. The mud and the smell were disgusting. She popped up with an awkward, shuddering heave.

"Ma'am?" the man yelled. "Ma'am!"

Stella lunged for the bank. It was easy to imagine the enormous sturgeon circling her feet, with their six-foot scaly bodies and their prehistoric, whiskery faces. She'd only caught shadowy glimpses of their submerged forms when Leon had occasionally pointed them out. But

February was too early for them to return. Surely that light brush against her ankle was a weed. A man crouched, reaching toward her. She clasped his hand. He yanked. He could have been a murderer, and she still would have allowed him to pull her out of the pond. She landed on the ground in a sodden pile. Stella spat, pushed her hair from her eyes, and emitted a high-pitched wail. Her fingers were already turning numb, and her limbs shook with cold.

"What," she said on a wheeze, her lungs still clenched, "the *fuck*."

"Bit nippy for a swim," said the man, smirking.

He had a Wisconsin accent like an overtightened guitar string. Stella hunched over herself on the ground, sopping wet and freezing.

"You startled me and made me fall," she said. "Who are you? Why are you here? No, never mind, I need to get warmed up. Just leave, now."

He frowned. "Whoa, there. I'm looking to speak with the homeowner."

"Did you try calling?" She pushed herself to her feet and hugged her arms across her chest. Her parka had absorbed about twenty pounds of pondwater. The stranger wore a puffy black coat with an embroidered shield on the breast, and Stella looked more closely. Wisconsin Department of Natural Resources. He looked like a half-baked cop.

"I'm attempting to make a home visit," he said.

The urge to contradict him was powerful enough to subvert her drive to get warm and dry. "Well, the homeowners don't live in the pond. You've missed your attempt. Or did you take a wrong turn along the driveway? Funny, I thought it was a straight shot. Too bad you ended up here terrifying me into the drink. Sure, yep. You'd best be going. I really need to get inside and get changed."

"Then I'll come with you up to the house and have a look—"

"No," she said. "Not right now. I told you I need to shower and change clothes."

"Ma'am, I am here on Department of Natural Resources business." He tapped the shield on his chest and firmed up his voice. "Bit of business regarding allegations of resource violations here on this estate."

She raised her eyebrows and tried to ignore the gross water dripping from each clump of her hair. "This *private* estate," she emphasized.

"Well, yes."

"Are you subject to the same laws that frown upon murder? Because I am freezing to death, all my internal organs are shutting down, the blood flow to my brain has congealed into jelly, and you're standing around talking to me about resource violations."

The man hesitated, one fingertip caressing the embroidered badge on his puffy coat. "What's your name? I need to speak to the homeowner. Is that you?"

"What's *your* name, officer? You're the one trying to get into the house."

"I'm a state conservation warden." The man sighed his impatience but reached into an interior pocket.

He produced a badge, which Stella squinted at. The credentials looked good enough, although she was unfamiliar with Wisconsin law-enforcement departments. "Thank you for visiting, Officer...Diettrich, and for pulling me from the water. Goodbye."

Officer Diettrich stowed his badge but again pressed a hand on his chest, and she suspected he was either having a heart attack or had an envelope in his breast pocket.

"Alrighty," he said. "My pleasure. Hang on for one more minute. What was your name again?"

"Why're you here if you don't know the name of the homeowner? Isn't the deed on file with the county?"

She cursed herself inwardly for her stubborn questions that prolonged the conversation. She was a Midwestern girl with good tolerance for the winter, and the whole season had been worryingly warm, but her fingers and feet were numb. She was shaking all over. She needed to finish with the man and get warmed up quickly.

"We're state, not county," he said. "I've got a lot of experience, but I'm new in this district. Started poking around the files, looking to earn my pay. I was surprised to note that, according to our records, this parcel hasn't had the resource survey done in over ten years. The data is missing. That's unconscionable on the part of Baybrook, my predecessor, and I mean to see it rectified this year."

"Survey data?" Stella asked. "Is there some sort of problem?"

"Probably nothing. Probably an oversight. I'm sure we can get this sorted out in the spring spawning season." He hooked his thumbs in his oversized belt. "The DNR requires annual access to relevant private properties for our mandated research and resource studies. For science, you understand, and the good of the species."

"That species being *homo sapiens*?"

He frowned. "No, the lake sturgeon. *Acipenser fulvescens*."

"You're telling me this is a whole fish thing," she said. "A fish problem."

"Likely not a problem, as I said. I'm sure you'll be fine."

"Such a non-problem that you paid us a personal home visit."

"Yep. I need to keep an eye out for small compliance issues before they become big," he said. "Such as illegal harvesting of lake sturgeon. Limit one tagged fish per person per season, yeah? And even then, you can't sell the caviar. You can give it as a gift. Odd present, right? Fish eggs?" He gave an exaggerated shrug. "People will give the strangest gifts with very little provocation. Pretty girl like you talks nice to a fellow, he might give you a jar of fish eggs. Anyway, still limited to a single fish. Anybody gets bigger ideas, we gotta nip that sort of thing real quick to protect the population."

Stella kept silent, shivering in her sodden clothes.

"It must be a mistake," he continued. "There's only one good reason I can think of that somebody would intentionally dodge the resource survey for ten years running, and that's if the protected fish we're meant to be counting are all, in fact, caught, killed, harvested for their eggs, and the product sold illegally. That would sure make *me* evade a simple annual count." He whistled a tone that rose and sank. "That would be bad. Not a misdemeanor fine, but a Class I felony, with sentencing guidelines ranging up to three-and-a-half years. But I'm sure you folks have none of that junk happening here."

"Right," Stella agreed lamely.

Felony. Even a whiff of prison was something neither Elizabeth nor Leon could tolerate. Surely a good lawyer could wriggle them out of any minor violations, but it would be expensive...and even worse, the stress would be detrimental to Leon's heart condition. She couldn't stand back and allow them to be trapped in Wisconsin by some power-tripping cop with a ten-year backlog of survey work dragging out the threat of a felony. A gosh-darned fish felony.

But it wouldn't come to that. Leon wouldn't have killed all the sturgeon. There was no way. His respect for the land was too great. She shoved the idea aside, but it floated right back, belly-up.

Elizabeth and Leon were so eager to get out of town.

"Ma'am?" the officer prompted.

"Yes." She had no more time to think, and she would take on the problem herself to make sure it didn't land on Elizabeth's shoulders. "I am the homeowner. That's me. Property owner. If you'll give me your card, officer, I'll make sure it gets handled, so you won't need to make another trip out."

"I'll do you one better." He unzipped his coat and reached inside, then brandished a slim white envelope. "This gives you an idea of the requirements. We'll be requesting another trip out during the spawning season, where we'll count the fish and sign off on everything. That'll bring this parcel back within regulations, and you won't need to look at my face again until next year. Alrighty?"

Stella clenched her jaw against the chattering of her teeth. She took the paper and held it between two fingertips to keep it dry. "Fine. I'll handle it. Thank you."

He gave her a jaunty salute and walked away. Stella waited, shivering violently, until she heard a distant engine start. Then she took off running for the house, pausing at her car only to retrieve her purse and duffel. Her legs were stiff, her wet clothing dragged at her knees, and her lungs burned. At the top of the lane, she veered away from the front door and stumbled down the exterior steps to the lower patio. She let herself in through the sliding door and dripped along the carpet. Then she rapped on the door to Everett's guest room.

When he opened it, he was dressed in dark denim and a forest-green long-sleeved shirt. His hair was damp but perfectly neat, and he smelled again of that faint herbal scent. Stella was immediately conscious of what a filthy, bedraggled mess she presented. *Oh well.* She was usually a mess, anyway. But with less shivering and much less pond muck. She let her bag drop with a thud near his feet.

"Hello. I thought you'd left—" He stopped abruptly, his eyes widening. "Holy shit, Stella. You look half frozen. Come here; take off that coat. Are you injured? What the hell happened?"

His mild profanity was oddly endearing. He seized her wrist and yanked at the cuffs of her parka.

"I'm s-so c-cold. Unexpected dip in the pond." She glanced over her shoulder and allowed Everett to strip away her coat. Her aunt and his uncle were upstairs in the kitchen, but she lowered her voice anyway. "I fell in. I was startled by a stranger, a m-man. He said he was with the Department of Natural Resources and had an important letter for the homeowner, but Everett—I said I was the homeowner. You don't think Leon and Elizabeth have murdered all their endangered fish, do you? Please tell me it can't be true."

Chapter 7

NEGOTIATIONS OVER LAUNDRY

Everett stared at her, her dripping coat in his hands. Stella thought he might close the door in her face or tell her she was crazy. That she was unbearably clumsy and leaving puddles on the carpet. Her shoulders tensed as if she were expecting a blow.

Instead, he retrieved her bag and entered the adjoining bathroom, where she heard the shower splutter to life. She stepped into his room, which was similar in its minimalist styling to the one she'd stayed in, although a bit darker without the east windows. And, of course, it was much tidier than hers had been. A leather duffel with a long strap was on the chair, and the bed had already been stripped of its linens. She should have thought of doing that.

"Your leg," he said when he returned. "You're limping."

"My knee is a little sore, but it's fine, I s-swear. I twisted it falling into about eighteen inches of water and three feet of mud, in a fine display of my usual grace. It's the c-cold that's going to kill me."

"Yes. Go ahead, the shower should be hot. What did you say to Leon to explain your condition?"

She entered the bathroom and left the door cracked open a scant inch. There was a dry towel in the cabinet, and she almost wept at the relief of peeling off her disgusting leggings. Everett had hung her wet coat on the hook.

"Nothing." Stella stared at her grimy face in the mirror. She'd lost an earring in the pond. She removed the remaining one, then hauled her shirt over her head and let it fall onto the tile with a sodden splat. "I came straight here. I didn't want to raise a big scene and send him into cardiac arrest."

When she stuck a hand under the shower's spray, the water was the perfect temperature. Everett had twisted the knobs; Everett had showered only minutes before. It shouldn't have felt... intimate, but it did. He had been nude right where she was standing. She stepped gratefully into the stall, and her lungs began to relax under the heat.

"You came straight here," Everett repeated. "To me."

His voice was muffled by the door between them and the rush of the shower. She imagined him standing with his ramrod posture, arms still folded.

"Yes because—" Stella cut off when her phone buzzed. It lay face-up beside the sink with her purse, and the tone was for her security system at home. Her frazzled nerves wouldn't allow her to ignore the sound. "One second."

She stepped naked from the stall and tapped the phone. It opened the video feed from her building's entrance and activated the microphone. A woman with ash-blonde hair she recognized from divination sessions was there wearing a stocking hat and an anxious expression. She looked haggard in the small image, but she was younger than her tired face would indicate. And worse, Stella even knew the woman's name, despite her sincere efforts to never learn any of their names. The woman was the sort of regular client who insisted that she and Stella had a cosmic, universal connection, so profound were the depths of Stella's bullshit insights. She came often and paid well, though, and she had left a generous gift at Christmas.

And her finger was poised to hit the buzzer again.

"Not a good time!" Stella said loudly. "I'm not there. Go away and come back tomorrow, Allison. Or don't."

"I'll be very quick," said Allison.

"I can't do this right now."

"Wait, Stella, please," she pleaded. "I just wanted to ask if you think I should speak to my husband about—"

"Sure, yes, if you want to. Honestly, we talked about this last time."

"But I found photos of a woman on his computer, and now I haven't even seen him for twenty-four hours, and I don't know if he'll even listen."

"Lots of men have photos of women on their computers. Ask him about it. No charge this time. Bye." Stella jabbed the red button that cut off the feed and ducked back under the hot spray of water.

"Stella," said Everett. "Wasn't that a customer? You took a work call from the shower. You were in fact *yelling* at a customer from inside the shower."

"From outside the shower." The inane normalcy of dismissing a needy client had the effect of reducing her stress. "And I was merely speaking at full volume. I needed to send her away or she'd keep buzzing. She'd probably be trying to break into my building by now."

"Are you—*really?*"

"No, no, Allison would have gone away. She's too docile to stage a break-in. But some of the others would."

"You have a very strange job."

Stella was glad she couldn't see Everett's face. He was probably frowning in vast disapproval. "I promise I won't tell my clients this address. They can't possibly find this place, so you won't be embarrassed by me. Anyway, I was trying to tell you that the Department of Natural Resources officer tried to downplay the problem, but I didn't like it. I felt...I don't know. I was left with the feeling that the lake sturgeon were murdered by Leon and Elizabeth."

She hurriedly scrubbed herself all over, then drizzled shampoo into her palm.

"I suggest you stop referring to it as murder and perhaps say *fished*," Everett asked. "They're fish. Maybe someone went fishing."

"The guy implied that overfishing would be a major problem. He showed me a badge."

Stella's icy skin began to warm up. She rotated, rinsed her hair, then turned again. She could have stood under the hot water all day. But Everett had more questions.

"You think he was legitimate?"

"Yes." She closed her eyes, let the spray cascade over face, and tried to put the feeling into words for him. "I lie to people for money, you know? All in good fun, of course. My clients are aware of the utter nonsense of the cards—at least, they ought to be. Anyway, I recognize a liar when I meet one. Although I don't accuse him of lying, he was underplaying. I don't think he was impersonating an officer. He was...it's so hard to describe, especially since I was a bit preoccupied by the possibility of frostbite, but he threw me off. Talking about gifting caviar, saying things like *I'm sure you'll be fine*, and then mentioning major crimes in the next breath."

"Are you telling me his vibe was off?" Everett asked seriously.

Stella laughed. Everett wouldn't recognize a vibe if it were lemon-scented. "Yes," she said. "Absolutely, the guy had weird vibes. You believe me, right?"

"Yes. What are you proposing that we do about it?"

The ease of that *yes* brought a lump to her throat. Stella shut off the shower and squeezed water from her hair. She looked around the edge of the glass divider at the mirror. Everett wasn't reflected through the crack in the door. He wasn't the sort of man to peep.

"I lied and told him I was the homeowner, and I took his letter," she said in a rush. "I dropped it on your bed. I propose we handle this ourselves. Keep the old folks out of it."

"Good. Listen, Stella, you did the right thing. It had to be done. If Elizabeth and Leon want to make this place our responsibility, we might as well start now. Thank you for coming to me."

"Oh," she said. "You're welcome."

The remaining choices in her overnight bag were slim. Her pajamas were silky and sheer. The crumpled orange dress held no appeal, and anyway it was none too clean. She hadn't brought a second casual outfit. Asking Everett to borrow a t-shirt seemed much too personal. Sharing clothing was a step further than suggesting marriage, apparently, in the strange corners of her uncooperative mind.

But she did have another dress. It had been her backup choice when she was getting ready, shoved into her bag without thought, in knee-length jade jersey with an asymmetrical neckline. It would have to serve for the short trip back to Chicago. She donned her bra from the night before, then shimmied into the dress and flung open the door.

Everett wasn't standing rigidly in the center of the room, where she'd last seen him. Instead, he was sitting on the edge of the bed, elbows on his knees, spine curved forward, with the unopened letter in his hands. He looked... worried.

Then he shot to his feet, his face perfectly composed, any trace of vulnerability erased.

"Zip," Stella said, twisting her damp hair aside and presenting her back to Everett. She pretended she hadn't seen him slouching because she didn't know what to make of it. "Please and thank you."

He zipped without comment on her fancy costume change and without brushing her skin with his knuckles. His customary poise was restored. "Shall we?" he asked, extending the sealed envelope to her.

It wasn't quite a question.

Stella slid a finger under the flap, extracted the single page, and skimmed the text. It was printed on official-looking letterhead with the same shield logo she'd seen on the man's coat.

"Sturgeon population inspection and management strategies," she murmured as she skimmed, picking out what seemed to be relevant phrases. "Cooperative research unit. Funded by a federal grant in perpetuity. Isn't 'perpetuity' such a nice word? Minor river tributaries, unique genetic populations, spawning locations, assessment of reproductive success. Call to schedule a mandatory three-day window of inspection in the spring. This," she concluded, looking up at Everett, "is all about counting fish."

"I concur." Everett was suitably somber. "A fish census. I'll call the department's office number on Monday morning to verify it's real."

He entered the bathroom and rolled his shirtsleeves up to his elbows. Was he revealing his forearms to distract her? If so, it was working. She stood and leaned in the bathroom doorway. Everett turning back his cuffs was nearly the equivalent of a striptease from another man, and she was permitted to watch. She tried not to ogle him, though, since he'd been so gentlemanly about not peeping in on her shower. They were excellent forearms, with dark hair and ridges of muscle and vein. His hands looked strong for a man who worked a desk job. She glimpsed calluses on both thumbs and suspected there were more at the base of his fingers. He retrieved her damp towel from where she'd dropped it and used it to dry the floor and the edge of the sink. Stella re-gathered her concentration.

"Elizabeth serves fresh caviar each year. For the vecherinka," she said. "I assumed it was made responsibly. Legally."

"That's what I understood," he said, bundling her wet clothes with the towel. "But you heard them both suggesting that we shouldn't continue the vecherinka. Stella, what if we've been handed a muddy mess? Is this new circumstance merely unpleasant, or very, very bad?"

"A question I often ask myself in life," she said. "Every time my phone rings, and usually also when the doorbell rings. When I open the mail. When I have a sore throat or a headache. After watching the first ten minutes of a new movie. When the shoes I ordered online are pinching my heels."

When he exited the bathroom, it was dry and spotless, like the rest of the bedroom. "Disagree," he said. "Both of us know you're not a pessimist, so don't try to make me think the merely unpleasant has a grip on your imagination. A pessimist would never have proposed marriage to me. Now come along," he said firmly, "and try to be serious."

He opened the bedroom door and walked out. She watched him, a bit dazed by his matter-of-fact dismissal. He was right, of course. She wasn't a pessimist; she liked to peer into the dark corners of life, but she did not reside there. But Stella hadn't realized Everett understood that. She followed his broad back down the hallway.

"All right, point taken. I'll be realistic. We needn't make this any more difficult for ourselves," she said, marshalling herself back to the immediate problem at hand. "We'll allow Leon and Elizabeth to go on their merry way to Florida without mentioning this officer's visit. Because I care about them, and I'd do nearly anything to protect my aunt. And we'll let the DNR dude do whatever he wants to survey the damned fish, because I do not care about the fish whatsoever. They can send a hundred half-baked faux cops with fishing poles to swarm the entire property. Hell, they can put on their trunks and swim in the pond if it gets Name Estate off their naughty list."

"Those fish," he said, "are following an instinct coded into their genetics over millions of years. They have returned to this exact spot since the retreat of the last glaciers to continue their generations over countless cycles. They live for decades, and the females aren't fertile until around fourteen years at a minimum. We have killed them en masse and dammed and polluted their habitats ever since seizing the last of the lands from the Potawatomie in the mid-nineteenth century. And you can't bring yourself to care about them even a little?"

"They're just not that cute," Stella said. "With those weird tendrils on their faces. Ugh."

His silence on that point was eloquent.

"But you missed the main flaw in my idea," she continued. "If my dear friend at the DNR performs the inspection and doesn't find what he's looking for, then Leon and Elizabeth are on the hook. Pun fully intended."

Everett opened a door and entered a room she'd never explored, which turned out to be the laundry room. He opened the washing machine and moved a clump of clean, damp bed sheets into the dryer, then tossed her dirty things into the basin, added detergent, and pushed a button to start the cycle.

He'd surpassed the total laundry effort she'd exerted in the past two weeks. The noise of the washer buffered their conversation.

"You don't have to clean up after me," she said.

"I'm not," he said. "I'm the one who stayed in that guest room. It's my responsibility."

Stella examined his face for the implied *you're a messy houseguest and a terrible niece* but saw nothing besides his usual flawless symmetry. Although she still couldn't read him very well.

"Well," she grumbled halfheartedly, "don't clean up after me."

He shook his head. "I can't promise that."

The idea of competent, serious, rational Everett looking after her held a certain appeal. Not that she wanted him doing her chores, but he made laundry look good. Stella valued her independence, although once in a while... It would be nice for someone to care for her occasionally. She certainly didn't always take very good care of herself. And he seemed willing to play along with the clanging of her gut instincts about the DNR officer. He believed her, and he sounded so reasonable. Steady. Part of her wanted to relax into that feeling. What would it be like to have a real partnership with such a man based purely on free choice? She would never know. But she could take the fraction of good parts he was willing to offer.

She was caught off guard by the direction of her own imagination when she envisioned, quite unexpectedly, what might happen if she hopped up to sit atop the rumbling tumble dryer. Dress hiked up, thighs spread, heat seeping into her backside. Would Everett step between her legs and circle her waist with his hands? He could take care of her from up close. He would smell good. She would thread her hands into his hair and leave it hopelessly mussed, and she would slide all the way forward to twine her ankles together behind his hips.

Stella turned away before he could glimpse the flush on her cheeks.

"Uh. So?" she asked, unable to look him in the face. "What do you think of my suggestion?"

He rolled his shoulders and was silent for a moment, and she had a panicked, senseless worry that he somehow knew about her vivid imaginary scene atop the dryer. He didn't, of course. He was focused on the matter at hand.

"You're suggesting we need to get Leon and Elizabeth off the hook for their suspected misdeeds. If there's something going on—"

"You can say it," Stella cut in. "Something *fishy*."

Everett frowned at her. She smiled innocently.

"I don't want to mention this to Leon," he said. "I can't accuse him of mismanaging the land after they were so generous to offer it to us, especially while his health is fragile."

"I agree. Maybe the fish are out there, and we need to find them during the spring spawning season. We'll look for them. I don't want to lob accusations of fish murder like hand grenades."

"Didn't we agree to stop saying *murder?*"

"That was unilateral." Stella poked him in the center of his chest. "You-nilateral."

Everett didn't budge. "But we need to acknowledge it's possible. Perhaps the lake sturgeon population endured a natural die-off. It's a hardy species, right? Maybe the population has since recovered, and they'll reappear this spring. If they're here, we will find them."

Stella nodded slowly. On the wall beside her was a rack of brooms, dustpans, mops, and a squeegee on a long pole. She had already considered how much work went into maintaining the spotless fundamentals of floors, walls, and glass. The way Everett spoke, this was simply another chore to be administered. "And if we don't find them? He cited a felony charge."

"*What?* He did? How did this violation go on for so long that it's come to the point of criminal charges? Didn't he say we would be fine? Or *pay* a fine, I don't care."

"Apparently, this is a new agent. Different guy since last year."

Everett's brow furrowed. He spun around and began compulsively aligning the multitude of detergent jugs, cleaning sprays, dryer sheets, and aerosol cans on the shelf mounted over the washer. "If there are no fish, then the trouble goes through me and not through Leon. I would do nothing to jeopardize Leon's faith in me. That man has been more of a father to me than my own at times in my life." He turned around and faced her again. The cleaning products were evenly spaced, labels front, and the shelf had been dusted. "You're free to step away and let me manage the matter by myself."

"Nope. I'm already in this because I lied to that officer about being the homeowner. I won't let you push me aside."

"I'm not trying to steal your inheritance—"

"Never said you were. I think you're trying to shoulder the whole burden. Maybe I shouldn't have showed you the letter, then handled it on my own."

"I never want you to regret telling me the truth, Stella."

"Fantastic. Then you're going to have to bend an inch."

He sighed. "Together we find the fish and extract ourselves and Name Estate. Pay whatever trumped-up fines are levied, get rid of the agent. A fresh start, legal and clear. Agreed?"

He met her eyes steadily and spoke in a strict, even cadence.

"You'd better be a property owner, too," she said, ignoring the chaotic thudding of her heart. How many times could she propose marriage to Everett Novak? Until he said yes, apparently. "I know you never wanted me...my—this complication," she fumbled. Everett looked on warily. "But here we are. Jointly and severally. Earlier on the beach, you wanted time to reconsider. I hope you had time to think, because it sounds like you want to marry me for my troubled inheritance."

He twitched. "Correct. We'll continue the agreement as discussed last night and take over ownership of the property together."

"Good." She exhaled. She didn't feel triumphant at his acquiescence, just tired. "And now, I am going home."

"Thank you. Now that we are in accord, I, too, am going home."

She turned and left behind the warmth and linen scents of the laundry room for the hallway with Everett beside her. "And yet, apparently, we *are* home. Or it will be soon, anyway. Ain't it sweet?"

"Grand. And Stella?"

"Yes?"

Stella looked up at the forced note in his voice. Everett's cheeks turned a delicate shade of rose pink, which caused her some alarm. Had he inherited Leon's heart condition? He stared back, then put one hand in his pants pocket.

"May I. Uh." He extracted something and held it out to her. His phone. "May I please have your number. In case anything arises with the house while we're away this week. Or if I learn anything interesting after speaking with the DNR's headquarters. Or with our relations. Ah. Our respective relatives. Leon and Elizabeth. Or if you have any questions or, for example, concerns."

Stella stifled a grin. He was blushing and practically stuttering. The poor man. Had he never asked a woman for her phone number? They weren't exactly strangers flirting at a bar. She was tempted to allow him to continue, to see what further contortions he might ramble into, but she relented and sent herself a text from his phone. Then she inserted herself into his phone's contacts as 'Stella Woodward (Very Attractive, Inheritance)' and added three pink hearts.

Chapter 8

REINFORCEMENT

Almost a week later, Stella was back in her car, drumming her fingers on the steering wheel and idling outside her best friend's townhouse on a narrow street in Chicago's Little Italy neighborhood. She was anxious, apprehensive. She was on her way back to Name Estate, or she would be if Michaela Jones ever appeared.

But in a moment, everything was better because Michaela finally emerged from the house, rushed down the sidewalk, and threw herself into the passenger seat. They were running late, as usual. Michaela had many wonderful qualities, and among them was not promptness. If Stella was ten minutes late for everything, Michaela was usually ten minutes behind her. They were a terrible and wonderful pair.

"Sorry," Michaela breathed out noisily as she buckled her seat belt. "Is that the heater running? Why is it so hot in February?" She wore a long wool skirt, a tweed vest, and a trench coat with capacious pockets. She looked prepared for an archaeological excavation of dubious colonial provenance in Egypt rather than dinner and an overnight stay at a modernist mansion in Wisconsin. She and Stella had been friends since freshman year of college when they both played outfield on the intramural softball team and become so bored, they'd walked away between innings to go out for drinks. Stella was accustomed to her friend's fashion sense.

Stella turned down both the heat and the radio, which tended to overstimulate Michaela's already high-strung nerves. She did not comment that Michaela was wearing at least three layers of clothing. "I brought you a fancy fizzy water. The one in the cupholder. I think this one is meant to sync the vibrations of your mind with the moon. Grapefruit-agave-mushroom. How are the kids?" she asked.

Michaela had married a year out of college after a whirlwind romance and had her two children relatively soon and in quick succession. Raising toddlers at her age would have led Stella to feel like some sort of relic of the patriarchy, but on Michaela the young mom life seemed rather counterculture and cool.

"I don't know. Alive." Michaela cracked the can of carbonated water and swigged it. "Henry is taking them to the park to look for squirrels. This is delicious, thank you, I feel fully moon-synced. I owe him a hundred sexual favors for letting me get out of town this weekend, but he owes me two hundred, so it's fine. I haven't been able to work late all month."

Her work was as an artist's assistant at a private studio near the Art Institute. Her boss was a sculptor with vision, reputation, and arthritis. Michaela was a trained artist in her own right, and Stella often thought the arrangement took unfair advantage of her skill by putting another man's name on the works. But apparently it was more common in the fine art world than Stella had ever realized, and the steady paycheck provided Michaela with stability and more time for her kids.

Stella headed north along the lakeshore. The same water that slid along the rocky beach at Name Estate was barely contained here by the city's concrete breakwaters. The shallow parts should have been frozen. Friday-afternoon traffic clogged the roads as they made their way out of the city, and Stella drove slowly. Her mind drifted to Everett and the weekend ahead. She hadn't heard from him all week. They had not discussed what to say to their friends and family. It wasn't up to him, anyway. Stella decided to stick to the truth, but a somewhat streamlined version. It would do no good to freak out Michaela.

She would have to persuade her friend, somehow, that she and Everett actually *wanted* to get married for normal reasons. It would be good practice for conversations with her mother and the rest of the family. Stella could play her part. The tricky piece would be getting Everett to cooperate. He was unlikely to unbend his stiff personality long enough to convince anyone that he liked Stella enough to speak to her, let alone marry her. Maybe she could use that reflexive blush against him.

"And that's when their heads were chopped off and their guts were slit open," said Michaela.

Stella startled. Michaela had been speaking for some time, but Stella hadn't been paying attention.

"*What?*" Stella said. "Sorry, what?"

"Just testing you," said Michaela. "You failed. I was saying Kira's preschool doesn't have a daycare opening for Jackson until the summer session."

"Oh. Right. That, uh, that's..." What was it? "That's stressful?"

"All right." Michaela folded her arms, shifted sideways in her seat, and glowered. She was always beautiful, but she was especially glorious when she was annoyed. She was tall and lean, with light brown skin, straightened hair that shone, and expressive eyebrows. She had often made Stella collapse into laughter with a single well-timed flick of those brows, but presently, her face was drawn into a tight frown. "I can tell you have a lot of other things on your mind. Tell me."

"Sorry," Stella said again, striving for a casual tone. "So, uh, Mickey. You're right. There's a guy I want you to meet." But *guy* wasn't the right label for Everett. "A man."

"Who?" Michaela demanded immediately. "Where did you meet him?"

"He's related to my Uncle Leon. You'll meet him when we arrive."

"Wait. He's your cousin?" Michaela asked in a rising screech.

"No!" Stella death-gripped the steering wheel. "No. He's no blood relation to me, only to Leon. Elizabeth is my aunt, remember?"

"So, then he's, like, your step-cousin?"

"Absolutely not. Is that a thing? No. His uncle is married to my aunt. I only met him a couple of times over the years. And again, last weekend."

Michaela remained unconvinced. "I'm gonna need you to draw me a family tree to really grasp this."

"Sure," said Stella, "except it would be *two* trees, because his parents are not related to my parents. Believe me?"

"Uh-huh. What's his name? Is he cute?"

"Everett. Cute is for horsies and puppies. Everett is... You'll like him. He's a real adult with an actual job and a keen sense of responsibility."

"And this actual grown adult man seems to like you in return?"

Stella glanced away from the road long enough to affect a wounded pout. "Ouch."

"The point remains." Michaela was unabashed.

"Unfortunately, you happen to be correct. I don't think he *likes* me. But there's something tangible between us. Maybe you can make him think that I am actually super awesome."

The tangible something was a solid concrete mansion and a family legacy, but she wouldn't explain that yet.

"Very intriguing." Michaela had that puckish, pixie note in her voice, the one that made her irresistible and had trapped Stella in her orbit so many years ago. "All right, count me in, you actually-super-awesome saucy bitch."

"Good," Stella said. "Thank you. I'm inviting the neighbors for dinner tomorrow night, too, since I seem to be spreading my cards on the table."

She winced inwardly at her own turn of phrase. She'd brought her oracle deck, along with an enormous suitcase, her computer, a jumble of charging cables she suspected Elizabeth and Leon did not own, and a stack of books. She was beginning to think about staying permanently at Name Estate, although she hadn't yet got around to renting a moving van. There was still plenty of time.

"You mean Auntie Liz is doing the inviting," said Michaela. "As the hostess."

Stella nodded, lost in her own lies. Really the dinner invitation was an excuse to ask the neighbors if they also had to undergo an annual DNR visit, since the same stream ran through their property. If the adjoining property had documented their lake sturgeon recently, it would be a huge point in favor for Name Estate. She hadn't told Michaela she was taking over possession of the mansion. She and Everett, together. Elizabeth wouldn't mind if she began issuing her own dinner invitations. "Right, yes. Auntie Liz."

"Ri-ight," said Michaela, drawing the word into two suspicious syllables.

Chapter 9

AN EMPTY HOUSE

Stella's left knee bounced restlessly as she turned off the road and stopped before the locked entrance to Name Estate.

"As in, like, No-Name Estate?" Michaela asked, squinting at the sign in the headlights' beam. "Is that the joke?"

"That was my guess, too." Stella rolled down her window and punched zero-five-zero-eight into the security box. The device emitted a red light and a disapproving bleep. "Damn," she said. "I don't have the current gate code. Let me text my uncle."

But after two minutes of idling, when Leon hadn't replied, she instead opened a new message. Everett. It had been dark for two hours already, and she didn't want to wait for Leon.

Hi, she wrote, then erased it.

She stared at her phone, at the blinking cursor.

"I'm getting out," Michaela announced.

"Fine," said Stella. "Sorry. One more minute."

Michaela climbed out of the car in a whoosh of wool skirt and disappeared into the darkness. Stella abandoned the blank thread and dialed Elizabeth instead. Her aunt didn't pick up on her cell or the house's ancient landline. She couldn't see far enough up the lane to know if Everett's black SUV was already parked out front. A fine job she was doing so far at caring for the house when she couldn't even *access* the house.

Leon still hadn't replied, so she dialed him, but with no response. Stella stiffened under the first frisson of worry. They knew she was arriving. It was unlike them to be unreachable. And who had changed the code?

She jolted at a sudden movement only a few inches from her head, beyond the opened window. Her heart rate doubled in an instant. Michaela was bent at the waist, staring into the car, her face on a level with Stella's.

"There's a gap in the stone wall over there," Michaela said. "Let's leave the car here and walk up. I need to pee."

Stella steadied herself with a deep breath and unbuckled. She had no excuse for being so jumpy. "Okay. Right behind you."

Michaela walked away. Stella reopened the blank thread with Everett.

Hey, I'm at the house. You know which one. Do you have the security code? I should have the code. Please share. Leon isn't picking up. Anyway, I'm leaving my car outside the gate. If you're all inside sitting down to dinner, ignoring me, I'm going to be irritated. I'll be the banshee banging on the window in about five minutes.

Send. There, easy. She rolled up the window, locked the vehicle, and left it. The rear bumper was safely clear of the state route, and traffic was sparse.

0508, Everett replied promptly.

Not that one, the new-new one, she sent back.

When he didn't begin typing an immediate response, she hurried and caught up with Michaela, whose expedition outfit was looking more and more appropriate by the minute. The only natural light came from the waxing moon behind thin clouds, filtered through bare deciduous trees in branch-broken shards. A few dozen yards from the gate, they both shone their phone's flashlights at a tumbled-down section of the stone wall. It wasn't meant to be an egress. Perhaps that was how Officer Diettrich had entered. Stella exchanged a glance with her friend, who gestured for her to go first. It was the best they could do.

Stella climbed over with her phone clamped between her teeth like a pirate with a cutlass. The operation was not graceful. Repairing the fence would have to go on Everett's to-do list. Was he the type of man to do it himself or hire a handyman? She recalled the tendons in his forearms and decided he'd probably insist upon performing the stonework himself. Once on the other side, she extended a hand to Michaela, who climbed over princess-fashion with her skirt hem lifted a few inches.

The woods were dense. Stella paused and considered. With the road behind them, and the lake ahead of them, she couldn't possibly become lost. They'd follow the inside of the fence back to the lane.

"Grumble," said Michaela. "Whine."

"I know, I know," Stella said. "Sorry, come on."

She traipsed back the way they'd come, one hand trailing along the cool, mossy stones for balance and a sense of security. But after only a few strides, she realized the fault in her plan. Thick vegetation crowded against the stone wall. Branches and thorns snagged her at every step. She veered away from the wall to avoid an impenetrable bush, then moved east again around a fallen tree. They were hampered by darkness and the shifting, blueish lights on their phones.

"Shouldn't this be farmland or something useful?" said Michaela. "Why are these shrubby things in my way?"

"It's not far to the lane," said Stella.

"I have to pee."

"You already mentioned that." She glanced at her phone. No texts, no calls. "Less complaining, more walking."

"Wait. Do you even have a key to the house? What if we walk up there and can't get in?"

"I'm sure everybody is inside. They must have silenced their phones for some reason. Or maybe the music is turned up loud."

"All right. So, you don't have a key. I'm going to urinate behind that tree. Hold the light for me."

Stella spun and angled her phone in the opposite direction. "I'm not going to illuminate your stream. Oh, look!" She pointed at a silvery glint visible through a break in the undergrowth, although behind her she heard Michaela's skirt rustling. Her friend was busy. "That's the pond. There's a trail from there to the lane. We're getting close. I'm going to go find the end of the path."

"Don't go too far."

"I won't."

Stella made her way toward the pond, then circled around the murky bank. After a moment, she heard the crunching of footsteps. Michaela was following.

She came across the exact location where she had stood the previous week and fallen in. It seemed more and more likely that Diettrich had entered via the same gap in the stone fence. She beamed the phone's light all over the ground, half expecting to spot her missing orange earring, but found nothing. The ground was steeply sloped in the place where she had tumbled. It really wasn't the warden's fault, although she wished she'd reached out and pulled him in after her. Stella turned away from the pond to follow the trail.

In the darkness, mere steps away, Everett loomed. He looked huge, his face shadowed, and Stella had never been gladder to be tracked in a forest by a man. Somehow, she wasn't even surprised. He was supposed to be there, just like she was. She shined her light into his face. It had been nearly a week since she'd last seen him, which was preferable to the decade that had gone before. Still, six days was a long time, too. The anxious band around her stomach relaxed. He squinted.

"Hi," she said.

"Stella," said Everett, and briefly his lips parted like he might add something else. But the moment passed. "Are you attempting to fall in the pond again? It's dangerous to tromp around in the dark and allow strange men to lurk behind you."

"I don't tromp, and you don't lurk. I thought you were Mickey, anyway. You didn't text me back."

"Because I don't know any code newer than zero-five-zero-eight. Who's Mickey?"

More crashing sounds emerged from the undergrowth, accompanied by a pinprick of light. "Stella?" yelled Michaela.

"That's Michaela," Stella told Everett. "Under no circumstances will you make you're-so-fine jokes."

"Believe me, I had no intention of doing so. I'll stick with Michaela."

"Very wise," she said. Then, loudly, "Over here. I found Everett."

"I found you," he said. "Technically."

They waited a moment while Michaela crashed her way in their direction.

"What's in your hand?" Stella asked Everett, aiming her flashlight at the brown paper bag he carried. "And how are we going to get the cars past the gate?"

"I have a call into Leon for the new code."

"So do I."

"He'll call me back," he said.

"You dare to imply that he wouldn't call me back?" she said. "Leon, playing favorites? You, maligning the reputation of my dear uncle? He would never. And don't think I didn't notice you dodged my question about that bag."

Everett suddenly grinned, a flash of white in the gloomy forest. He pulled his phone from his front pocket and answered it.

"Hello, Leon. So good of you to return my call," he said.

Stella rolled her eyes at him.

"Yes, she's here with me," Everett said into the phone. "Six-nine-seven-two. Roger. Both the house and the gate? Are you inside? It sounds noisy." He fell silent, listening, and Stella watched his face. "Understood. Yes. Yes, I'll tell her. All right, bye. Thanks."

Michaela appeared at Stella's side, grumbling under her breath and decorated with a few dead leaves.

"Hello, strange man in the woods," Michaela said loudly. "Status report?"

"Code acquired," said Stella. "He's going to open the gate, then we'll move the cars. Will you meet us up at the house?" She grasped Michaela's elbow and pointed her in the right direction. "Follow this trail to the lane." Stella needed to speak to Everett alone for another moment.

But Everett, as usual, navigated around her ill manners. He extended a hand to Michaela as if the dark forest were a wallpapered drawing room.

"Everett Novak," he said. "Welcome to Name Estate."

Michaela's foul mood dissipated. She beamed her irrepressible smile and shook his hand. "Michaela Jones. Stella mentioned you. I'll have to get a better look once we're all inside."

"A pleasure to make your acquaintance. The house access code is six-nine-seven-two."

Michaela nodded. Then she leveled a finger at Stella's forehead. "You'll be carrying my duffel bag in from the car as repayment for my many indignities."

"Yes, ma'am."

Michaela departed along the path in a twirl of wool. Stella held out a hand to prevent Everett from following.

"Leon and Elizabeth aren't home," she said. "I could tell from your voice on the phone. Where are they? And who changed the gate code?"

"Must have been Leon. He's been a bit paranoid lately. I changed it for Leon last week, then he did so again. Elizabeth laughed at him and said that no one was poaching his sturgeon via a land invasion."

Stella considered. "*You* set it? Zero-five-zero-eight."

"Now it's six-nine-seven-two."

"The one before the new one. Zero-five-zero-eight. You set that one?"

"Yes, last weekend. But if you keep repeating the old one, I'm going to forget the new one."

"The eighth of May is my birthday," she said.

"I wanted to make it easy for you to remember, although I didn't realize Leon would promptly override me."

"You know my birthday."

He shifted his feet. "That's a normal fact for one person to know about another person."

Everett knew her birthday. His face was a pale smudge between his dark hair and his dark coat. Stella resisted the urge to shine her flashlight at him again to see him clearly. "You're the one who left the note on my steering wheel with the new code?" she asked.

"Yes. Now it's the old code. And you should lock your car."

"Clearly there's no need while it's parked inside this fortress. Which means you're the one who filled my gas tank! And cleaned my windshield." Stella realized she sounded accusatory, rather than grateful, and softened her tone. He was the breed of gentleman who would perform a chore for a woman he didn't particularly like. "Thank you."

"You're welcome. It was no trouble."

"Listen, Everett, I had to tell Michaela that I thought there was something between us because she's a romantic and she cares about my feelings, so I'm hoping that you and our aunt and uncle will please play along with—"

"They're not here," Everett said. "Forgive me for interrupting you."

Stella blinked, wishing again she could get him into better lighting. "Oh, right. Where are they?"

"The hospital. Uncle Leon had another instance of heart trouble earlier today."

"Shit." Stella wrapped her arms around herself and squeezed. She couldn't hug Everett. "And I was babbling about my birthday code. Should we...should we drive to the hospital? Is it bad?"

"To your latter question, I don't know. He sounded tired, but anyone would be in that situation. And to your first question, they're already on their way back. He's been released. They should be here in an hour."

"All right," she said quietly. "I guessed that something like this might have happened when no one answered my messages or phone calls, but I didn't want to let myself wander down a pessimistic path. Hopefully, Leon will get some rest. Tell me if you hear anything else before they get home, all right?"

"Yes."

He gestured for her to precede him onto the trail. Stella reached for his elbow and casually linked her arm through his, safely muffled under layers of clothing. She didn't have to rub up against his skin. They could walk together, and she could beam the light at the ground before their feet.

Except Everett gently disengaged her hand from his coat sleeve and stepped aside to put another foot of space between them. He was so polite about it that Stella didn't realize what he'd done until the maneuver was complete.

"If you don't mind," he said, "I've had a long day, and I've already eaten. Please extend my apologies to your friend Michaela. Give me your keys, and I'll move both our cars, drop your bags in the entrance hall, then turn in early. Perhaps my absence will encourage Leon to do the same. All right?"

"Sure." She passed him her keys as requested. There was nothing she could read in his expression, although clearly, he didn't want to spend the evening hanging out with her and Michaela. Why would she have thought otherwise?

Everett nodded once and strode into the darkness, and Stella made her way alone along the path.

Chapter 10

MEETING THE NEIGHBOR

Stella and Michaela slept back-to-back, as they often had after late college nights, in the same guest room Stella had used before. In the morning, Stella awoke first and showered and dressed quietly. She nudged Michaela awake.

"Let's walk over to the neighbors' house," she said, "and invite them to dinner."

"Mmph," said Michaela.

Stella had decided at some point during the night that she wouldn't bother Everett all day. The memory of him unlinking their arms the previous evening was clear in her mind. The less she asked of him, the better. Elizabeth and Leon had arrived home late, with Leon weary and leaning on a cane. He'd gone straight to bed. Stella had sat up with her aunt drinking herbal tea. When she'd tentatively mentioned calling upon the neighbor, Elizabeth had agreed.

"Oh, Marvin? Yes, you must meet him. He's lived next door forever." She had looked distracted. "He's been a good neighbor. Very quiet and mainly keeps to himself. A bit odd, in truth, but harmless. A houseguest is staying with him presently, so make sure to include his guest."

"But with Leon's incident today," Stella said gently. "Maybe another time would be better."

"No, I insist," Elizabeth said. "Anyway, I wanted to let Marvin know we're going away."

So, Stella decided to proceed with her plan. But she wasn't foolish enough to go alone. If the neighbor was weird or unfriendly, she'd have Michaela for backup. Well, maybe not *backup*. But she'd have Michaela to sprint away with.

Stella wore straight-leg denim with frayed ankles and a gray t-shirt, which was about as much fashion as she could muster for a Saturday morning, while Michaela pulled together an ensemble from an overnight bag that didn't seem large enough to hold so many pieces. It was a white corduroy skirt cut in a voluminous circle, a white buttoned-up blouse, and a vest—a *different* vest from the previous day—in black and cinched by a brown belt. With it she wore matching brown knee-high boots and a plaid newsboy cap.

Michaela looked incredible. Stella double-knotted her sneaker laces and zipped her purple hooded sweatshirt.

"Ready?" she asked brightly.

They caught no sign of Everett on their way out of the house, but his black SUV and her red hatchback were snuggled up together on the concrete parking pad, his charging on a high-amp line running from the house. The sight flustered Stella. Those cars spent the night together.

It was a ten-minute walk up the road to the next private turn-in. The morning was cold and shivery with mist, and both Michaela and Stella sipped from insulated mugs of coffee as they walked. Stella regretted that she had no bribe of muffins to offer. The neighbor's place was blocked by a gated vehicle entrance like the one at Name Estate, but nearby it also had fancier human-sized access. Two tall black doors with old-fashioned lanterns on either side were shaded by cypress trees. Stella exchanged a glance with Michaela, then pressed a buzzer.

After a moment, the speaker crackled to life.

"Hello," came a man's voice.

"Hi," said Stella with her best chipper charm. "Is that mister, um. Is that Marvin?" She cringed. Elizabeth hadn't given his surname. "I'm Stella Woodward, and I'm—well, my aunt is Elizabeth Novak, who lives down the road. I was hoping to introduce myself and—"

"You just did. Introduce yourself. Sorry, can't come out, still in my pajamas."

Stella forced a laugh and leaned closer to the security box. "Yes, absolutely right. In addition, I wanted to invite you—and your, um, spouse or other members of the household, whomever—to dinner this evening."

Silence. Stella thought for a moment the connection might have failed. She had a flash of empathy for the customers she often left cooling their heels outside her apartment. Then the box squawked again.

"Woodward, you said? Dinner at Name Estate?"

The conversation might have been easier if conducted on the front stoop, as Stella had imagined, or even face-to-face outside the gate. But at least they were in no danger of being abducted, and she needed to learn whatever she could about the DNR survey. She leaned so close to the speaker she could have licked it.

"Yes, tonight, Name Estate," she said. She couldn't tell Marvin she was moving into the house next door to him when she hadn't even told

Michaela yet. "I'm the new, um, I'm her niece. Elizabeth's. I wanted to introduce myself."

"Already said that."

"True."

A long silence.

"Caviar?" he asked gruffly.

Stella glanced at Michaela, who shrugged. "Yes. Seven o'clock."

"Fine," came the quick response. "You found my weakness. Could never resist. Two of us will attend. I will bring wine."

"Perfect," Stella exclaimed. "Looking forward to it. Wonderful. Thanks so much for your time this morning, and we'll see you tonight. Have a nice day."

Michaela made a gagging face in response to her exaggerated sweetness. There was probably a camera nearby pointed at them, so Stella carefully did not react.

"Fine," said the neighbor again.

Stella waved awkwardly, then turned away.

"Who are you waving at?" Michaela asked.

"Them." She gestured vaguely back toward the speaker. "You know."

"You didn't get his guest's name."

They walked slowly back down the road under the wide winter sky. The air smelled of composting remnants of the previous harvest, dirt, and fish.

"I know," said Stella. "But on a positive note, I think he sounded nice. You know me, always friendly, right? Love to meet new folks. People, humans, all sorts."

Michaela chuckled into her coffee.

Chapter 11

DESTROYING ART

Everett was in the kitchen with Elizabeth and Leon when the women returned. The three of them all looked faintly grim. Stella exchanged a glance with Michaela and tossed her jacket over a stool. Everett stood beside the island and wore a stark white button-down shirt with black pants. *That* was his weekend attire? Elizabeth fretted a tea towel around and around between her fingertips.

"Good morning," Stella said, leaning down to hug her uncle. "You remember my friend Mickey. How are you feeling?"

"Fine," Leon grunted. "Damned nuisance. Hello, Michaela."

Michaela greeted Leon while staring intently at Everett.

"Why are we all standing around?" Stella asked, pouring herself fresh coffee. She felt Everett's eyes on her as she added too much cream and sugar.

"Stella," Everett said, "Elizabeth and Leon will need to fly back to Florida later tonight for another appointment with the cardiologist tomorrow."

"Tonight? That's quick," said Stella. "But if you're sure it's necessary."

Elizabeth nodded. "The local ER sent over the lab results, and Leon's cardiologist wants to see him immediately. He's meeting us at the hospital on Sunday."

A premier cardiologist taking a short-notice appointment on a Sunday. Stella did not remark aloud on the severity of that action, but she saw the deep lines of worry in her aunt's forehead. Elizabeth knew.

"Therefore, it has to be today," Everett said. "If we are to proceed. Please forgive the inconvenience, but I do believe it's best for Leon's health."

"What has to be today?" Stella asked. "Their flight?"

"You're Everett Novak," Michaela blurted. She pointed at Everett like she was identifying a crook in a police lineup.

"Mickey, put on your normal behavior. We all know who he is." Stella reached over and swatted her hand.

"Yes, we met outside last night," said Everett with careful courtesy. "Although it was quite dark."

"I remember where I recognize you from—a photo in the gallery's catalogue. You're *Everett Novak.*"

"Ah," he said uneasily. "Yes."

"I've seen your stuff for sale. I want to see the *before* version. Not the gallery version."

"What stuff?" Stella asked. "The gallery where you work?"

"Not my gallery, a different Gold Coast gallery."

"You never mentioned it to her, son?" Leon asked.

"Are you a fan of Everett's work, Michaela?" asked Elizabeth.

"Well...ah, no. I said I've seen it, not that I *like* it. I can't believe anybody likes it. Sorry, no offense. Nothing personal."

"That's art for you," Everett said dryly. "Famously impersonal to the artist in question."

"I mean, other people like your art, clearly," said Michaela with a tinge of apology.

"What art?" Stella nearly screeched. "What are we talking about?"

"It's nothing, really," said Everett. "My hobby."

Michaela coughed out an indignant laugh. "Is that part of the act? Is that how you pull it off? Everett Novak, the modern artist, the sculptor. The hobbyist."

Stella looked back and forth between Everett and Michaela. Their conversation remained beyond her comprehension. "He's an accountant for a manufacturer in Milwaukee. Right, Ev?"

His *hobby*, he'd said. But Michaela looked certainly, stubbornly correct, and Everett had his eyes pressed closed.

"Yes, that's right," said Everett.

They were both true, Stella realized. The accounting job, the hobby. "And?" she demanded.

"And the fancy gallery in Chicago that has my boss under contract also represents him." Michaela jerked her thumb in Everett's direction. "*This* man. They sell his piles of dust and shards and plaster."

Stella shook her head. "What is going on. Piles of dust? As in garbage?"

Elizabeth clicked her tongue. "Everett's art challenges the viewer."

"He sculpts things in plaster, then smashes them before anyone sees them and sells the remains." Michaela rolled her eyes extravagantly. "To be honest, I can't say whether I'm annoyed or impressed by the scam."

"It's not a scam," said Everett flatly. "It's just something I do. I don't force anyone to buy my pieces."

"*Pieces* is right," said Michaela. "Like a million tiny pieces. What does it *mean?*"

Everett was silent for a long moment. Stella's mind had not properly processed any of the new information. Was she now supposed to understand that Everett was an artist, a sculptor, in his spare time? She considered again the calluses on the sides of his thumbs and the tendons in his forearms. His big, shiny car. He made things, smashed his own work, and sold the bits as art. It would take her months, maybe *years*, to fully ponder that new facet of him. She could think about it forever.

"It's my comment on the dual nature of the soul," Everett said finally. "Or its lack."

"No, that can't be right," said Leon. "You told me it was your comment on the superficiality of internet culture."

"Really?" said Elizabeth. "He once said to me the work was a statement on the elasticity of time."

"Yes," said Everett in general, frustrating agreement. Michaela laughed.

"But...but you're always so prim and uptight," Stella said, and Everett leveled a look at her that only proved her point.

"None of this is relevant for today," he said. "Which, as I said before this digression, must be our wedding day."

Stella's knees went watery. She shoved her sweatshirt off the stool and eased herself onto it before she toppled.

"Hang on," said Michaela. "Wait. What?"

"You definitely did not say that earlier," Stella said, ignoring Michaela's protest.

"Such a nuisance," Leon said. "Sorry, Stella. But I need to get to my doctor in Florida. And your aunt wants to make sure this place is handled, as you two kindly agreed last weekend. In case I don't ever—"

Elizabeth emitted a tiny sound, a muffled squeak. *In case Leon won't ever be coming back.*

"My mom's not here," said Stella. "No. She should be here. I can't get married without my mother knowing anything."

"I don't know anything, either!" shrieked Michaela. "I do not give my permission! You can't do this without telling me."

"Well, you didn't tell me Everett was a weird modern artist until two minutes ago," Stella said sharply.

Michaela scowled. "It's not my fault you didn't perform any basic online stalking of the guy you apparently intend to secretly marry."

"It's not a secret, I just needed somewhere in the range of six months to six years to really think about what the hell we're doing."

"Sorry, sweetie, but we don't have the time," said Elizabeth, cutting through the bite of their exchange. "You can do the formal, legal side of things now. The paperwork. Have a reception for all your family and friends later, if you want. For today, think of it more as an elopement. People do that all the time, right? More often in Las Vegas than Racine, Wisconsin, I suppose. We'll simply swing by the courthouse." She said it as breezily as running errands. Pick up dry cleaning, get married, buy groceries. "I know a fabulous judge. Then to our lawyer's office. He'll come in on a Saturday for us. Draw up the papers, fill in the gaps in our will. Name Estate will be officially yours. Both of yours."

"*Yours?*" Michaela turned and whacked Stella's shoulder. "Somebody had better paint me the full picture. You're marrying your cousin? For the inheritance? *Today?*"

"We're not cousins," said Everett. "But as for the rest of it... Mostly correct. Yes."

Michaela didn't look at him. Her gaze was locked on Stella, and she raised those perfect, expressive eyebrows.

Stella flinched. "Yes. Sorry, Mickey. I told you there was something tangible between us. It's this house."

"Well, muchas gracias for the update," said Michaela, and Stella didn't have to be her best friend to hear the acidic sarcasm. "So nice to be back in the loop."

Chapter 12

PRACTICE

Stella retrieved her hoodie from the floor and walked to the patio doors with her chin held high. She felt wronged, somehow, but it was clear that Michaela did, too. She needed a moment for her brain to catch up—and to give her friend some space.

"Everett," she said. "Outside, please."

He slid open the glass panel and followed her onto the terrace.

"You're a sculptor," she said as soon as the door was closed. That fact seemed more immediately important than their impending meaningless marriage, which would be little more than a piece of paper with a notary public's seal pressed into it, left to gather dust in a drawer. It was significant only because it would enable her to unburden Elizabeth. "You never told me."

"Not a lie but admittedly a small omission," he said. "I do work in the accounting department in an aluminum fabricating shop in Milwaukee. We fabricate parts for golf carts, ATVs, motorcycles, and—"

"And you also make art out of plaster, then crush it."

He shrugged. "Yes."

Stella studied his expression. She had intuited there was a well-hidden passion to him that not many others would notice. She saw it in the intensity of his eyes, his watchfulness, even the way his body was so engaged with his surroundings. He was solidly there, absorbing everything around him. No wonder some part of him reflected art and creativity back into the world. And to think she had found him interesting when he was merely a stuffy accountant.

Behind him, inside, Michaela was talking with Elizabeth. It would take a few minutes before Michaela would forgive her. Maybe as many as ten minutes. It was one of her friend's best qualities. Anyway, Michaela loved drama, so the prospect of a quickie wedding would jostle her out of her annoyance. Stella toyed with the metal tips of her sweatshirt's hood cord. "People really buy the bits? The...the smashings?"

He made a noise of amusement deep in his throat. "That's what I call them, too. The smashings. And yes. I usually write a paragraph to go along with it, something about what the statue had been before I destroyed it, and the gallery puts the smashings in a nice bowl on a pedestal. I used to suspect that customers bought the smashings to get the nice bowl, but my gallerist assures me that is not the case."

"How do you do it? The destructive part."

"I usually first throw the piece against the floor," he said. "Or knock it over, if it's large. Then hit it with a sledgehammer. Then finally, stomp it with the heel of my boot."

"Wow." Stella pictured Everett wielding a heavy tool, with sweat on his brow, raising it overhead and bringing it down hard. "That sounds intensely satisfying. Really. I wish I'd known."

"Why?"

"Because I—" She stopped. Why, indeed? Did it matter? He owed her nothing, not even a complete depiction of himself. "Does it bother you if I think you're interesting? If I like knowing you better?"

"No, of course not. But Stella, you already know me better than most people."

If that were true, then very few people had glimpsed his inner self. "There's a connection between the work I do and what you do, you know," she said. "We're both selling what's not truly there. The fully disclosed con. Even though you don't respect what I do." She lobbed the comment in his direction like a hedgehog. Prickly and indignant.

"Yeah."

She hadn't expected him to agree so easily. "I sell fake fortunes, and you sell broken sculptures," she explained.

"I know. I see your point." He slid his hands into his pockets and looked out at the lake.

"Then how can you harrumph about my dumb job and not your own?"

"I do not harrumph. I'm not an elderly Victorian clergyman."

"Disagree, vicar."

He pivoted to face her. "Because you don't like it," he said abruptly. "You clearly don't like what you do. If you were proud and relished the challenge or enjoyed helping people or...or even felt glee in fleecing your marks, I would have no concerns about your odd career. But it makes you feel like a crook and a liar, and you don't enjoy it. So, no, I don't approve. That's all. Although you don't need my approval, obviously."

She swallowed. "Meaning, by correlation, that you do love your art."

"Well, yes," he said, as if it were obvious.

They had veered too close to the vein, somehow, so Stella mustered a carefree smile. "Especially the smashy-smashy part, I'm sure. Is there any other unusual hobby you'd care to disclose? Taxidermy? Are you a closet harpist?"

"None. I don't believe a harp would fit in most closets. Running, you already know about. I read books. The usual. Sculpting takes up most of my free time."

"Can I help you do it sometime? The destruction."

He raised his eyebrows. "You want to destroy my art?"

"I thought the destruction *is* the art, Ev. I want to break things. Doesn't everyone?"

"Nobody has asked before to participate. No one's even seen the unbroken pieces, as far as I can recall. Maybe. Let me think about it."

Stella *hmphed* in her throat and promptly felt like an elderly Victorian vicar. "That hasn't been our style, has it? Taking time to think things over. For example, we're apparently getting married today."

"I won't force you." His broad shoulders hunched up around his ears like he expected a blow. "I won't even try to talk you into it. Tell me now, please, if you're ending the agreement. Perhaps there's still another way to free Elizabeth and Leon of the problems brewing here. Although I called the DNR's headquarters, as I said I would, and the person who answered the phone confirmed the warden's name and everything in the letter."

"Have you thought of another way to assume responsibility for the estate?" she asked. "Something else that allows our relatives to fly away feeling as if they've happily done us a favor?"

Instead of leaving us with an open investigation and a threat. But Leon and Elizabeth weren't doing it on purpose—they must not know. She had told them nothing. They couldn't be blamed, nor would she want to accuse them.

"No," he said. "I have not. Especially nothing that we can do so quickly and that aligns with their wishes. I'm sorry."

She should have been grateful for the opportunity to lock up a huge inheritance and a polite husband. She'd proposed to him twice, after all. *At least I didn't beg,* she thought wryly. Regardless, Stella wished he would have devoted a moment to persuading her. One sentence from him would have cleared away her apprehensions. She had a dozen important thoughts and feelings she probably should have said aloud, but she and Everett were so far from accord on all of them, her doubts were too embarrassing to venture. *Is there any part of this relationship that could have been real? Can I trust you? Is this house, this land, too much obligation for us to shoulder together? What if we fail our families?*

But all those emotional queries would have created only dismay in practical-minded Everett.

"I don't have anything to wear," she said instead.

"It doesn't really matter what you wear," he said.

Stella turned away. She would have to practice better hiding the sting of his total disregard. And his indifferent insult came right after he'd offered once again to release her from their agreement.

"Because—" he said hurriedly. "Because. I did not intend to dismiss your wardrobe concern as irrelevant, but only to imply...otherwise. Because you're always lovely. Lively. You're always you."

Stella faced him and scanned his features. He stood close to her, eyes steady but his shoulders still raised. She slowly removed her hands from her pockets. His rather stilted comment didn't make much sense.

"Lovely, or lively?" she asked. "To clarify."

Everett, however, didn't take the bait. "No woman should marry—" he paused, swallowed. "Nobody should marry unless they want to."

"Except us. We don't want to. But we *need* to."

"Yes," said Everett. "We need to."

"All right. Shall we go now?" She put on a breezy, smiling face. It wasn't easy to talk about how much Everett felt compelled to marry her. "I'm not busy."

Everett stood as motionless as the craggy shoreline the house had been built into. "Stella, if it alleviates any of your concern, please know that I won't—I would not presume to kiss you at our...at the courthouse."

"Oh, please," she snapped. It seemed much past the final insult she could be forced to endure. He must have been pretending not to know or guess anything about how she really felt. Everett could not be so dense. The restraint of her temper was insufficient for his false nobility. She narrowed her eyes and glared hard. "Don't kiss me, then, but don't play it off like you're doing so for my benefit."

His mouth opened, then closed again. Then he spoke. "There will be other people present."

"Yeah? And? That's how government buildings generally operate."

"I didn't think—although I should not have assumed, I now understand—but I didn't think the, ah, traditional kiss-the-bride moment would be something you would want considering our unusual circumstances and the fact that we have no...no practice. I have never held your hand, much less kissed your lips, and I don't believe a fluorescent-lit office in the Racine County courthouse will be the most conducive location for a first attempt. As you so bluntly noted only minutes ago— did you not call me prim and uptight? —you may prefer not to kiss me."

She listened to him enough to follow the gist of his complaint, but her lungs tightened when he said *you may prefer not to kiss me.* It was far from true. But somehow, impossibly, Everett didn't know.

He was standing so close. Stella reached out and braced two fingertips and her thumb against his sternum—warm, solid. She stretched up onto her toes, searched his eyes for an objection. When no objection made itself apparent, she leaned forward, puckered her lips, and smooched him. Right on the kisser. With a tiny, damp, smack. *Smooch.*

She leaned back and opened her eyes, looking at him unrepentantly.

"There," she said. "Now you can't say we haven't practiced."

Everett, however, glowered with undisguised anger. Stella smothered a tinge of unease. Maybe she should have obtained a signed permission slip before daring to kiss Everett Novak.

"That?" he said. "Is *that* how you practiced your tennis or piano lessons?"

"I didn't take tennis or piano," she said.

"Clearly," he replied. "Because *that* was not practice. What you did was a mockery that scarcely approximates the full potential of the experience. You think I became a skilled sculptor by practicing like that?"

"No," she shot back. "I have no reason to think you ever did become a skilled sculptor, considering you've smashed everything you ever made."

"You are—"

Everett tilted his head back and stared up at the sky. Stella examined the fascinating contours of his throat. She watched him swallow. When he lowered his chin, his jaw was tight, with a twitch in one small muscle. She found that was fascinating, too. Even when he was annoyed with her, everything about Everett that he couldn't control was of the greatest interest to her.

"You're right," he finished. He glanced at the transparent sheet of glass that separated them from the kitchen. "Come this way."

He turned on his heel and walked away. Stella, helpless, followed him. He disappeared around the corner of the terrace, and she pursued him down a flight of concrete steps. At the half-turn landing in the stairs, where the stone corner was filled with moldering leaves, he stopped.

She paused on the last step. "What are we—"

"Practicing," he said.

He reached for her. With an almost-mocking expression, he put three fingers on her sternum, as she had done to him. But his big hand took up the scant room between her breasts. Her sweatshirt was unzipped, and her t-shirt did nothing to insulate her from the weight of his touch. Stella shifted, but his hand stayed in place. Her rear end collided with the cold concrete barrier of the staircase and stopped. Everett came closer. She caught his scent, the expensive smell of a well-mixed cocktail, except this time it was served with a slosh over the rim. She wasn't afraid of him, but she also didn't recognize him. In that moment, he was tempestuous, unpredictable. He was a unyielding challenge she could never have declined. Her lips parted. He flattened his palm flush against her, and she was certain he must have felt the pounding of her heartbeat.

"You." His breath was no more than a feather on her face compared to the heaviness of his hand. "You induce rash decisions in me."

"Yes," she said on a rushed exhale, although she didn't know what exactly she was agreeing to. Stella hardly remembered who she was, and she certainly knew nothing about him. Who was this stranger making her pulse race, making her hips twitch, making her knees weak? Who was she marrying?

He slid his hand up slowly from her chest to her neck, rucking her thin shirt as he moved. With Everett's hand light on her throat, his thumb pressed under her chin, Stella couldn't have looked away if she'd wanted to.

But she didn't want to. He was glorious, and as he bent his head toward her, a few strands of his smoothed hair fell forward onto his forehead. His gaze moved from her eyes to her mouth. He kissed her slowly, and she couldn't keep her mouth from opening the barest fraction. Everett angled his head and touched the tip of his tongue to the silky inside of her lower lip. Stella made the most embarrassing noise, but Everett didn't seem to mind. She was kissing, *actually* kissing, Everett. It was an occurrence she had imagined so many times it was awful to contemplate, but the likelihood of real kissing had always been zero.

Was it even real, though, if he said they were practicing for future veracity before their audience of county employees? Surely, he didn't care about that. His clever mouth wasn't behaving as if the moment were meaningless. It felt real to her. He left a zingy tingle on her tongue like he'd come to her straight from his toothbrush. Her mouth probably tasted of coffee—or like her usual dollop of cream and sugar, if fortune smiled on her. There was no way she could have guessed upon waking where that morning would lead. She had advanced straight to intimate familiarity with the razor-shorn prickle of stubble under his lower lip.

He inhaled hugely so his chest expanded to meet hers, and he snaked his free arm around the small of her back. With a quick jerk, he snugged their bodies tight together from mouth to thighs. He was tall, and there was no give in his hips. The connection didn't feel quite right, but it certainly didn't feel *wrong*, either. Stella's hand was caught between them, and she grabbed his belt. The tang of the buckle bit into the soft pad of her thumb. The pain was a nasty contrast to the pleasure humming in every other inch of her body.

"Ouch," she mumbled against his lips.

Instantly, Everett moved away, and a rush of chilled air flowed over Stella.

"Apologies." He pushed the fallen strands of his hair back into perfect alignment. "I—I may have taken liberties you didn't intend to—"

Stella waved a hand in front of her face, both to stop his unnecessary words and to hide the blush rising in her cheeks. She hadn't meant to complain. "No, sorry, it wasn't anything you did, I only...I stabbed myself on your belt."

It sounded ridiculous. Everett's brow furrowed. "My belt."

"Not because I was unfastening it," Stella said swiftly. "I reached for it, and the pointy end of the..." She examined her thumb. There was a teeny, insignificant mark on it, already fading. "Never mind."

"All right," he said.

He gestured toward the house, and together they started back up the stairs. Stella wasn't certain, but Everett seemed to be standing closer to her than usual. His arm brushed her jacket sleeve.

"You were right, though," she said, hoping to coax a smile from him. Or at least a loosening of the tension in his neck. "We did need practice. I hope to avoid further injuries. We should probably get ready to leave." *For our wedding*, she could not say aloud.

"Yes," he said. "I believe Elizabeth intended to arrange for a judge and set a time."

Stella's brain was still swimming in thoughts of kisses and weddings and belt buckles. "I hope we're not too late getting back," she said. "This morning, Mickey and I walked to the neighbor's house—well, to the gate, past which I was not admitted. He seemed nice but odd. The man accepted my invitation to dine here this evening." She paused, frowned. "That was before I knew it would be our wedding dinner."

"Thank you. We'll ask him about his experience with the resource survey." He nodded toward the enormous house atop the hill with a faint smile in his eyes. "Honestly, having no one but Michaela and the odd neighbor at dinner probably suits our unusual sort of marriage."

Stella laughed. "It does, doesn't it? And don't forget the weird neighbor's houseguest."

"Excellent. Perfect. I hope they bring their pet marmoset or closet harpist or whatever else to keep things lively. I don't suppose you have a hidden passion for cooking?"

"No," she said. "But I know where the caviar is stored."

Chapter 13

BELLS

Back inside the house, Stella found that Michaela was ready to forgive her and move on with the wedding, on one condition.

"This is your aunt's wedding dress," said Michaela, flourishing a creamy white gown swathed in a plastic dry-cleaning bag. "It's forty-five years old, it's fantastic, and you're going to wear it."

Elizabeth was with them in the primary bedroom's walk-in closet, so Stella did not want to mention that while the dress was surely fantastic, it also had long, diaphanous, chiffon sleeves and that Elizabeth had always been at least six inches shorter than Stella.

"Wow," she said.

She had taken aside Michaela and quietly explained in more detail that she and Everett were marrying to make it easier for Leon and Elizabeth to gift them the land and house, and she'd mentioned Leon's health concerns. Michaela remained wary, but she knew Stella would do nearly anything to help her aunt. Stella had said nothing about the missing sturgeon or the estate's simmering legal trouble.

"I can make a few quick alterations," said Michaela. "Stop making that face. Just trust me on this. You're not going in your stretchy pants to your wedding."

"At the county courthouse, Mickey, I must emphasize," said Stella. "The other female wedding-types will probably be wearing chic pantsuits."

"Brides, we call those," said Elizabeth. "Female wedding types. I wore a lace choker with that dress, if you'd also like to borrow it?"

"Um," said Stella. "Maybe I'll wear Mickey's faux pearls."

"Yes," Michaela agreed, and Stella let out a careful breath of relief. Everett would have laughed his charming laugh if she'd appeared wearing a seventies-era lace choker. "And my nude pumps. I have a retro-mod vision."

"Right. Got it," said Stella. She did not have a retro-mod vision, but she did trust Michaela's fashion sense.

It felt to her like only a blink of an eye before she and Michaela climbed into her red hatchback, and Everett escorted her aunt and his uncle into his SUV, for the short drive into town. Michaela piled the dress in her lap, and she scolded Stella to brake more smoothly because she was still frantically stitching up the alterations. Stella kept glancing at Everett's black vehicle in her rear-view mirror. Was the cargo section covered in plaster dust from transporting smashed sculptures? No, she decided. Likely not. He probably vacuumed it clean every time.

Stella did not have any preconceived notions of a fancy courthouse, but the building's exterior turned out to be rather wonderful. It had severe, geometric art deco lines and rose to a grandiose height. The windows were stacked in double columns, and the state and national flags whipped from atop poles studding the wide approach. The place was apparently very busy on Saturday afternoons, and she and Michaela circled the adjacent lot in search of parking.

A pickup truck cut her off as she signaled for an open spot. For the first time, Stella considered indulging in a bridezilla tantrum. *Let me park in the front, I'm getting married!* she would screech. *I deserve good parking because he doesn't even love me!* She didn't, of course, but it would have made Michaela laugh and Everett cringe.

She watched Everett park on the other side of the lot. He emerged and waited patiently for Elizabeth and Leon's slower steps. Stella caught his eye, and he raised his chin in the direction of the entrance. *Go on.* She nodded.

Michaela linked their elbows. The vintage dress, apparently now held together with enough thread to satisfy her, was draped over her other arm. "Let's go get you changed. We don't want to keep the judge waiting. Or your...uh, Everett."

Stella squeezed her arm. "Thank you, Mickey. For not saying fiancé. But seriously, thanks for being here with me. And I should have asked you this already, but will you please be my maid of honor?"

"Delighted. I'm not doing your hair, though. Not my area."

"Understood."

"And you owe me free childcare on a weekend of my choosing."

"Well, hang on, now," Stella said teasingly. "*Both* kids? They weren't my idea. Maybe we can consider this your penance for those green-and-gold slip dresses all of us bridesmaids had to wear at *your* wedding."

Michaela ignored this old complaint. "And a margarita for altering a dress on zero notice."

"All right, all right."

They climbed the steps together, and Stella pulled the heavy door open so Michaela could enter sideways with her armful of white fabric. "The best thing you could do for me," said Michaela softly, "is find some way to be happy in all this weirdness. And, let's be honest, you also need to view Everett's sculptures before he smashes them to get me a photo."

Stella smiled. "I'll try, I promise."

They commandeered an empty women's restroom off a quiet second-floor hallway by bolting the door. Stella stripped to her bra and underwear, then Michaela lifted the dress over her head. Beadwork on the waistline and hem made it heavy. Stella quickly realized that Michaela had removed the poofy sleeves, leaving only narrow straps that hugged the outer curves of her shoulders, and raised the hem to tea length. The neckline was square and low, and the waist was fitted, but overlaid was a sheer chiffon jacket of sorts that fastened with three pearl buttons.

Michaela unhooked Stella's utilitarian pink bra, maneuvered the straps down over Stella's elbows, and tossed it aside. She smiled, and Stella was surprised to see a glint of moisture in the corners of her eyes.

"Feeling sentimental, Mick?" Stella asked.

Michaela said nothing but grasped Stella's upper arms and spun her around. Stella stared at her reflection in the streaky mirror over the row of sinks.

"Oh," she said.

The dress fit. In fact, it suited her perfectly. The wide neckline emphasized the stubborn set of her collarbones and offered a hint of cleavage. White fabric made her complexion seem less pale—which was essential, considering her cheeks were bloodless. The beaded waistline flashed under the sheer overlay. With some lipstick, blush, and

Michaela's necklace and shoes, she'd be fine. Better than fine, she might even manufacture some poise, if not total confidence.

She turned and hugged Michaela. "Thank you," she said. "Aunt Elizabeth will be pleased."

"So will Everett," said Michaela.

"He doesn't care," said Stella. "As long as I don't show up naked or, like, smudged in literal dirt, he doesn't care."

Michaela eyed her briefly, then turned away to clear up their mess. "I agree he wouldn't like one of those options. Now twist your hair into a chignon, please."

A few minutes later, Stella was as ready as she could be. Michaela unbolted the door, and they exited past an elderly woman whose impatient glare showed she had been waiting to enter the restroom. Stella offered her a smile, and the woman's scowl faded to misty pleasure.

"Best wishes, dear," said the woman. "Good luck. I hope he's worth it."

"Thank you," said Stella. It wasn't Everett's worthiness she was concerned about. At least she could offer him half a substantial fortune along with herself.

They returned to the first floor and the county clerk's office. A happy couple was leaving, so Stella and Michaela shifted aside, but the pair didn't even notice them in their excited haze. Inside, Everett stood very straight with his hands at his sides and his shoulders squared to the door. Elizabeth and Leon stood when Stella entered.

Elizabeth exclaimed in delight upon looking her over and was soon crying in earnest. Leon gave her a gruff hug and patted her arm.

"You look very nice in that old dress. Looked better on my Lizzie, of course," Leon said loyally, "but nevertheless."

Everett approached and grasped her hand. Stella forced herself to meet his eyes. If she unclenched her jaw, she was certain her teeth would begin clattering from nerves. He offered her no compliments, as she'd expected.

"All right?" he asked quietly.

"Yes," said Stella. "You?"

"Yes."

The woman working behind the counter, armored in a navy blazer and pragmatic haircut, cleared her throat. "One-hundred dollars," she said, "for the license, and twenty-five for the rush. Cash."

Leon reached for his wallet, but Everett held out a hand to forestall him. "I'll handle it," he said, and Leon stepped back.

Once the license was settled and signed, they all followed the clerk through a warren of interior hallways paneled in a dark wood that smelled faintly of fried food. Outside the judge's chambers, the title *Hon. Ramseyer* was engraved on a very nice nameplate. She opened the door to the clerk's knock. The judge was grandmotherly, kind, with a wicked sparkle in her eyes. Stella was relieved she wasn't wearing the imposing black robes but rather black jeans and a luxurious cashmere sweater.

"Madeline," said Elizabeth, as she and the judge exchanged cheek kisses. "Thank you so much for coming in on a Saturday."

"Anything for you, Liz. But I won't forgive you for leaving town on such short notice. Chris and I will call you when we next get down to Miami."

"Please do."

"And now, to the business." The judge braced her hips against her enormous desk and folded her hands, then looked Stella in the eye for a moment before shifting her gaze up to Everett. Stella still had his hand clasped in a hold that was making her palm sweat and was surely causing him some level of pain, but she had no intention of releasing him. "I assume you two must be Stella and Everett. Do you have your own vows, or shall I do the standard set?"

"The standard, please, your honor," said Everett, unfaltering. "Thank you."

Stella's sensory inputs faded to static. She nodded at several points where it seemed relevant, repeated the necessary words when prompted, and maintained her clutching grip on Everett's hand. They had no rings to exchange, so that section was omitted entirely. It turned out that rings were a tradition not required by any law. It didn't matter. Stella neither processed nor retained any sensation other than the perspiration gathering under her armpits and the wobble in her knees. She could not pass out. If she fainted, Everett would have to hoist her upright, and she would leave damp sweat stains on his white shirt.

In what felt like scant minutes, however, the judge seemed to be drawing to her inevitable conclusion. *Pronounce you husband and wife* et cetera.

"Wait," Stella blurted. "I do have something to say."

Judge Ramseyer paused, an indulgent smile on her face. "Go ahead."

Stella felt the collective eyes of her family, Michaela, the judge, and Everett all weighing on her. "Do I have to say it to all of you or just to him?" she asked.

"Whatever you'd prefer."

Stella returned Everett's steady gaze. A faint furrow appeared between his eyebrows. She swayed close to his ear. "I promise," she whispered, "that I will try not to fuck this up."

She leaned back, satisfied. Everett pressed his lips together and nodded once in acknowledgment. A muffled snort emerged from Michaela, and Stella suspected her whisper had not been quiet enough in the small office.

"Excellent," said Judge Ramseyer. "I do love romance. We're done here. I now present the new husband and wife!"

Chapter 14

AN ACCORD

Everett stepped toward Stella, moving one palm to the small of her back. His touch was solid, gentle, and her strain faded for the first time since they'd arrived. She tilted her head back, as they'd practiced. She lifted a hand to his collar, where the top button of his shirt was open. A small triangle of bare skin appealed to her. She pressed her fingertips against the base of his throat and felt his pulse. He met her eyes; she saw a question there. *Yes?* In response, she lifted onto her toes.

He kissed her simply. No pressure from his hips, no tongues, no hand against her breastbone. Not like when they'd been alone outside, earlier at the house. But after a few seconds passed and she shifted her weight to end their embrace, he pressed his fingers against her spine and kissed her for another moment. Not long. Not *too* long. Then they both straightened. Everett had a smear of red lipstick on his mouth, and she reached up with her thumb and smoothed his lip clean. They turned to face their small audience.

"Oh," said Elizabeth.

"Mm-hmm," said Michaela.

"Now that's done, let's go out for lunch," said Leon. "Before visiting the lawyer's office."

Everett shook the judge's hand, and Stella gave the woman a quick hug.

"I'll ride with your aunt and uncle," Michaela said as they left the office. "You go with Everett."

Stella nodded. She didn't know what to say to Everett, but she should think of something.

He was, after all, her husband.

She glanced over at him, incredibly handsome in stark black-and-white, and quirked her mouth. They'd done it. His somber expression softened to something approaching a smile. At the tall doors leading outside, he reached for her again, and they exited the courthouse hand-in-hand. A few onlookers applauded and whistled. Stella found herself grinning. Even if her marriage had been arranged for reasons of inheritance and the protection of her family, the wedding itself was real enough and had turned out to be quite perfect for them. They paused on the grand steps for Michaela to snap a few photos.

Elizabeth, Leon, and Michaela separated themselves with waves and blown kisses, promising to meet them at a restaurant Leon specified. But at the edge of the parking lot, Everett stopped abruptly. He looked at Stella with the uncertain pinch of befuddlement in the faint brackets around his mouth.

"I'll...I will go bring the car around?" he suggested. It was posed as a question, not his usual assertive tone. "You'll wait for me here?"

"Why?" Stella looked across at his black vehicle, no more than a hundred yards distant.

"Because... Because I should, right? Because you're my...you know."

"Yeah, I know. Or is it because I'm wearing these high-heeled shoes? They don't pinch my feet. I'll walk with you."

He nodded, looking relieved. "Right, yes. That's good. We'll walk."

Stella, amused by his uncharacteristic hesitancy, laughed. Was this how it would be to be married to Everett? Would he be carefully considerate of her comfort, wary of stepping out of place? Was he, like her, trying not to make a total disaster of their new relationship in its first hours? With a new dose of uncertainty making him less perfect and more approachable, she might be able to see them as equals. She looped her arm through the crook of his elbow, and they walked.

He opened the SUV's passenger door for her. The car's interior was immaculate, which she'd come to expect from him, and it smelled of Everett and leather.

As he belted himself and started the engine, Stella gathered her courage. They had only a few minutes alone together. "So, Everett," she asked brightly, "how shall we proceed?"

He was silent for a long moment, and Stella didn't mind. She liked that he contemplated his words before speaking.

She did not, however, expect his reply.

"I know that you despise me," he said. "And I'm sorry for it."

"*What?*" she gasped.

"Because of what happened that spring before I graduated college," he added quickly. "At the vecherinka. I know I was standoffish and hurt your feelings, but in my defense, you must have been no more than sixteen. And I had received some bad... I was in no mood or condition for conversation with my aunt's little niece."

"Stop," Stella said on a groan. "Please, stop. It's also been blocked from my mind. In fact, I believe it was the vodka that handled disposal of that evening's memory on my behalf. I can only imagine how awful I was, and I'm so sorry."

"*You're* sorry?"

"Yes."

"For what? For once being a teenager, or for despising me?" he asked.

"Everett." Stella drew a deep breath. "I just *married* you, for heaven's sake. You did the right thing by ignoring me a decade ago. I am, however, a little miffed that you think I'd carry around a decade-long grudge against a man I rarely saw. That sounds like a lot of work."

"Then why do you despise me?"

"I don't." The familiar feeling of uncertainty came flooding back. She couldn't tell him that he was too good for her. That she wanted to be great at something and instead was forced to pretend that she was amused by her own ridiculousness. That she was hurt that he didn't like *her*. Maybe someday she'd find the right way to explain those complications. But on their wedding day, all she needed him to know was the simplest version of the truth. "I don't despise you," she repeated. "I like you very much."

"What do you want from me?" he asked. "Tell me."

Stella laughed. *Everything I can't imagine having with anyone else.* If only it were that easy. "Yeah, right. Nice try. Your turn. What do you want from me? From this joint venture? At first, we'll work together on finding our valuable fish, thus defanging the DNR. I want to live in the house, but I suppose you don't need to. After the legal problems are resolved, you could live in Milwaukee and visit once a month to check the pond and the shoreline."

"No, the estate requires more attention than that. I need to close up my place in the city, but I'll be moving in," he said.

He wanted to live simultaneously in the same house with her. Granted, the place was a mansion, but they really should have worked out these details.

"All right," she said slowly. "If you want to be roommates, I could leave you in peace apart from twice-daily encounters while crossing paths in the kitchen. I could avert my eyes while your girlfriends enter and exit. I could buy your favorite cereal while grocery shopping."

She waited for him to repeat something similar.

He did not reciprocate. "There will be no women coming and going," he said. "That's not...that is not my preferred pattern of behavior."

"No?" She hadn't stopped thinking about kissing him. Not recalling the nice embrace in the marriage office, or remembering their practice session that morning, but ruminating upon the *next* time she might kiss him. "Then what is?"

Stella watched with interest as his hands tightened on the steering wheel until his knuckles turned pale. It was too easy to imagine him squeezing her hip like that, pressing her closer.

"This," he said, and he released his iron grip on the wheel long enough to gesture back-and-forth between them, "is not what either of us expected for our futures, of course. I do not intend to be your roommate, Stella."

"You said you wanted—"

"I had always assumed I would have what everyone else has," he said in a murmur. "A relationship, a partnership. Trust. A wife in all senses."

Stella inhaled slowly, quietly, so he wouldn't hear her indrawn breath. She meant it to calm the quiver in her stomach, but it didn't help. She smelled his irresistible scent, and she saw the slight flex of his thigh as he braked at an intersection.

Because her mind was hazy, though, she needed to make sure she understood. "You mean, for example, all five physical senses. Such as seeing, hearing, and, for example, touch."

"And taste." He understood. He never pretended to be stupid, and it was one of her favorite aspects of all she'd learned of him.

They were both talking about sex. She was talking about embarking on a sexual relationship with him. With her husband.

"Well then," she said with a carefree smile, "here I am!" She lifted her palms and splayed her fingers wide. An offering. An invitation.

A week ago, it would have been about the bravest thing she'd ever done. But since then, he'd pushed her against a wall and kissed her until she couldn't think straight, and he'd hardly let go of her hand all day. They were married. Things were different.

It wasn't different enough, however, to make her forget that he'd said he had no reason to speak to Stella apart from the estate. But wasn't she delivering on that reason? She was bringing value to the marriage, and Everett seemed sincere. Maybe the unique beauty of Name Estate would convince him that acquiring a wife in the bargain wasn't all bad.

Everett glanced over at her with a slight angle to his head before returning his gaze to the road.

"Are you certain?" he asked.

Her heart lurched. "Sure. Yeah. I mean, despite my job, I don't believe in predictions for real life, and it's too soon to know if you'll want to murder me within a month, but I always wanted..." *You.* "The same things you said. The things everybody wants from life."

She swallowed hard and tugged at a piece of itchy lace on her upper arm.

"All right," he said. "Yes."

"Yes?"

Everett, miraculously, reached across the center console, and she interlocked their fingers. "Yes," he repeated firmly.

They had been saying *yes* to each other, Stella recalled, at every turn. *Yes* to inheriting the house, *yes* to the marriage, *yes* to finding the sturgeon, *yes* to taking a real stab at...at what? Were they dating?

It didn't matter if the answer was *yes*. She laughed, then raised the back of his strong hand to her lips and planted a kiss there. *Yes.*

He returned her fierce grip. But then he disentangled their fingers and, instead of retreating, as Stella dreaded, he advanced. He moved his hand to her thigh, covered as it was in fine, shimmery fabric, and pressed his fingers into her pliable flesh. The material of her wedding dress slid against her skin. Stella bit her lip and shifted her hips down a fraction. As if he understood what she wanted, he let his hand drift higher on her leg. Stella exhaled softly. He was dangerously close to the juncture of her limbs, where she was suddenly desperate for the pressure of his palm against her warm, damp crotch.

A tiny noise escaped her lips.

Everett looked over, and an arrogant smile flirted with the corners of his mouth.

"Wife," he said quietly.

"Husband."

The accord between them stretched to a moment, then to a minute. Everett shifted. He brought the car to a stop at a red light. His expression changed to a glimmer of pain, like someone wearing stilettos had stepped on his foot.

Well, shit, Stella thought, watching him closely. Their shining, glossy marital accord hadn't lasted very long, and the throbbing demand between her legs remained unsatisfied as he clenched the steering wheel at ten-and-two.

"Although we don't yet know each other very well," he said. "Or all the most important points."

"You know most of my medium-important points," Stella said with a forced laugh, desperate to extend their number of perfect minutes at least into double digits. She smoothed the rucked-up panel of her dress.

"Exactly," he said. "Our unusual circumstance is what created this marriage. We will find a way to coexist within our new boundaries."

She sighed. Perhaps he needed time. A few more flirtatious smiles from her, a few more of their practice kisses. He was a man of rigid honor and regimented behavior, after all, and she'd come along and blown up his life with little warning.

"We will," she said with the full power of her nonexistent foresight. "I know we will."

Chapter 15

LEGALITIES AND NEW REALITIES

Leon bought them all lunch at a place that fell midway between a pub and a dive bar. The walls had exposed plywood in several places and displayed deer heads preserved by an indifferent taxidermist, but the floors were clean.

Stella stood beside Michaela. "This is a strange place to be wearing a wedding dress."

Michaela clasped her hand and gave a defiant stare to another patron. The music changed to a fresh pop song, and the waitress led them to a table by the windows. Leon, apparently in a jovial mood, waved to an acquaintance. Stella felt...different. As if changing her status on a piece of paper had changed her brain chemistry. Everett pulled out a chair for her. He inquired about her preference for a beverage (diet pop) and asked if anything on the menu looked appetizing (crunchy chicken salad).

It was all faintly surreal, perhaps nothing more so than the tension of Everett's arm and shoulder alongside hers. Stella wondered if the man ever relaxed.

"Do you own sweatpants?" she whispered to him while they waited for their food. Elizabeth, at the other end of the table, was threatening to drag Leon to the Florida condo's health club for a fitness class called Aqua Merengue. Leon, in return, waggled his eyebrows and said he would only attend wearing the swim briefs he'd purchased in Rio de Janeiro, which made Elizabeth squawk in protest. Michaela was egging them on.

"Yes," Everett said. "But I decided not to wear them to my wedding."

Stella turned and stared at him. His mouth curved slightly. It was a *joke*. She nudged his arm with her elbow. "Probably a good decision," she said. "I would have, personally, but Mickey wouldn't allow it."

"I would have liked to have seen that," he said.

Stella laughed, mostly at the playful twinkle in his eyes. He would never be particularly hilarious, she decided, but neither was he as entirely serious as she'd once thought. She could tell he was trying his best to be lighthearted.

"Don't turn around," she said, "but the woman behind you...I just watched her sort envelopes into three piles and put them back in her tote. One for envelopes, one is all catalogs of glossy ads, and one has coupons for baby clothes." An image rippled across Stella's imagination of the woman, a middle-aged brunette with red eyeglasses, laying a messy spread of cards. The imaginary woman then palmed two of the nearest cards and made them disappear. "She's been stealing her neighbors' mail. Between that and the short tip she left for her waiter, I suspect she's been overdoing the shopping and has dipped into shoplifting. She's looking for a new thrill in this petty thievery."

Stella, of course, was merely enjoying the brand-new thrill of showing off to her brand-new husband. Everett quirked his eyebrows.

"And how would you advise her, if she were your client?" he asked.

She shrugged. "I'd tell her to transfer all her balances to a low-interest card and learn skydiving. And I'd tell her not to take out her mistakes on the waitstaff."

He laughed. And later, when the multimillionaire Leon left a scant ten-dollar tip, Everett put another twenty atop the bill as they walked away. Nobody saw him but Stella, and he said nothing.

After lunch, at the lawyer's office, Stella struggled to concentrate on the discussion. Huge assets and her future were at stake, but details of the tax withholdings and the fund for estate maintenance were too dry to hold her attention. Her interest was solely fixed on Everett. She could easily grow accustomed to his hand wrapped around hers.

The papers were quickly drawn up confirming that Stella Woodward Novak and Everett Novak were the owners of Name Estate. Elizabeth and Leon were using up much of their lifetime gift-tax exemption. Stella and Everett were not required to sign any detailed partnership agreements because of the one important document they'd already inked and filed— the marriage license. Under the law, they'd have to figure out their own ways of working together.

And if anybody was going to jail over violations occurring at the estate, it would be them. That, at least, was a relief. But Stella had no intention of letting it get that far. Together, in the spring spawning season, they would resolve their obligations to the state and be free of worry.

Outside the lawyer's office, Stella was ready to go home and change out of her fancy, vintage dress and back into something modern, breathable, preferably made of stretchy fabric. Everett still looked crisp in his white shirt.

"A moment, if you would," he said quietly.

They were alone. Michaela, superfluous to the meeting, had driven Stella's car back to the house, and Elizabeth and Leon walked ahead toward Everett's SUV.

"I would," said Stella.

The law office occupied an unlovely block, but it did have a broad-trunked, leafless tree along the parkway and a waist-high brick partition edging the property. Everett stopped her so they were partly secluded behind the tree and peered at her.

"We did it, you know," he said.

"Yeah." She tugged her coat higher around her neck. "Kinda feels like we got away with something criminal." She had seen the figure her aunt and his uncle had allocated for the maintenance fund. She didn't deserve the house, the inheritance, or such generous relatives.

He nodded. "You did well today, Stella."

"I did?"

"Yes."

She couldn't think of a single thing that she'd done especially well. Besides not fainting, perhaps, which was a low hurdle to have cleared. "Uh, thanks. What did I do?"

He reached out and traced a finger under her ear, along her jaw, to the point of her chin. "You were beautiful, which is a bride's prerequisite, is it not? You satisfied Elizabeth of your good intentions for her legacy, and you persuaded your best friend that you're not making ill-advised alliances. You impressed both the judge and the lawyer," he said. "And you impressed me."

She let his words wash through her and soak in. Everett's approval felt like the fresh air in her lungs was enough to float away on, to get high on, to live on forever. She could never let herself strive for his approbation, in fact had courted his disapproval, and here he'd casually delivered such compliments as she might have dreamed of. It was intoxicating.

And he'd called her beautiful.

"Thank you," she whispered, reluctant to let any space into the moment. She wanted that same air in her lungs to sustain her. "So were you, as always. Don't you ever get tired of being good?"

He leaned forward slightly, his weight on his toes. His fingers under her chin urged her head to tilt up. "Oh, yes."

"And what then?" she asked.

He reached for her waist with his other hand, his eyes warm and heavy-lidded. There were people elsewhere on the street, but a pack of lions could have appeared, and Stella wouldn't have looked away. He was going to kiss her again. Everett rounded his shoulders toward her and bent his head until their lips were nearly touching, until she was stretching up to meet him.

"And then," he said, "I am very, very good."

He kissed her hard. Stella inhaled the smell of him, the heat of his mouth and his skin. He moved both hands to her hips and snugged her up close. They'd had practice, after all. Stella looped an arm around the back of his neck. She angled her hips closer to feel the hard ridge of his erection. He was arrogant but correct—he *was* very, very good.

They broke apart a moment later. Everett grasped Stella's hand, and she flipped her skirt to resettle the fabric where he'd crushed it. Her breathing slowed. A couple in their early thirties was approaching on the sidewalk. The woman smiled knowingly.

"Newlyweds?" she asked.

Stella glanced at Everett, who wore happiness only she would have noticed. It was apparent in the creases beside his eyes and the faint tint of red lipstick on his gorgeous mouth.

"Yes," said Stella. "We are."

"Let's go home," Everett murmured in her ear.

"Yes."

Chapter 16

DEPARTURES

They drove back to Name Estate with Leon and Elizabeth in the backseat. The older couple were chattering, both clearly feeling carefree after having divested themselves of their largest responsibility. Stella's mood was dampened only by the knowledge that her aunt and uncle had a late flight to catch from Milwaukee.

"Don't forget about the binder on the shelf behind the desk," Leon said to Everett. "And the hanging file drawer. Those have manuals, warranties, and the number for my best plumber. There are old blueprints in a box in the basement. Oh, and I dragged my electronic files into that cloud folder you emailed me."

"Good," said Everett.

"There's an entire chicken in the freezer," said Elizabeth. "Too late to defrost it for tonight, of course, but please do use it. And a tray of lasagna. Remember the chest freezer in the garage if you want to stock up. Who knows what's in there, probably antique ground venison, but I'm not moving all that junk to Florida."

"You already said all that," said Leon. "Forget about the damned chicken. Did you tell them about the truck?"

"Yes, the truck," said Elizabeth. "Monday. But you don't need to be here to supervise."

"You told us," Stella confirmed. Elizabeth had hired movers to collect their personal effects, although some of the larger furniture was staying with the house.

"Because everything," said Elizabeth, "is working out perfectly. Just as I'd said."

"You were right, Lizzie," said Leon. "Everything."

Stella craned her head over her shoulder. They were holding hands in the backseat like middle-school sweethearts and sounded smugly pleased with themselves. Stella wanted to get them sent off so she could be alone with her husband.

But her wedding mood dissipated as Everett drove through the gates. In the long driveway, the headlights illuminated Michaela standing beside Stella's hatchback—which was pointed toward the exit. Her overstuffed bag was on the ground by her feet.

"What is she doing?" Stella blurted, although Michaela was clearly leaving. Stella hopped out of the SUV before it had completely stopped.

"Mickey," she called out.

When she got closer, she saw Michaela's face was scrunched into a tight, worried frown. "Stella, I got a call from Henry—"

Her husband. Stella halted, a hot ball of dread curdling in her stomach. "Oh, no. The kids? What happened? Is everyone all right?"

"Yes," said Michaela. "No. Mostly fine. Henry is with Jackson at the emergency room to get stitches in his lip. He apparently fell, although under what circumstances are unclear because Henry *somehow* didn't *witness* what happened to injure my two-year-old *son*. Who now needs four stitches in his perfect tiny baby mouth."

Her biting tone made it clear what she thought of Henry's loose supervision. "And Kira?"

"She's fine. Henry has her with him at the hospital, so I'm going to go pick her up and take her home while Henry stays with Jackson."

Chicago was over an hour away. The plan didn't make much sense to Stella. "What, now?" she said. "Are you sure you need to go? We were going to have dinner. They'll have Jackson patched up soon, and Kira probably has wi-fi on her tablet. Henry will—"

Michaela shook her head. "I need to go."

Elizabeth and Leon were leaving, too. Stella would be left with Everett...and the two neighbors she'd invited. It would be awkward. Everything was more awkward without Michaela. "It sounds like Henry has things under control. It is my wedding, after all."

"Not the kind of wedding with an RSVP for the steak or the fish." Michaela restlessly shifted her feet, then darted a glance at the waiting car.

"But I need you to help me!" Stella heard the whine in her own voice yet couldn't stop herself. "What am I supposed to do with—"

"Stop." Michaela raised both hands and spread them wide, parting Stella's objections like abandoned toys strewn on a rug. "Please step aside. Tell Everett to reverse out of the way. You don't need me, but my kids do. This is your life, Stella, so figure it out."

Stella had already crossed the line. She felt indignant anyway. "But you're taking my car."

Michaela pinned her with a stare. "Yes. I am. Move, please, before I decide to call you a selfish bitch, so I can get back to my children."

Stella surrendered. She hurried back to the driver's side of Everett's vehicle, where his window was already rolled down. His eyebrows were raised in a question, and in the backseat Elizabeth leaned forward. She could see they hadn't heard enough to know anything.

"Will you please back up and let Michaela get by?" she asked.

"Is she all right?" Everett asked. He already had the gear shifter moved into reverse. "No emergency, I hope."

Non-emergency, Stella thought sourly. How easy it was for her to slide from anticipation into self-pity. Yet another of her failings.

"Yeah, she's fine," she said. "Minor injury to her younger kid."

Everett stretched one arm across the headrest of the other seat, craned his head around, and smoothly reversed the big SUV out of the driveway. Stella stepped off the gravel and into the grass, and her heels (Michaela's heels) sank into the dirt. Michaela rolled by without pausing, without a word or a glance. The abruptness of her absence was like stomping through the nonexistent thirteenth step on a twelve-step staircase. Something as innocuous as *I'll call you tomorrow* would have been nice.

The taste in Stella's mouth was salted with abandonment. She thought she had done something meaningful, something real that day. A step toward the kind of adult life Michaela had already embraced. *Not the kind of wedding with an RSVP*, Michaela had said, as if her kind of wedding didn't really count. Her best friend had better places to be.

Stella turned and walked alone up the driveway in her wedding dress and her muddy heels. She stepped aside again as the black vehicle passed her. The forbidding, squared-off façade of the house was cloaked in afternoon shadows. It matched the dull, achy tiredness in her eyelids and in her mind. The wild swings of the day's events and emotions left her feeling like she'd attempted a marathon and failed to finish. If only she could go to bed and sleep until morning. But she had to help Elizabeth and Leon get organized and turned around for their flight, then she had hostess duties.

Everett was waiting by the steps when she walked up. "I am sorry about your friend," he said.

"It's not your fault," she said, with a shrug for falsified nonchalance.

"I know that. I meant I am sorry for the disappointment you must feel."

He was annoying, and he was investigating her feelings too closely. "Why should I be disappointed?" she snapped, turning her chin aside from his inspection. He wouldn't empathize with her most selfish instincts. "Obviously, Mickey needs to go be with her kid."

"Obviously," Everett repeated. "All right." He reached for her elbow, but the motion of his hand was tentative. A start, a hesitation, a jerky misdirection. Without conscious decision, Stella shied away. It was only a single step backward, although she saw his mouth tighten, and his hand returned to his side.

She didn't want his sense of *obligation*. The man was an absolute glutton for doing the right thing. She didn't want to be that to him. Let him reach for her when he couldn't resist her. Let him reach for her in desire and companionship and trust. But he didn't trust her, and she couldn't even trust herself not to cry over the tiniest, most insignificant slight, which Michaela had probably already forgotten.

She turned, stepped inside, and slammed the front door behind her.

Chapter 17

AN EMPTY BEDROOM

The front door promptly opened again. Everett was planted in the doorway, pinning Stella in place with his flinty frown and a pair of creases between his eyebrows.

"No," he said. "No, you don't. I do not endorse door-slamming and unexplained fits of temper on our wedding day or indeed in our married life."

She glared right back at him. "I won't be a recipient of your bottomless well of obligation and reluctant gestures of nobility." She shoved the panel, but the door didn't swing. Everett had his forearm braced across the outside.

"Good, because that is not at all how I am feeling at the moment," he said. "Move aside, let me through, then follow me. Leon and Elizabeth need to pack their bags for the flight, and we will allow them privacy in their own space for their last time as residents here."

"I'll go to my room and stay out of their way—"

"No. Come with me."

"Bossy."

"Come." He angled his shoulders and slid past her into the house, removing his overcoat with a shrug.

With him out of the way, she saw Elizabeth and Leon making their way up the sidewalk from the parking pad, arm in arm. They did appear wrapped in their own world. Stella groaned and, after dropping her coat and heels in the entryway, followed Everett as instructed.

He surprised her by leading her downstairs to her guest room. He knelt beside her bag and looked over his shoulder at her.

"May I?" he asked, pointing at the zipped duffel.

"May you what?" she asked, blinking.

He slowly slid open the zip of her battered canvas bag, and Stella shivered as she inadvertently imagined him undressing her with the same expression of focused intent on his face.

"You can't wear that dress all evening," he said gruffly, riffling through her clothing, which was crammed in haphazard fashion. "Although it looks nice. It's making your arms itchy, and you need sturdy shoes if we're going to the pond."

She studied the back of his neck. "To look for fish."

He pulled out a fuzzy pink sweater and a pair of black yoga leggings that Stella had never worn to yoga. "Here, put these on. Yes, to look for fish. Unless you prefer to take another refreshing dip. Do you want this bra?" A piece of frilly lace dangled from one of his fingers.

Stella pressed her lips together before mustering a response. "Have I mentioned you're bossy?"

"Quite recently. Do you need help getting out of that antique?"

She grabbed her clothing. "Michaela would tell you to call it *vintage*. No, thank you."

She faced the wall and shimmied out of her wedding dress, aware that it was the second time she'd undressed with him in the room in the last week.

"While you were first arguing with Michaela and then pouting over her departure," Everett said, and she could pinpoint the direction of his voice well enough to know that this time, he watched her, "I pulled this note off the security box at the gate."

Stella fastened her bra and pulled her sweater over her head. He'd picked one with a wide neckline, and it slid off one shoulder. She passed him her wedding dress in a frothy clump in exchange for a thin manila envelope with a neon-yellow sticker on the front. *DELINQUENT*, it screamed. Stella was familiar with the sort of sticker from several occasions when she'd fallen behind on her cellular service bill.

As interested as she was in the new letter, something else Everett had said caught her immediate attention. "Pouting?" she repeated. "I was *pouting*?"

He shook the wrinkles and folds from the dress, then went to the closet for a hanger. "Focus, Stella."

"Yes, I am, believe me. You assigned a derogatory word to my behavior." She was perversely energized by his assessment. Her astonishment even overcame her wounded pride...and he was probably correct about the pouting. "You're mad at me for being mad about Michaela."

"That's ridiculous." He hung her dress from the clothing rod.

"Tsk, Everett! Rude again. You must be really, truly pissed off." A fragment of her card-reading skillset pushed its way to the front of her mind. He was an irresistible subject of analysis, especially when the corners of his mouth tightened in a way that invited torment. "Let's consider. Why would that have made you angry?"

"I was not...Listen, I should not have said you were pouting, all right?" He exhaled noisily. "Please accept my apology for using such a rude, if apt, gerund for the way you stuck out your lower lip when you failed to get your own way."

"That was a terrible apology. But let's get back to you." Stella tapped a forefinger on her lip, the same one Everett was complaining about. His eyes dropped to follow the movement. "I think you were mad that I was reacting to Mickey's—"

"Some might say *over*reacting," he said.

"—To Mickey's departure," Stella continued, "because in the shadowed hallways of your mind, it reflected poorly on you, somehow. It wasn't about Mickey, clearly. You don't care if she stays or goes."

"I like Michaela, and I hope her son is feeling better soon," said Everett.

"Sure. But that's not enough to upset you. She abandoned me, I felt sorry for myself, then I hated myself for feeling sorry for myself. Then I hated myself for hating myself. It's a boring whirlwind of self-loathing. What kind of off-brand toaster pastry of a human being lacking any common sense or perspective pities themselves after marrying a nice, extremely handsome man and inheriting a huge asset? I do, apparently. Therefore, I'm irritated. But then, interestingly, *you're* irritated. Why do you think that is?"

"You tell me," he shot back.

She sat on the edge of the bed, tossed the envelope aside, and set her mind to untangling him like a Sunday crossword. "I got irritated with myself. Michaela left, and I felt alone. Abandoned. Therefore, I humbly suggest that you were irritated because my reaction negated your presence entirely, as if you weren't with me at all, and you don't like feeling negated." And Stella was pierced by a dart of understanding. She had hurt him. In her thoughtlessness, in her mistaken belief that she couldn't hurt him because he couldn't possibly care what she thought or what she said. But perhaps he did, after all. She winced. "For which I am actually-factually non-ironically sorry."

"You're not alone, and you're not abandoned," he said in tacit acknowledgment of her accuracy. "Look, Stella, I apologize, too. Today is already an earthquake of a day. Give yourself a fragment of grace for feeling rattled, and I'd ask the same for myself. I can't bear you analyzing me any further. I tremble at the thought of your powers of observation when you choose to devote yourself to a goal," he said, meeting her eyes again, "if you are so astonishing now with little effort."

Stella snorted. He was absurd. But he had managed to gently jostle a piece of truth from her, and she was relieved. "Please do tremble. That sounds like something I might like to see."

"I want to return to an important point you made a moment ago," he said.

"What?"

"*Extremely handsome.* That's a direct quote. I thought you expressed that idea very nicely. You were eloquent, succinct, and relevant." He raised his eyebrows, clearly baiting her.

Her amusement expanded into a full laugh. "I retract. You are awful, and I extend no forgiveness to you for repeating a compliment given in a moment of abstraction."

"No?" The dark focus of his gaze dropped to her mouth. "Let me earn it, then."

Stella had no reply. Everett closed the bedroom door.

He edged closer, erasing the gap between them.

"What did you have in, um—" she began. He raised his eyebrows and touched her bare thigh, a whisper of a fingertip on her skin. Her muscles relaxed like he'd hypnotized her, and her knees fell open. She hadn't yet managed to don her leggings. He leaned forward. His hands closed hard on her waist and lifted her backward until she was centered on the bed.

The house was quiet except for the distant noise of waves that matched the low pressure of her heartbeat. He bent his head and smoothed his lips across her exposed collarbone, and she shuddered with both nerves and pleasure.

"Oh," she said.

"No, you're right, we can't do this now," he muttered. "I said we were going to look for fish. Maybe later, after we have the house to ourselves, we can—"

"No! I mean yes. We can do this now." Stella reached up to take his face between her hands. Her knees urged him closer. She wasn't even sure what *this* was, but she was confident there was no better time. "You have to earn your compliment."

She slid her sweater over her head and raked the static out of her hair. Everett studied her like there would be a quiz afterward.

"You said you have three tattoos," he said.

She twisted her torso and showed him her shoulder blade. "One," she said, indicating a small flower with a yellow center. "For my dog Daisy, who died when I was nineteen. I had her through most of my childhood, and I think she was the only reason I survived my parents' divorce.

"Two." The marking was on the back of her neck, a thin vertical chain like an ornate lamp pull. It was usually hidden by her hair. Michaela had a similar piece. They'd gotten them together on spring break in Las Vegas.

"I noticed that one," he said.

"That's the one I don't really remember picking out, but I still like it. And..." she turned back to face him. "Three."

She unhooked her bra, slid the straps off her shoulders, and let it fall. Her third and most recent piece was a geometric, art deco diamond that stretched between and beneath her breasts. The lines were simple and clean, with swathes of tiny beads and a circle at the center meant to represent a full moon. It was new enough, only about eight months old, that no one had seen it except her tattooist and Michaela. And now her husband, on the day of their wedding.

"Do you like it?" she asked.

Everett appeared dazed. "I don't know," he said. "I haven't finished looking yet."

Stella laughed and reached for him. He gripped her waist and glided his thumbs over her tattoo. With another inch, he was fondling her breasts, and Stella arched against him. He kissed her shoulders, her throat. It wasn't long before she wanted him so badly it made her stomach hurt. The buildup of her impatience felt like more than the minutes they'd been alone together, or even the short time since they'd become involved. It felt like ten years of impatience, of frustrated desire for Everett Novak, clenched in her belly. It was powerful enough to overcome the insistent voice in her mind that said *he can't really like you.*

She became aware of the amorous nonsense he was whispering in her ear, silly mumblings about how she was lovely and delicious, about how she smelled like caramel, about how he couldn't possibly do all the terrible, wonderful things he wanted to do to her. He whispered once that she was utterly perfect, which was how Stella knew he didn't really hear what he was rumbling about, much less mean it literally. She threaded her hands into his hair and pulled his head closer so she could hear more of his sweet lies.

When she finally had him where she'd wanted him, she felt impossibly good. They felt impossibly good together, and his desperate whispers in her ear told her he knew it, too. She reached for his belt buckle, this time on purpose.

"Stella?" came a call from upstairs. "Are you downstairs?"

Stella ignored her aunt. She tugged the tang free of the leather and unfastened Everett's trousers. His breath was hard against her ear.

"Stella? Everett?" Elizabeth repeated, a strident yell.

"Don't," she whispered to him. "Don't even think about it."

"I'm not, I promise. I can't." he said.

She kissed him with the fervor demanded by such acquiescence.

But then, a moment later, Elizabeth's slow steps tapped on the first few wooden stairs. Her tread was light and tentative, unlike her voice.

"Stella?" she called. "I need you for something. Are you down there?"

Stella squeezed her eyes closed, released her grip on the waistband of Everett's trousers, and sighed in defeat.

"I am," she yelled back. "What do you need?"

Everett winced at her volume so close to his ear, all his weight braced above her on one knee and both elbows.

"Bring up the two big suitcases from the closet in that guest bedroom, please," said Elizabeth.

"All right. In a minute."

The sound of Elizabeth's steps paused, then reversed. Everett heaved himself upright. His hair was mussed. Without a word he went to the closet, hoisted the luggage, and set it down. His shirt hung open, exposing his pale and tempting torso, and Stella wished she were capable of resisting her aunt.

"We were discussing," he said, "I believe, the letter I found on the mailbox."

Based on his tone, Stella was resigned that he would not be rejoining her in bed. Not immediately, anyway. She swept an arm across the duvet until she came upon the discarded envelope. "Yes. We were."

"You'll be the one going to jail for fish crimes, so you get to read it first."

"*I'll* be—?" she squawked. "Why would *I* be the one to—"

She then saw a spiky glint of devilry in his eyes. A joke. An olive branch to smooth over the awkwardness of their unfinished interlude.

"Humph," she said, mirroring his mischievous humor. "If I am ever sent to jail, it will be for pummeling you in the stomach."

"No jury would convict you after any minor acquaintance with me, I'm sure." He took the envelope and extracted a single sheet, which he passed to Stella.

Stella read. "Polite exhortations couched in bureaucratic terms," she said. "Very repetitive, honestly. Violations of state regulations, mandatory inspection. These people are hot about sturgeon."

"I'm glad no one was here when they stopped by," said Everett. He retrieved the second suitcase from the shelf. Stella glanced up to watch the play of muscle under his skin. She found her bra, sweater, and leggings, and dressed again.

"Me, too. Can you imagine Elizabeth's face reading this garbage?"

"I was envisioning Leon's blood pressure skyrocketing."

"Stella?" Elizabeth called down again. "Did you find those suitcases, sweetie? They should be on the top—"

"Yes," said Stella hurriedly. "Yes, sorry, one minute."

Everett buttoned and tidied himself to perfection—apart from a pink mark at the base of his neck, visible inside the notch of his collar, that Stella had left upon him. He took both pieces of luggage and schlepped them up the flight to the main floor.

Stella left the door open to the guest bedroom and followed him, after a final forlorn glance at the empty bed.

Chapter 18

FISHING RETREAT

"Right there, yes, thank you, dear," said Elizabeth, directing Everett to leave her luggage in the hall. "What were you two doing down there for so long? Anyway, we're almost done packing. A bit more time should do it. Will you drive us to the airport? Stella, what's that letter you have? Did you find that in the guest closet, too? I didn't think we had anything else down there."

Stella moved her hand behind her back. "It's nothing. Junk mail."

"I'll be happy to drive you," said Everett. "Give me a shout when you're ready."

"We're going out to look at the sturgeon pond," said Stella.

Elizabeth frowned. "Why?"

"To fish for caviar."

"Not in February, sweetie. But have fun. Bundle up." Elizabeth wheeled both suitcases toward the north wing of the house, where she and Leon had their primary bedroom.

"Let's go." Everett handed Stella her coat, and she stuffed her feet into someone else's rubber galoshes. "We're trying to keep all this away from them, you do recall," he said.

"Yeah, except I'm inexperienced in conducting covert operations. I told Elizabeth I'd be here to check on things after their moving truck has departed, although really, I want to look for fish." He opened the door and gestured, and she walked outside. "The last thing we need is the DNR tracing Elizabeth and Leon to their Florida address. Staring into the pond feels like something I can do to help. Even though I know looking for fish is not the same as summoning fish."

"I doubt we're allowed to sprinkle fish flakes. Ecologically speaking."

"Aren't you going back to Milwaukee? For your work." It was odd and pleasant to talk to Everett like a coconspirator, like a friend...maybe almost like a boyfriend, given the way they'd been making out in the guest room.

"Yes, I have to go into the office, and I need time in my studio for a sculpture that's been on my mind...but it's only an hour from here. However much this place feels like a far corner of the earth, it's really not. I was thinking of..." He gestured vaguely at the house, although part of his wave seemed to scoop her up, too.

"You want to drive back here? In the evenings?" she asked to be certain. Otherwise, she wouldn't believe it.

Everett glanced at her, then returned his attention to the uneven mulched path. "Didn't we already discuss that I want to live here? Yes, I would, if you don't mind."

"No, no, I don't mind," she said. "I misunderstood that you meant... immediately. As in, like, this week."

"You could get irritated by having me around all the time."

"I might," she said. "I might not."

"You could become bored of me."

"Anything's possible. It's also possible that *I* will aggravate *you* like a pebble in your shoe," she said. "Like a papercut on your pinkie."

He inclined his head. "Like a song I can't get out of my mind," he said.

She dropped her chin to her chest. He still seemed unreal, and she cared too much. It was tempting to forget she'd overheard how little he really felt for her. She put some distance between them with a quick step, then another, hurrying along the path.

But Everett stayed right behind her. "Stella," he said. "Wait." He touched the inside of her elbow. She stopped, turned, almost without thinking. She wished she could resist his slightest impulse. He urged her under the heavy, spreading branches of a bare maple. "We were interrupted," he murmured, leaning closer.

"We don't have time," she said through the buzz in her brain. "You'll have to leave soon to make their flight."

"There's no traffic." He whispered it against her cheek, then pulled at her coat's zipper, exposing her throat to his mouth. "The roads will be clear."

"Hmm." Stella didn't feel the chill. The faint scent of him was a relentless tease. "You would break the speed limit? Not very responsible, Everett. In fact, you should probably leave now to be safe."

"I'd rather stay," he said.

He was hot and cold. Too much, too confusing. She understood him not at all, and she was accustomed to understanding nearly everyone. "But you left me in the bedroom, minutes ago."

"Only under duress, and I regretted it immediately."

She squeezed her eyes closed. "Everett, I can't think."

"Then don't. All you need to remember is that we were married this morning. You're my wife. I want to know you everywhere."

What *he* wanted. How was she supposed to respond to what he wanted when she didn't understand herself? It lit a brutal defensive fire in her, and she leaned forward. "Are you sure?" she said into his ear. "After all, for that you'd have to get close enough to me. And if it weren't for the enticement of owning this estate, you would have no reason to speak to me at all."

Everett twitched once, then fell motionless. He opened and closed his mouth.

Stella smiled tightly. She was certain she had quoted him nearly precisely. The terrible words he had said to Leon had seared into her brain, after all. She'd might as well put the memory to use if it was going to haunt her anyway. They had to address the truth of his opinion of her if they were to proceed with any sort of honesty.

"You—" he said finally. "What do you mean? Did you..."

"Yes, I overheard you speaking to Leon." She crossed her arms. "On the terrace. I was barely even eavesdropping."

"You heard that, and yet you said earlier you don't despise me. I can't believe it." Faint pink smudges appeared on his cheeks. "Stella, it's not what you think. Allow me to explain."

"Everett?" Leon shouted from somewhere beyond the trees. "Time to go."

"Shit," Everett muttered. "Five minutes," he yelled.

"Nope," said Leon loudly.

Stella waited and affixed a firm smile on her face. It was rather pleasant to see Everett squirming under the weight of his own bad behavior, for once, rather than herself.

"Stella, please," he said. "I'll be back in an hour. We'll talk then, all right?"

"Of course, dear," she said. "I would never dream of disobeying my husband." She rezipped her coat and brushed past him.

Chapter 19

RELUCTANT HOSTESS

Stella tried, she really tried, to restore her mindset before dinner. She drank a cup of tea. She daubed the dirt from Michaela's shoes and set them aside to be returned. To a certain extent, those normal actions were effective. After slipping into her own clothing, she felt much more like herself.

But the problem was *herself* wasn't a great feeling. The wedding, the inheritance, and most of all, Everett—they had helped her see the possibility of becoming someone different. Those types of good, important, notable events and people didn't generally happen to her. But her familiar preoccupations came creeping back. Had she seriously thought for a moment she could make all this work? Everett was too smart not to see that she wasn't cut out for someone like him. He said he had some explanation for the cruel remark he'd made to Leon, but Stella couldn't envision anything that would persuade her.

So, she had smiled, distributed hugs, and wiped away a few tears when Elizabeth and Leon departed. They both promised that Stella and Everett could call with any questions about the house or the land. The offer was sincere, Stella was certain, but the older couple had their own lives to focus on and Leon's medical issues to manage. She didn't intend to bother them. *This is your life, Stella, so figure it out.*

After what felt like a week of goodbyes, she had the house to herself.

It was fully dark when Everett returned a bit later than he had said and carrying a cloth grocery bag. In the kitchen Stella was assembling a tray of appetizers from Elizabeth's pantry and attempting to arrange her selections artfully. She wished she had Takis Fuego to add a pop of color. There wasn't much else to do, really. She threw a cheerful top-hits playlist from her phone to the kitchen speakers. The floors, countertops, and powder room were already clean—did Elizabeth employ a cleaning service? Stella had never thought to inquire. It was a lot of house to keep tidy. She was a new lady of the manor without maids or footmen.

Everett set the bag on the counter. He watched her, as cautious as a wolf surveilling a twitchy rabbit he intended to catch. "That looks great," he said.

"Thank you," Stella said calmly. She kept her head down, focused on the platter before her. "What do you have there?"

One by one, he extracted a pint of fresh blackberries, a fifth of bourbon, a package of gingerbread cookies, and a half-gallon of vanilla ice cream. "Ingredients for the most delicious milkshake neither of us has ever had," he said. "Peace offering. There are a few things I want to tell you, Stella. One thing, really. I should have told you before we...before today."

She couldn't bear to raise her head. "I really don't need a lot of explanation for your low opinion of me. You're entitled to it. I can't even tell you you're wrong. But we're married now, so I thought it was better to put the truth out in the open. Maybe I'll be able to change your mind about me, one day. But in the meantime, you don't have to pretend anything you don't feel. And you don't owe me white lies or excuses."

Everett pulled a blender from a deep shelf. He scooped ice cream into it, then added the fruit, cookies, and a splash of alcohol. The resulting purplish-beige concoction he poured into a glass.

He passed the glass to Stella, who sipped cautiously.

"It's both more and less complicated," he said, "and it's not entirely about you. Come here. Please."

She was already within his arms' reach, but he didn't grab at her. He let her step forward. She kept one hand on her shake, raised the other to his shoulder, and he settled his hands on her waist. The playlist changed to a wistful crooning. They swayed together.

"Then what is it?" she asked.

He rested his chin atop her head. "How's the Stella?"

"How am I?"

"No, the milkshake. I christened it the Stella."

"Unusual. Can't say the color would look good on a menu board. But it's really very tasty."

She felt his smile.

"Then it fits its namesake," he said. "The truth is that ten years ago, before that memorable vecherinka we both attended, I...well. I don't talk about it very much, to anyone, really. I received some news that was bad on top of bad, and it felt like the end of something that never really started. The new reality was a much-narrowed scope of future choices. But I—"

The gate security system chirped twice from a box mounted on the wall. Everett twitched and straightened. Stella glanced at the clock in the microwave. Marvin and his visitor were right on time. She stepped reluctantly away from Everett and set aside her sweet drink.

Everett tweaked his cuffs, although his sleeves were perfectly straight. He'd changed at some point from his starchy white shirt into a starchy blue shirt. "I will go deal with our guests," he said, all business, his secrets unrevealed. He pressed the button that activated the gate's hydraulic arm.

Stella gritted her teeth. She could do this. She *had* to. She'd already signed up for the life, and she sure as hell wasn't crawling back to Chicago, to her terrible superintendent and the clients she could never respect and her friend who had a separate, adult life to lead. She could have dinner with the neighbors and her husband, who had something he clearly didn't want to tell her.

Besides, the oven was already preheating. Wasn't that a sign of her fantastic organizational skills and graceful hostessing? She chose a glass jar of Name Estate caviar from the fridge, positioned it on her tray as the final touch, then picked up her wineglass and followed Everett.

Everett had made it halfway along the hall, intending to open the door alone, but he paused. He looked at Stella. She dropped her eyes to the stemware in her hand, then he was back by her side.

"You can trust me a little bit, you know," he said.

She studied his earnest expression and said nothing.

He raised his hand slowly toward her face, as if she might flinch away, but Stella remained still. He smoothed a few strands of hair behind her ear, his hand lingering. "We're on the same side now."

He was offering her the loan of some of his terrible competence. She exhaled slowly, then leaned her cheek into the cup of his palm. A part of her had wanted to marry Everett for exactly this reason. He could do anything, and she could ride along beside him. She didn't have to be perfect; she just had to be on Everett's team. It didn't matter if he *liked* her. He would always behave with utmost propriety at a dinner party.

"You're not going to enjoy having these strangers in our house, are you?" she asked.

"Good lord, no," he said, recoiling as if she'd suggested committing a white-collar crime or buying grocery-store sushi. "Not in the slightest."

"Thanks," she said, and she meant it. *That* reaction had been honest, at least. They had something in common.

They answered the door together. It would take a few moments for the guests to proceed along the lane to the house. But after Everett swung the panel wide, admitting a chill evening breeze, he remained planted squarely at the threshold.

Through darkness pierced by the porchlight, Stella made out two figures approaching, one stout and stooped, the other of average build. Everett draped an arm around her shoulders like they'd been accustomed to such casually intimate maneuvers for years.

"Good evening," Everett announced. "Everett Novak."

The shorter man wore a smile and held a bottle of red wine, while the other hung back a step and flicked a cigarette butt into the shrubs.

"Hello." The stout man exchanged a handshake with Everett. "Thanks for the invitation. Marvin Fehr. Dinner at Name Estate? Didn't even try to resist. And you must be Stella. Kindly rang my bell this morning."

Stella smiled and inclined her head. The man's accent wasn't of Wisconsin origins but rather had taller vowel sounds, something shipped in from the east coast. The half-dome of his forehead overwhelmed the rest of his features. His speech was clipped, aggressively casual, like what he said was so clearly obvious to all involved it didn't require effort. It was time to invite them inside, rather than continuing introductions on the stoop. Everett had not stepped aside from the doorway, however, so she nudged his ribcage. He did not move.

"And, ah," said Marvin, gesturing to the person beside him, "my friend and associate, Sergey Golubev. From out of town and staying through the season."

"Hello," said the taller man, with a faint aspiration on the front of the word. He was dark-haired and handsome with a shadow of beard scruff on his chin and cheeks. The two men were a mismatched pair, and Stella couldn't imagine what Sergey found to entertain himself along their chilly, isolated coastline. "You are very beautiful, Mrs. Novak. Your husband must be charmed."

"Call me Stella," she said with a light laugh. She decided to ignore his flirtatious remark. "We're still in the darkest winter. I would have thought the tourist season was July and August, Mr. Golubev."

From Sergey came a hard, furtive scowl so brief Stella would have missed had she not been watching. His expression cleared almost immediately to politesse. "I would be pleased if you both would call me Sergey," he said in perfect English with a minor eastern European accent. "My business often takes me away from the tourists and into the truly beautiful places in the world. But in my country, this winter would be called mild."

"It's mild here, too," said Stella. "Far too mild. Anyway, pleased to meet you."

"Sergey," said Everett, inclining his head. "A pleasure. I must admit, however, that we've had a bit of a complication in our schedule this evening."

Stella elbowed him in the ribs again. What on earth was he doing?

"My wife and I," Everett continued, and he flexed the arm that was slung around Stella's shoulders, "are amidst an important conversation. Not a fight but a topic of marital importance that I really hate to postpone."

"Everett," Stella murmured warningly. It was odd for her to inhabit the *responsible* role.

"Oh." Marvin's genial smile faded. "We interrupt. Did I have the time wrong? Or date? Stella mentioned this evening, yeah?"

"No, no, it's not your mistake; it's my fault entirely," said Everett. "However, I do wonder if you'd be so kind as to reschedule for next weekend?"

It was so breathtakingly rude and yet spoken so *politely* that Stella could not restrain a laugh of disbelief. He wanted to cancel their dinner plans on the spot in order to continue a conversation with her? "Everett," she gasped. "That's ridiculous. Please, Marvin, Sergey, forgive my strange husband and come inside."

She shoulder-checked Everett. He shifted no more than an inch.

Marvin remained on the stoop, and flat malcontent settled over his face. "Wouldn't dare to intrude. Clearly, you're busy. We'll go."

"Hold on, please." Stella glared up at Everett. They had to talk to Marvin about the DNR survey. That was why she'd invited him in the first place. If he had any knowledge of the agency or the research project, it could cast much-needed light on the legitimacy of the officer's threats and how to resolve them. "We can resume our discussion later, Ev. Don't forget we had a few questions to ask our neighbor about his experiences living in the area."

Everett was unmoved. "Which we can ask another time. After we've finished our conversation."

Sergey muttered something inaudible.

"All right. We are leaving," said Marvin. "We walked over. Might as well walk back."

"Wait."

It was a light, tremulous, female voice. Marvin and Sergey both turned around, and Stella peered into the gloom beyond them. From the scrub along the edge of the lane, a figure emerged and came closer. Stella squinted.

"Wonderful," Everett said under his breath. "*More* people. Why the hell do we even bother locking the gate?"

She didn't respond. It wasn't *people*, despite his complaint, but rather a single person, a petite woman. When the woman crept within the porchlight's glow, Stella required a moment to process whom she was looking at.

She stepped over the threshold and squeezed between Marvin and Sergey. "Allison?" she called out. "Allison, is that you?"

It was her client from Chicago, the woman who had buzzed her apartment while Stella was in the shower the previous weekend and been summarily turned away.

"Yes." Allison's thin voice grew slightly stronger as she ventured closer. "I'm so sorry."

"How did you get—" Stella stopped. She must have slipped inside the gate behind their guests. "*Why* are you here? How did you find this place?"

"I really need to talk to you, and you would barely speak to me last week," Allison said, pitching very close to a whine. "I intended to catch you on your way home, honestly, I tried to avoid causing any inconvenience, but then I realized it wasn't you driving your car. It was someone else. Did you know that? Was your car stolen by that...that woman?"

Some fearful, pathetic note in Allison's question implied *that Black woman*. Stella gripped her temper by the leash. "That woman is my best friend. You, on the other hand, I don't know at all. You shouldn't be here, Allison."

"You do know me better than anyone. I said I was sorry, but you didn't respond to my emails, and now you've been away two weekends in a row. I need to talk to you again about my husband. I was nearly into the city when I realized that wasn't you driving your car, and I came all the way back here. I'm so tired."

"Then you should go home," Stella said abruptly. Name Estate was supposed to be a haven from her clients, safe from the work that embarrassed her. The night's wintery stillness was broken only by the humans around her and a coyote yipping twice in the distance. She had promised Everett that her customers wouldn't find this address. That promise had only survived a week.

From the men on the porch, however, the awkward silence became noisy. Someone coughed, another was shuffling his feet—not Everett, he was not a fidgeter.

Everett cleared his throat. "It is getting rather late," he said. "Perhaps we should all go inside for a drink."

There was a moment of hesitation, and Stella thought Marvin was too offended and would refuse. But Sergey said, "Fantastic!"

Allison was already hurrying toward the house. Stella groaned and followed her.

At the porch, Everett shepherded their guests inside. Stella narrowed her eyes and stopped. She waited a moment as Marvin handed off his bottle of red and disappeared into the kitchen.

"You," she whispered to Everett, "cannot banish invited guests simply because you prefer to continue arguing with me instead."

With one foot wedged against the sill and his back against the doorframe, he looked adamant enough to hold up the walls of the house through sheer willfulness. "Yes, I can," he said. "And I'll do it again. Any argument with you is more important than any guest. You, however, seem to have a customer service problem in your business. Primarily that you have not displayed any intention of offering your customers any service."

Stella shook her head. "Allison doesn't need customer service; she needs to use her own noggin for once. I'll talk to her briefly and send her home. And you don't know anything about my customer service."

Everett compressed his lips but said nothing. He vacated the doorway and gestured for her to enter. Stella brushed past him. Although she was annoyed with him, she couldn't help but inhaling his now-familiar scent. They needed to get through dinner, then they'd have time to themselves. Everett could finish explaining himself. Two hours until then, maybe three. Nothing more. She drew back her shoulders, expelled a rush of air, and settled a pleasant smile on her face. Everett touched the small of her back with hesitant fingertips, skimming across the fabric of her shirt. It agitated her. She wanted his palm pressed hard into her spine, or he may as well leave her alone.

"All right?" he asked softly.

She nodded once and took hold of Marvin's wine. "Fine. Let's get this over with."

Chapter 20

THREE READINGS

In the gentle light of the kitchen, the three visitors made a cozy scene. Coats were discarded over the backs of chairs, and the guests were snacking from Stella's carefully assembled platter. Her smile slipped only a fraction before she recovered it. She wasted a moment wishing desperately for Michaela, who would have been funny and charming and snarky and made the party tolerable.

The only bit of oddness was that Sergey and Allison were standing close together, and while Sergey wore a benign smile, Allison blinked too often and looked befuddled. She quickly stepped sideways as Everett and Stella entered.

"So, Marvin," Everett said genially, as if he hadn't attempted to turn away Marvin at the door only minutes prior, "I understand that you've lived on this stretch of coastline for quite some time?"

Marvin wafted a cracker through the air, sketching a long line. "Decades," he said. "House belonged to my grandparents, in fact. Much older than this modern monstrosity. No offense."

"Hmm," Everett said.

Stella went to the wine refrigerator and stashed the bottle Marvin had brought, then pulled out a chilled white. She poured some for the others but none for herself. Her brain already felt swampy, like she was operating through an aquarium filter, and alcohol would not help her mood. She hefted the tray of Elizabeth's homemade lasagna and slid it into the hot oven. Beads of sweat gathered almost immediately along her hairline.

"Leon called yesterday saying he'd be off to fairer shores," said Marvin. "Didn't know it would be so quick. Sad to see them go, of course. Hard to find good neighbors. But fresh blood is nice."

"And it's so kind of you and your wife to assume the care of this place," Sergey said. "So many things to consider. I can imagine it would become burdensome for the elderly." He flicked a glance at Stella. "You two have been married long?"

Everett made a strange sound in his throat that might have been a cough or a strangled laugh.

Stella busied herself with adding more cheese to the rapidly disappearing pile. Allison slathered Name Estate's delicate caviar over a cracker like it was chunky peanut butter and put the whole thing in her mouth. Stella was absolutely *not* cracking open a second jar of caviar for them. Let them fight over the last few nibbles on the tray. Allison closed her eyes and moaned as she chewed.

"Not long," Stella said. "Not very long at all. Feels like just yesterday. Right, my love?"

She said the endearment with enough sweetness that Everett turned his glittering eyes toward her.

"Doesn't it?" Everett came around to her side of the counter and circled one arm around her waist. He squeezed her against his hip and planted a noisy kiss atop her head. "I'd say it almost feels like today. Anyway, Mr. Fehr—"

"Marvin, please."

"Marvin," Everett acknowledged with a nod. "Do you have experience with the state DNR's annual resource survey?"

The neighbor blinked, apparently not expecting that topic. Stella was discomfited, too, but for other reasons. Everett's arm was still around her midsection, and he showed no sign of releasing her. She squirmed slightly and somehow ended up plastered even closer against his ribcage. Allison, at the end of the island, leaned forward onto her elbows. Stella became aware the woman was trying strenuously to make eye contact, but Allison could wait.

"Yes," said Marvin. "Great annual fish count? Heard plenty, no direct experience. If only I were so lucky. Nobody wants to look at my piddly, useless section of the creek. Minor hassle, so long as your fish are present and thriving. All for the best."

"Did Leon ever mention anything to you about it? Complaints about the process or the conservation wardens, anything?"

"Nope. Why?"

Stella managed to escape from the heavy weight of Everett's arm. He was very annoying and warm. No one should be expected to stand complacently beside him, least of all his wife. She moved to the safety of the far cabinets.

"The DNR is implying that Leon killed all the sturgeon," she said.

Everett turned his head sharply toward her and widened his eyes. Combined with the fractional tilt to his chin, she understood it as a silent rebuke.

"Did he?" Sergey asked.

"I would not say they implied that," Everett said, facing Marvin again. "We're getting caught up on delayed paperwork and trying to get accustomed to the new circumstances."

Marvin nodded. "Nothing to it, really. You grant access to the property. State vehicles will clog up your lane. Because we're so isolated, the officers might ask to use the powder room. A pot of coffee wouldn't go amiss. Couple of days at most, I'd guess. Again, though, no spawning pond on my land, so that's my basic impression. I'd trade your plot for mine if I could in a flash. Long as the fish weren't all taken." He chuckled. "A protected species? If they were, whole host of other problems."

"The sturgeon could not have been overfished," Everett said calmly. "I'm sure the survey won't be a problem. Thank you for sharing your insight."

While they talked, Allison had been shifting her weight like a toddler who needed to pee. The woman clearly had no interest in fish murder. She was bursting with impatience to address whatever dire need for fake fortunetelling had compelled her to stalk Stella and trespass at her home.

"All right, Allison," Stella said heavily. "You've got my attention for ten minutes. Do you want to talk here or privately in the study?"

Allison straightened up and ran a hand over her limp hair. "Do you have your cards?"

"Cards?" Sergey repeated. He had been listening patiently to the fish conversation, but he stirred at the change in topic. "Would that be business cards, or...?"

Stella turned to Allison with the intention of herding her out of the room, but it was too late.

"Stella," Allison announced, "is talented in cartomancy. She senses things about people, about the future, and interprets the cards. Her readings for me have been nothing short of miraculous."

Everett knelt in front of the wine fridge, opened the door, and rattled among the bottles.

"Very, very, interesting," said Sergey. "What an incredible woman. Will you perform a reading for me? I would not dare to ask a doctor to examine a bad toenail at a dinner party, but..." He shrugged expansively, then pushed both sleeves up as if preparing to get down to serious work. "I must venture to ask. Do you ever mix business with pleasure?"

The comparison of divination cards to an infected toenail was apt. Neither was appropriate to display at a table surrounded by strangers and guests.

"Her reading is not," Allison said with stiff formality, "a carnival trick. The insights gained take quiet concentration to process, and the deep nature of the questions is too personal for a group setting."

Stella grimaced. Allison sounded much like a carnival barker, despite her disavowal. All she needed was a cape. *Ladies and gents, step right up to be conned out of a nickel.*

"You only intrigue me more, ma'am," said Sergey. "Now I will cut before you in the queue of people who want to speak to your spiritual advisor. Stella, may I insist? What is your rate for a session? I know you are a professional."

She did not look over at Everett, but she knew his shoulders and back were stiff. He liked this no more than she did. It was Allison's fault for showing up, for raising the topic. Stella directed her frown at the blonde woman. It seemed too much effort to put up a major fuss, and her eventual concession felt inevitable. She could agree to read for Sergey, compel Allison to wait a little longer—and, if she dared to be honest with herself, show off her odd skill in front of Everett. He wouldn't approve, of course, but he might be impressed anyway.

"Fetch my deck," Stella commanded. "In the nightstand drawer of the first downstairs guest bedroom."

"Of course." Allison turned obediently toward the stairs. "Because Stella does not handle the cards," she explained to the room. "To maintain their purity."

Her footsteps were a light tap as she scurried off on her chore. Sergey exchanged a glance with Marvin, eyebrows raised. They'd surely find much to discuss later at home about why the mistress of the house with her apparently happy marriage kept personal possessions in the guest bedroom. Stella's twitchy mood had her palms sweating. Everett opened the oven and rotated the pan of lasagna, then turned up the dial. She didn't like the extra heat, but the sooner the food was hot and served, the sooner they could usher everyone out.

"Should I dim the lights?" Everett asked dryly. "Play eerie harpsichord music, find some candles?"

"No," said Stella, "and if you choose to be bothersome, you may take yourself elsewhere."

"I have never been bothersome a moment in my life," he replied. "Are you sure you're in the right mood for this work?"

"Never better."

Allison returned, slightly breathless, eyes alight, with the tattered old deck in her hand. "Here," she said, sliding the cards onto the countertop.

Stella locked eyes with Sergey. Her customers found strong, unbroken eye contact to be unnerving. "Spread the cards," she commanded in a low voice.

He laid them slowly, face down, in a neat grid. Stella, as usual, did not care about the cards. She only watched her client. He asked no questions and requested no further instructions.

Face down, a man who did not reveal himself easily. Grid, oriented toward himself, obviously an organized mind. But uncreative, lacking in empathy. His evident fascination with cartomancy was because he found people to be entirely unreadable. But he was decisive, confident.

"Flip," she directed.

He used the tips of his fingernails to lever up a corner of each card from the smooth counter. The cards' edges were furred from years of use, so they shouldn't have been too difficult to turn. To Stella the use of his nails implied a certain unpleasant violence. Once, a client had unthinkingly licked her thumb before turning each card, as if she were turning the pages in a paperback novel, which Stella had divined as a desire for a baby. Correctly, as it happened.

When Sergey was done, he put his hands on the marble, wider than his shoulders, and shifted his weight forward onto his palms. He noticed her looking at his stance, rolled his sleeves down, and resumed the same posture. Aggressive, defiant, challenging. This didn't bother Stella, but clearly Everett felt it, too. Without a word or a change in his expression, her husband placed himself nearer to Sergey. Stella restrained a slight smile. She doubted Everett consciously realized what he had sensed, or what he had done in response. But he was an artist at heart, not as thoroughly logical or impassionate as he tried to portray himself.

She forced her mind away from the interesting topic of Everett and back onto Sergey.

"Your question?"

He shrugged. "None. I am merely curious to hear your perceptions."

She did not look down at the cards. The cards did not matter. They never did.

"You are very boring, sir. Only in terms of the revelations in your upturned images, of course." This was calculated to irritate him into revealing something more. "Call your mother less frequently. You upset each other and do no good. Birthdays and holidays, no more."

Sergey rolled his eyes. "A middle-aged Slavic man has a difficult relationship with his mother? How utterly common. No wonder you call me boring. Forgive me if I fail to detect a supernatural talent at work."

"Did I claim to be supernatural?"

"Yes," breathed Allison.

"No," said Stella sharply. "There is nothing here. I am nothing. Do you understand me? This is no ancient tradition, no religion, no link to a universal consciousness. If anything, this is your mind revealing itself to you. Or it is nothing." She shrugged. "I've seen both. And you feel that you have seen so much of the world that nothing matters anymore. Nothing new, nothing of real pleasure. It's your loss and your error. It's why you were so eager to lay these cards. It's why you ate barely a scrape of our astounding caviar. You arrive early for flights and roll around—metaphorically, you understand—in the worldly irritation, the superiority."

"Y'do get to the airport too early, my friend," said Marvin.

"Many people do," said Sergey.

"If you want advice from me," said Stella, "it's to do what you came here to do. Without taking for granted your circumstances, without superiority or irritation, without hurrying to be off somewhere else."

"Unspecific," said Sergey.

"Oh, for heaven's sake," Stella snapped. "Obviously, Marvin has some social or business connection you need, so do that, all right? You're using him, so make it quick. Don't flirt with him unless you mean it. And I suggest you stop coloring your hair and embrace the natural gray. It's thick enough for you to be vain about it, so go for it. You're trying—and failing—to quit smoking not for your health but because your father was a shitheel who made those old burn scars on the insides of your forearms. And to be totally honest, I cannot foretell good results for whatever venture has brought you here. It's not in the cards."

"You predict bad results?"

"No. I see no results."

Sergey opened his mouth, closed it again, then nodded once. He cleared the cards with a swoop of his arm. "You're not the only person who gleans details from careless words." He pulled a pack of cigarettes from his breast pocket, tapped them against his palm, then hid the packet away again. "Others do the same."

She had silenced his objections, but Everett did not appear to be dazzled. Some cutthroat demon in her would not allow the moment to pass. She should have known better. She had so often settled for leaving a bad impression on Everett because striving for his good opinion was a fool's errand. But since marrying him that morning, she'd become even more foolish over him.

"And you," she said to Marvin, contradicting one of her own core principles, "may as well give him what he desires now, because you won't have the strength of will to resist."

"Haven't laid the cards," said Marvin.

"If you think that's an impediment, then you weren't paying attention," she said.

Everett frowned.

"Why are you doing him anyway?" asked Allison. "I thought it was my turn next."

Stella exhaled. She was thoroughly sick of Allison and her whining. "A dinner party is meant to be entertaining, Allison, and I'm not sure your many woes will qualify."

"Stella," said Everett, "I recommend you take your client into the study for privacy."

But Allison continued, apparently unconcerned by secrecy. "I came all this way, you know, and you said we could—"

"What do you want to ask me?" Stella interrupted.

Allison took the deck from Sergey and began a meticulous pyramid arrangement. "I think it's good news. That photo I found on Lawrence's computer, of a hot woman apparently named Raquel, wasn't sent to him. Rather he has sent it *to* other men. That's good, right? He's not dating Raquel. But why is he doing...that?"

"He's catfishing those men, Allison. There's probably an email or social media account you can find if you dig. Next question?"

Allison looked bereft. "Oh. That would explain the deposits I saw. But that doesn't mean he's leaving me. I want to know if my husband still loves me enough to—"

Stella did not think. She hardly even listened. "Oh, no," she said flippantly. She did not assess Allison. Stella's own husband did not love her enough for anything, and it made Stella careless. "He surely does not. Why should he? Why should anyone? You don't know where you're not wanted, and you eat caviar like a child eats playground dirt. Is that really why you came all this way? Next question."

A terrible silence fell. Stella heard her own words ringing in her ears, and her voice was ugly. Her intentions were ugly. Allison stopped laying the cards and set them aside. Stella looked at her, and the woman's red face crumpled.

Marvin scuffled his feet. The oven's fan clicked on and whooshed them with a blessed veil of white noise that covered the horrible snuffling coming from deep in Allison's throat.

"Um," said Allison, nasal and quiet, "yeah, that was all. You know what, um, it is getting late, and you're right, I really shouldn't have—I'll just be...yeah."

Stella turned to face the glass doors and the lake beyond. She could not bear to look at Everett. The lake, at least, was placid. She wondered how long it would take to run down there and drown herself in it.

"Allison," said Everett gently, "I will get your coat."

"Yep," said Marvin. "Time for us to shove off, too."

"I do apologize for intruding on your evening," said Sergey formally. "Thank you for the appetizers and the drink."

"My regards to Leon and Liz," said Marvin. "Sure do miss them already. Miss them heaps. Good neighbors."

Stella did not follow as Everett escorted the others out. If only Allison had not been so annoying; if only Sergey hadn't challenged her. If only the day hadn't been so long and draining already. Surely Allison knew she had only been joking. She even wished she were drunk, so that she wouldn't feel her own mind so sharply and tomorrow she could blame the wine. After she heard the door open and close, Everett would reappear. She whirled toward the stairs, eager to be alone.

"Stella."

She stopped. "You want to pick up our earlier conversation," she said to forestall his disapproval. "You wanted to explain why you told Leon you wouldn't speak to me, except for the enticement of the estate."

When she looked up into his face, she saw he was not distracted from his path.

"No," he said. "No, I am not in the mood to continue that discussion. How could you have been so rude to Allison? She is your client."

Stella attempted a laugh. "Oh, I'm sure she knew I was teasing her. I was joking! Reluctance is all part of my persona for the job, the tortured spirit at work. It's what I play at, and they eat it up. They know it's a farce."

"You underestimate your influence on Allison. I saw her face, and your comment was no joke to her."

"*You* were rude to Marvin and Sergey, you know. You practically tried to throw them off the doorstep." Stella put her hands at her sides and clenched her fists.

"I am not addressing that right now." He stood with his shoulders squared. "I'm talking about you, Stella."

That was the last thing she wanted. "You saw yourself how pathetic Allison is. She came here uninvited, she has a terrible husband she can't seem to stop talking about, and she is irritating."

"Can you see that the events of today change your position relative to hers?" Everett pushed a hand through his hair. He turned and paced across the kitchen. "Do you think she also inherited a multimillion-dollar mansion today? Heaven help us, listen to me. You force me into the regrettable mode of Mr. Knightley. You cannot be rude to a person who is so friendless in Chicago that she would drive to this secluded place simply to speak to you. I'm sorry to lecture—you called me uptight, and you're not the first to think me too rigid—but *goddammit*, I care about you too much to keep quiet. I'm going to say what your parents or Aunt Elizabeth or Michaela or *someone* should have said to you years ago: You do yourself a disservice. This act that you perform, this farce, it's beneath you. You know it. But when you extend the damage to others, you go too far. People believe in you and trust you, and by making the job into a joke, you betray that trust time and time again. Even worse, you throw away any chance to do real good—not with divination, but by connecting with people who need someone to listen. You have something to offer. Please don't neglect that responsibility."

Stella began crying silent tears while he was in the midst of his reprimand. She faced the cool glass door again and pressed her forehead to it. Her defiance faded, leaving her with the whole-body ache of regret and embarrassment. She might have stood staring out at the lake for an hour, except the oven timer chirped, a cheerful, homey sound. She turned, thinking she would begin a sincere apology to Everett, but he had gone.

She was alone in a room she'd driven everyone else away from.

Chapter 21

ESSENTIAL REPAIRS

Stella slunk back into Chicago on the Sunday midday train feeling like a kicked dog. Everett probably expected he'd rarely see her back at Name Estate again. Leaving the station on foot, she examined every lamppost expecting to see signs with her photo on them. *Lost Idiot, Do Not Approach, Justifiably Cancelled.*

When she'd emerged from her guest chamber around dawn, the house had smelled of burnt lasagna and Everett was already gone. Of course. His instinct to avoid her was the correct one all along. Part of her wanted to ignore him for another ten years. That was what she'd done before, even if she had to admit he'd never really been banished from her mind.

She tiptoed through the lobby of her apartment building even though Philip didn't usually work on Sundays. A contrarian corner of her mind, the same tender spot that knew she had behaved badly, was readying a totally different response, and she couldn't get sidetracked.

Because Everett had said, as if he almost couldn't stand to let the words out, *I care about you too much to keep quiet.* Because of that, she would try almost any sort of song-and-dance to repair the damage she'd caused. And ignoring him for a decade was not a routine she could tolerate.

For the first time in her life, she had some idea of what he might extend in return. Everett's approval was the most difficult goal she'd ever grasped after, and surely the most valuable. She was excellent at some things, perhaps not marriage or customer service, but she had a depth of excellence that people tended not to expect from her. Her mother, her teachers, even Michaela and Elizabeth, they all maintained a dim view of Stella's potential for grace and wisdom. Everett was right—she was better than that. She intended to demonstrate her capability. While shielding her aunt and uncle from nuisance and legal trouble, she would amaze her husband, fortify their marriage, do some aquatic environmentalism, and make the mansion she didn't deserve into their home. She wasn't sure exactly how she'd go about doing all that, but if she could pull it off, she'd impress even herself.

And as another benefit, in her shining excellence she could raise the bar for Everett, too. He still owed her an apology and an explanation for the awful things he'd said about her to Leon.

Her first appointment the following afternoon, therefore, was the one she was most dreading. She had emailed Allison and asked her to stop by.

When the buzzer sounded, Stella pressed the button and admitted Allison promptly. "Please come in." Allison looked tired and wary, and she was over-bundled in a puffy winter parka, hat, and scarf. As if she wanted extra padding to defend herself against Stella. "Let me take your coat."

Allison peeled off her layers one by one. "To be honest, I didn't expect to hear from you. You're so nice to email me. I know you're incredibly busy and maintain your privacy. I didn't even know you were married."

"Yeah. Listen, Allison, I'm so sorry about Saturday night."

"Please don't be, I shouldn't have barged in on—"

"No, I mean it." Stella inhaled and let it out slowly. "Do you want a cup of tea?"

"Thank you."

A few minutes later, after they were both seated on the couch with their teacups, Stella crossed her legs at the ankles and gave Allison her attention.

"What's going on lately with—" she wracked her memory for the name of her client's husband, a man whom they'd spoken of many times. "With Lawrence?"

Allison tipped her head toward the drawer in the coffee table. "Do you want me to get the cards?"

"No. I do not."

"Really? You just want to...like, talk?"

"Sure."

"You were right about the catfishing, of course. I started feeling crazy and did more digging."

Stella nodded. "Does he still live with you? Weren't you talking about a trial separation?"

"I would if I could even get my own husband to prioritize talking to me at all. I *asked* him to prioritize us."

Stella recalled how Everett had tried to call off an entire dinner party to argue with her. He had not contacted her since that night, and she didn't know what to make of it. It was more than a little ridiculous to offer marriage advice when her own was such a mess. She smiled weakly at Allison and made a *go on* gesture with a wave of her teacup.

"He got super mad when I suggested we go out for dinner here in Chicago this past weekend," Allison continued, "because he said I was being passive-aggressive and not supportive of his work. But I really wanted to go out and have a real conversation. Or at least, that's what I thought I wanted, until he told me I wanted to make him feel guilty."

"So, he didn't come home at all this weekend? No dinner-date?"

"No."

"Then it sounds like he moved out without having the conversation about moving out," Stella said, sipping from her fragrant tea. "Which sucks."

"I think, maybe, yeah. We were on a video call—the one where I basically begged for a date night—and I made the mistake of mentioning wearing a new pair of shoes if we went out to eat. So dumb. I know I shouldn't have said anything; I like those shoes, and Lawrence likes when I make an effort to be cute. Or he used to. But then I had to justify the expense. I had a coupon, honestly. I mean, geez, right?" Allison puffed air upward at her bangs, which resettled like the down on a chick. "And he does this annoying thing where he puts his chin on his hand like the girls taking selfies, you know?" She demonstrated with her face perched atop her fingertips and a flutter of eyelashes. "He thinks it's vain, and he's basically accusing me of being vain. For buying shoes. But when I tried to say so, he turned it around and said *I* was always picking fights by assuming the worst of him. Which I am *sure* is either gaslighting or overgeneralizing or both."

Allison looked at her expectantly, waiting for Stella to confirm her diagnosis.

"Okay," Stella said in two, slow long syllables. "You're dealing with a lot."

"No kidding."

"What do you want? Not from me, from your husband. To repair things."

"Repair?" Allison snorted. "No. We're past that. Honestly, I hate this vague state we're in where we're neither together nor separated nor happy nor divorced. I hate that he won't even toss me the crumb of agreeing that it's over. I don't like being ignored and cast aside."

She gave Stella a sidelong glance from under her eyelashes, and Stella knew she was being subtly castigated for essentially doing the same to her. She didn't mind because it was deserved, and at least Allison had identified a decision within herself.

"Congratulations," Stella said.

"For what, the failure of yet another relationship?"

"No, for making a difficult choice. I didn't tell you what you should do about Lawrence, and the cards certainly did not. *You* decided because the right path seemed obvious to you."

Allison shifted. "Well, thanks."

"You'll get a hold of him eventually, and you'll initiate the conversation he was too gutless to manage. And Allison, you *can* do this by yourself. I hope you know that. There's nothing magical about our conversations other than having someone to listen—which, I suppose, can feel rather miraculous some days." She paused. "I'm getting out of the cartomancy and divination business because it doesn't feel honest to me anymore."

It was the first time she'd said it aloud. It felt good. She also had the gut-dropping sensation of letting go of the handrail on a wobbly bridge. She'd clung for so long to the idea that she could do her job while hating herself for it. If she quit the dumb job, would she be required to demonstrate self-respect?

"Really? But what'll I—what will you do instead?"

"Not sure yet. But also, Allison, I'm sorry to have to ask that you..." She didn't want to say it. Maybe Everett could have politely phrased the request she needed to make, but Stella could only think of rude things to say. "Do a teeny bit less stalking."

Allison laid a hand on Stella's knee. "Meaning please don't show up at your house uninvited or generally act like a weirdo?"

"Yes," Stella said with a laugh. "Yes, exactly."

"I promise. Since you're out of the business and all. Can I buy those cards from you? Your predictions and insights were really good."

"No, sorry. They belonged to my grandmother, so I'll return them to my aunt."

The next day, she gave Philip notice that she was terminating her lease.

"At the end of *this* month?" he complained. "But it's impossible to get good renters in Chicago in March."

They stood in the building's vestibule, around the corner from the mailboxes, where industrial carpet runners failed to keep the damp grime from residents' winter boots off the vintage tile.

"Not my problem, Phil," Stella said. "The lease has been month-to-month since after my second year here, and you have nothing to hold over my head. I always paid my rent."

"You paid late about half the time."

She shrugged and flipped through the stack of junk mail in her hand. Speaking to Philip reminded her that she needed to have her letters and packages forwarded to Name Estate by some extra-strength foolproof service, because she wasn't planning on asking him for favors. "Don't give me a hard time about it or maybe I'll find a reason to tell your prospective new tenants that the puddle in the basement laundry room is in fact a permanent mold farm. Did you give my aunt's address to anyone?"

"No! Which aunt? To who?" he sputtered.

He was lying. Allison had got her information from somewhere, and the envelope flap had been suspiciously loose on the copy of the documents that had arrived as a signature-required delivery from the lawyer's office. Stella had a good guess about whose signature the driver had received.

"My aunt who lives a few miles east of Milwaukee," she said, testing him. He would be unable to resist correcting her.

"Nothing is east of Milwaukee," he said. "It's closer to Racine—"

Stella rolled her eyes and backed away from him, setting her hip against the inner door to the elevator lobby and shoving it open.

"—But I didn't tell anybody."

"Sure. Yeah. I'm reserving the freight elevator for my movers this weekend. Don't give out my personal details to anyone else or I'll call the property owner."

"She said it was important."

"Goodbye, Phil."

More important than Philip, more complex than Allison, was her next visit to Michaela. Stella took the train downtown and got off a block from Michaela's gallery. The showroom occupied a small first-floor retail space in an old brick building. Next door was an Italian restaurant with fantastic homemade pasta, and the two units shared a long bay of windows set in black steel frames. A bell over the door jangled when Stella entered—necessary, Michaela had once said, because on some days they received no walk-in customers at all. Other days, they sold six-figure abstract oil paintings. Mostly, however, Michaela worked in the back room on projects of her own.

Stella waited in the open, white-walled space. The floors were of narrow oak planks, the ceiling was exposed beams, and the paintings were hung three feet from their neighbors to properly breathe.

Michaela emerged from the back, wearing a canvas apron and dusting her hands. She untied the strings and slung the apron over a wall hook. Her emerald-green blouse had a loose bow at the neck and turned-back cuffs, and her pinstripe wool trousers were cinched by a leather belt. Yellow paint smeared on one hip would be a real pain to remove. She looked so glamorous, so utterly familiar and beautiful, that Stella's heart clenched.

"Hey," she said.

"Hi there," said Michaela.

The tricky thing about Michaela was that she could tease and love and forgive and forgive and forgive, but those hurts built up. She'd seen Michaela sliced a thousand times before she eventually cut a bad friend loose, and Stella had no intention of being that type of bad friend. But Michaela also didn't like addressing grievances head-on, as if peeling back the gauze over her various pains gave too harsh of a view. Stella needed to convey her remorse and apologize without tearing away Michaela's careful layers of bandaging.

"How's Jackson?" she asked.

"Good. He's good. He's got the cutest fat lip. Reminds me of when he was a chunky baby. Kira seems to think the popsicles and milkshakes are for her, too, and Henry is powerless against her, as usual."

"Is he going to have a scar on his face?"

"The doctor doesn't think so. They're quick healers at this age. The stitches come out tomorrow."

"Poor little guy. I'm sure he was very glad to see you on Saturday."

"Oh, so now you think so?" Michaela said tartly.

Stella deserved that little sting. "Yes."

Michaela walked idly toward one of the gallery's paintings, a square canvas with a craggy vertical streak of red surrounded by blue, and Stella followed, cautious.

"What happened after I left?" Michaela used a forefinger to swipe dust off the top edge of the frame.

"Oh, I was a jerk. Big shocker, I know. Before you left, after you left," Stella said, which was as close as she would come to acknowledging she'd been selfish in asking Michaela to stay. "The neighbors seem nice. The weirdest thing was that one of my clients turned up at the house uninvited. I was monstrously rude to her at the time, but we talked yesterday, and she seems willing to forgive me. I'm lucky in that department."

"Good thing."

"And I had a chat with her about please not turning into a stalker."

"That is wild."

"Yeah. So, what do you think of Everett?"

That was the next phase of working her way back into Michaela's graces—she liked to be asked for her opinion, which was great for Stella, who respected Michaela's input in most areas of life.

"After knowing him for a day? He seems kind. Stuffy, but kind. Maybe he was nervous. Couldn't take his eyes off you. I would say he's outrageously handsome, but I don't want to make waves. How are things between you two?"

"Uh, not great. Reference my earlier comment about me being a general jerk."

"Don't mess this up, Stella. He's too good to lose over your goofy shit. Except...if the whole marriage attempt doesn't work out, you can come back to Chicago. You never exactly got my permission to leave me behind, you know."

Stella opened her arms and pulled Michaela into a tight hug. For Michaela to express a vulnerable feeling like that wasn't commonplace. "I'm sorry. I would never leave you behind. You can come visit me anytime, and I'll be back often for the superior tacos here in the city."

After a moment, Michaela squeezed her in return and stepped back. "You'll have to sleep on the futon. You are such a pain in my ass."

"I know. Speaking of my incompetence, would you be willing to go on speakerphone with me while I call my mom? She doesn't know about the wedding, unless Aunt Elizabeth spilled. I think your presence will keep her temperature somewhat lower than complete meltdown. She thinks you're a rational influence."

Michaela snorted. "She probably hasn't heard about the time I couldn't remember where I'd parked in that garage by the movie theater, and we spent twenty minutes walking around before you remembered I had come in a cab."

"I certainly did not tell her."

"Let's call her." Michaela extended her palm and flexed her fingers, waiting for Stella's phone to be placed in her hand. She cultivated an odd enjoyment of Stella's messy mother, who was likely to be either slightly sauced at noon or out indulging in the athletic pursuit of retail therapy. Or both. "Tell her it was an elopement, and I'll sound excited. It'll be fine. She'll want to have a big family party this summer."

A giddy sense of relief washed through Stella. Michaela was fully back on her team. "Yes, good. And drop off those pants tomorrow so I can get the yellow paint out of them, all right? They look too cute on you to risk at the dry cleaners."

"Thank you. They are cute, aren't they?"

"Very."

"But not as cute as your statuesque husband. Oh! That reminds me." She pulled her coat from the rack and threw it around her shoulders. "Before we call Mrs. Woodward, there's something you need to see."

"What is it? Can I have my phone back?"

"Come."

Michaela led her out of the gallery and back onto the noisy street. Stella followed in Michaela's inexorable wake. They walked only a block and a half before Michaela entered a storefront—another art gallery, more modern and less homey than the one where she worked. An employee looked up from behind the desk, but Michaela ducked through an open doorway into the next hall.

"We do not want to talk to her," she muttered to Stella. "Snooty and almost definitely overpaid."

Stella gazed around. In the long, open room, one entire wall was devoted to deep shelves displaying many *objets d'art*.

"What am I looking for?" asked Stella.

"This." Michaela stopped before a shelf and pointed to an oversized bowl.

Stella inspected it with slow-growing understanding. *Of course.* It was a ceramic footed bowl with a fluted edge, mostly cream colored but with thin bands of dusky purple running around the base of the foot and the rim. Inside was piled a mound of white dust and fragments. Some of the shards were small, curved pieces, others were as big as her palm, with jagged chips and knifelike points. The largest pieces gave intriguing hints about what the sculpture might have depicted while intact, with their curves and ridges, but not enough to see anything like a complete picture.

It gave Stella a sense of collected violence, like a pile of broken branches after a storm has passed, and the graceful tragedy of one of those ancient Roman goddess statues missing a limb or two.

Beside the bowl, a tented card was labeled *Tomorrow* in a tasteful serif font, with Everett Novak below, and a five-digit price that made Stella's eyes widen.

"For the smashings," she breathed.

"I interpret this piece as a statement on climate change," said Michaela. "The destruction of tomorrow, you know. All that. You want to buy it?"

"Is that your sales pitch?"

"No, my sales pitch is that his works have doubled in value on the resale market in the past two years. And the snobby saleslady will take a credit card."

Stella shook her head. Art business was far beyond her comprehension. "No, I definitely do not want to buy this pile of mess, thank you."

After a long pause, Michaela said, "What exactly do you like about him?"

Stella considered for a moment. It wasn't his handsome face, although she liked looking at him very much, or the warm memories of his kindness when they were children, or the gentleness with which he treated their aged relatives.

"His exactness," she said softly, "feels like a hard edge to scratch myself against. He relieves my itchy sense of ineptitude, and his approval makes me feel like I passed the hardest test in the world. If Everett likes me, even a little, then I must be someone quite good after all."

Michaela hummed. "I like you just fine, and I already know you're wonderful. His approval isn't worth more than anybody would pay for it, but you're aware enough to read your own cards. Now, are we sure we're not gonna drop a stack of cash for this weird art?"

Stella laughed and linked her elbow through Michaela's. She didn't like it enough to purchase, even if she'd had many thousands of dollars to spend. Observers thought he was making outrageous, bold, provocative assertions with his destruction, but he was obfuscating the truth. She recognized the signs because what she'd been dragging along through her false divination business, Everett was doing with his art. And she meant to tell him. He could work a little for her approval, too.

Chapter 22

HOME FURNISHINGS AND CONFESSIONS

Stella and Michaela spoke to Stella's mother. Christine Woodward was, as ever, bemused by her daughter's life decisions. Taking a scholarship to a smaller in-state college instead of a big brand-name university in California, wearing her hair too long or too short (sometimes both at once, in regard to a disastrous layered cut that Stella had to admit her mother was right about), living alone in the city when she could have lived rent-free at home in the northwest suburbs. Spending childhood summers and holidays with Elizabeth and Leon when she could have enjoyed the homey comforts of her parents screaming at each other. Christine's foremost decision metric was status, so Elizabeth got a lot of points for money and architecture, but none for the remote, rural location where no one was around to envy her. And Stella, who cared very little about most other people's opinions, was an utter mystery.

Christine's first question, upon learning about the elopement, was whether Robert, Stella's father, had been present. That would have been a sign of favoritism and a major crime. But Christine was genuinely happy that Stella received Name Estate in the deal, and Michaela eased the conversation by sending a couple of photos. As Michaela had predicted, Christine redirected the conversation by threatening to stage an elaborate reception for family and friends at the estate over the summer.

"I wonder if we put out those big gas heaters, like the Jehle's had for their daughter's wedding, although she did get divorced last year, if the guests might stay until dawn," Christine mused, having already verbally constructed a list of a hundred invitees. "On that big terrace, can't you imagine? The sunrise over the lake. It's too bad there isn't a pool. Your cousin Maggie had that lap-band surgery I told her about, so she'd be there in her suit looking adorable, I'm sure."

Stella found it was best to let her mother wander freely down her mental pathways, but there were some byways she tried to blockade.

"We'll see, Mom." Stella rolled her eyes. Michaela couldn't have seen her past the hand she was using to pinch the bridge of her nose. "Don't recommend medical procedures, all right? Unless you passed some sort of board exam I wasn't aware of."

"I didn't even think you liked him, you know."

"Everett?"

"He was nice to you when you were little, but you complained about him incessantly after we got back from that Bahamas trip. All I heard for a week was how awful Everett Novak was. Remember that? Didn't you dislike him?"

She recalled it very clearly. It was the first occurrence of Everett shutting down her worst impulses. "I just married him, Mom."

"You should have traveled with us; the service at the resort was fantastic, and they had a shark tube. Michaela, you know the one I'm talking about, right?"

"Mm-hm," said Michaela, who was opposed to mindless Caribbean tourism for colonialism-based reasons that would have confused Christine. She shot a hell-raising glance at Stella. "Did you get your picture taken with the locals?"

"Oh, yes," said Christine.

"Anyway, we've got to go," Stella said hurriedly. "I'll call you again soon."

"But you do like him, Stella?"

She sighed. She'd had Everett in her mind nearly every waking moment as she scurried around trying to be, as he commanded, *better*. The question was whether *he* liked *her*. "Yeah, Mom. I like him."

When she returned to Name Estate on Thursday afternoon, the gate accepted her birthday as the code and swung wide. Everett wasn't there. The first thing she did was crank open all the windows. The place was starting to smell like Stella's own, like the wispy ghost of her favorite perfume and the grapefruit countertop spray she liked to clean with. Cool, crisp air flooded in, and she inhaled deeply. She'd have to close up soon or risk running the furnace all night to reheat the whole house. The fresh evening scent was worth it.

The elder Novaks' movers had carted away all their personal effects and much of the furniture and left behind a pair of keys on the kitchen counter. Stella was glad to see the matching floral sofas were gone. Her own small box truck had been packed and was in transit with regional movers who'd set a Sunday delivery window. Hiring professionals to move her stuff was an extravagance she'd never experienced before, and the idea of her clothes and books and piles of bedding appearing in a new place was magical. For two nights, however, she was alone in a house that was scarcely furnished at all.

But she also had a generously funded account earmarked solely for *the transition,* as Elizabeth put it. It was under Everett's name as well, but he wouldn't mind if she got to work. In fact, she could save him a great deal of time and effort.

So, she found her tape measure and began planning an interior makeover, probably the first redesign the place had received in decades. The modernist architecture, expanses of cold glass, and concrete floors were all somewhat harsh, so Stella wanted luxurious textures and rich, muted colors. It was the first moment she'd felt the power of her new wealth. The house didn't yet feel quite like hers, and the dollar values she jotted down might as well have been fake money.

She spent another hour daydreaming about what to do with the long-disused bedroom suite on the mezzanine level, pacing back and forth across the empty room and considering what new pieces might complement the vintage chandelier. It was difficult, however, to plan furniture around the uncertainty in her marriage. Would she ever sleep there with Everett? Would it be presumptuous to buy a huge bed and make it up with French linens? Maybe it would be smarter to buy two twin mattresses. Stella snorted at the idea of sleeping three feet apart from him. It would be more practical to remain in the lower-level guest rooms.

As twilight deepened into evening, she considered ordering food. Surely at least one pizza joint delivered to her new address. She descended two flights and peered into the room where Everett had stayed a few nights as if it might reveal something about him. It did not, of course. It was only a spare room. There was nothing of him. She hadn't really decided to check the room; it had just happened. But the bed was neatly made up. She leaned forward to catch a whiff of the pillowcase, hoping for evidence he still existed. That it was his home, too.

Her phone buzzed in her back pocket. Stella straightened bolt upright, and her heart thudded like she'd been caught red-handed doing something indecent.

She fumbled her phone, caught it upside down, and rotated it to see Everett's name on the screen. He'd never called her before. She rushed upstairs where the reception was better. What if he was waiting at the top of the steps? What if he'd seen her sniffing his sheets like an obsessive, too-loyal hound?

She groaned aloud, but at least he wasn't lurking in the kitchen. The house was still empty.

"Hello?" she answered, breathless from the stairs and her own imagination.

"Stella," he said. "Are you exercising?"

"Never. How are you? *Where* are you?"

"I am...not fine, perhaps, but not far from it. I am somewhere in the vicinity of fine. In Milwaukee. Where are you?"

"Home," she said. "Name Estate."

"Really? I was there; you weren't."

"Just arrived a few hours ago," she said.

A silence. The last time they'd spoken, on the evening of their wedding day, he had been harshly chastising her. She wondered if he, too, was thinking of that moment. She would be quite happy if it was never mentioned again.

"There are pink hearts beside your name in my phone," he said.

The connection was so clear, his voice reached her ear like a whisper. "I confess nothing." She grabbed her coat off the back of a stool, opened the sliding door, and stepped onto the terrace. The air was still, and the lake was unsettled by disorganized waves tripping over themselves in the endless advance and retreat.

He exhaled audibly, and perhaps Stella's imagination was firing again, but he sounded exasperated yet...fond. He didn't say he'd *deleted* the pink hearts, and he clearly was not revisiting their previous discord.

"Unlike you, I do need to confess something," he said.

"Yes," she said instantly. She switched her phone from hand to hand as she shrugged into her coat. "Good. Unburden yourself of your sins. The worse, the better."

"It's not the fun kind of sin."

"Oh, that is so disappointing. Nevertheless, please continue."

"I called Uncle Leon to ask about the fish," he said. "About why they had evaded the state's mandated review for so long. And I told him we had received a visit from that warden and a threatening letter."

"Shit, Ev, I thought we wanted to shield them from all that trouble." Stella grimaced, imagining Elizabeth fretting in the background of that call. "What did he say? God, I hope it was an oversight, and they'd somehow just missed the resource survey."

"No, he knew exactly what I was referring to. He was indignant, and he did not appreciate being challenged. Then I asked him if all the sturgeon were dead."

"And? What did he say?"

"Nothing. He made a horrible noise, then said he had to go. The call cut out. I assumed he was too angry with me to talk further, and I felt bad about upsetting him. Aunt Elizabeth texted me two hours later and said he'd had another flare up of the atrial fibrillation."

"*Everett.* Holy shit, is he—how is he now? He must be fine, or you would have led with that. Right? He's fine."

"Yes. He's resting at home."

Stella released a noisy breath. "Thank God."

He was quiet for a moment. "I wish I hadn't pressed him on the issue. The stress cannot be good for him and surely is a large part of the reason why they wanted to give the place away. I called because I felt... Well, I won't make excuses for myself."

But Stella knew him a little better after a week of marriage. She had a suspicion about what he had almost said. "Because after last weekend, you felt alone and wanted someone else to share in the responsibility? Because after our argument, you felt—justifiably—that I wasn't going to be very helpful. So, you called your uncle, as you've probably done many times throughout your life. It wasn't unreasonable."

"We had agreed not to involve them. I didn't adhere to that intention, and it exacerbated Leon's heart problem. It's my fault."

"It is not your fault. We know he's been having these episodes. It could have been spurred by an especially bad rerun of that high-school singing show they like to watch. You did not cause a heart attack." Stella leaned over the barrier and looked north, toward Milwaukee, wondering how much the coastline curved toward her speck of land. On a clear night, could she glimpse the faint glow of city lights? The unforgiving edge of the wall pressed against her stomach. "Where is your place in the city?"

"What? Oh, on the southeast side. Somehow, I really thought you might be...furious."

Stella frowned. "With you? Because you asked Leon those questions?"

"Yes."

"Give me a little more credit than that. I'm not a get-immediately-furious sort of person."

"No, you're not." He spoke slowly. "My statement was more about what I thought I deserved than how I expected you to react."

Stella paid more attention to what he wasn't saying. "Because you're not a hypocrite." In line with his mood and his edging around the real issue at hand, she said nothing further. She didn't say *you chastised me and expected the same in return.* Her errors had been intentional, hurtful, whereas he had merely overstepped. They were not the same. "I'll call Auntie Liz this week and check in."

Silence fell between them again, and Stella began to consider that she might need to hang up. She couldn't sit on the line with Everett all evening, especially since she had nothing interesting to say. She couldn't tell him she'd spent the better part of two days apologizing to people.

"Why did you ask about my neighborhood?" he asked, and Stella was absurdly glad to have a reason to keep him on the phone.

"I'm on the terrace," she said, "looking in your direction. But it's too foggy to see as far as Marvin's house, much less to Milwaukee."

"Tell me what you do see."

She looked around herself. "Mmm. The little waves out there need a committee meeting. They lack unity. The moon is a smudge of gray. We have a crumbling section of retaining wall beside the path—you know the spot? We'll have to call someone about it, unless you're interested in staging a murder to look like a freak landslide accident."

"I'll call someone," he said. "I like the way you see things. I probably would have recited the temperature and the humidity and the species of trees in my direct view, but you're covering up murder and organizing a focus group for the lake. You see magic in everyday things."

She quelled a hopeful flutter in her chest. "Which gets me in trouble, too. What do you see where you are now? And don't tell me the temperature."

Amusement warmed his voice. "I'm on the balcony here looking south, but all I see is haze from my neighbors' truly prodigious efforts at reducing the worlds' supply of marijuana. I have liked living here, although I won't be heartbroken to leave the city behind. The real estate agent was here today taking photos for the listing. I'm packing up tomorrow with a couple of friends."

"Let me come help," said Stella impulsively.

He hesitated a moment. "All right."

"Really?" she said, with a thrill of anticipation. "I was planning on coming into the city tomorrow to go shopping anyway. How about I meet you for lunch, then help finish up whatever packing you have left?"

"Yes."

"You can put stuff into the back of my car. And you can come look at a sofa I've been ogling online. I want your sign-off before I spend our transition funds."

"You've been ogling a sofa?"

"Yes. Fluttering my eyelashes, biting my lip, the whole deal."

He laughed. "No respectable couch would stand a chance against you, and neither can I. I'll text you the address of my favorite place to get a bratwurst in Bay View."

Stella found she was grinning. "Perfect. See you at noon."

She ended the call, then spent another minute admiring the foggy view over the water before heading inside to order herself a pizza. She had to get to bed early so she was well-rested for a first date with her husband.

Chapter 23

LUNCH WITH GENTLEMEN

Stella was in the car and on the road before nine o'clock the following morning, with an insulated mug of coffee jammed in the cupholder and her coat thrown across the passenger seat. She wore a wide-necked taupe sweater that made her cheeks look rosy, and she turned up the radio to sing badly.

After visiting a handful of stores and sinking her hands into any number of fine upholsteries, she was only a little late for lunch. Bay View was crowded with shoppers, and the sandwich place was bustling.

Stella approached the frazzled hostess. "I'm meeting my husband," she said. "He's probably here already. Have you seen him? Tall, dark-haired, and handsome."

"Heck, yes," the woman said. She added another pen to the three already clipped to her shirt pocket. "Good for you. He said you were coming. They're on the patio. Follow me."

Stella wasn't thrilled to hear *they*. Everett must have his friends with him. And it was quite chilly to eat lunch outdoors. But, as she followed the hostess, she saw the sun was shining, the covered patio had gas heaters blazing, and the space was a great deal less crowded than the indoor seating.

Everett spotted her and rose as she approached. "Hello."

The two other men at the table hastily shoved their chairs back and stood. They were both smiling and good-looking, but Stella couldn't take her eyes off Everett. He took one step toward her, stopped, then clasped his hands behind his back.

Stella advanced on him. His wool coat hung open, and the breeze ruffled his hair. Her instincts told her that he wouldn't have divulged to his friends the complicated details of their situation. She wanted to shove her hands inside his coat and wrap her arms around his midsection, but she stopped a few feet away. He might not have even called her his wife. She was willing to guess their eyebrows had shot up when Everett mentioned a woman would be joining them for lunch.

"Hey, Ev," she said casually.

The staff person handed her a menu. "I'll grab another chair."

She hurried away, and Stella noticed for the first time the table had only three seats. Everett gestured to where he had been sitting.

"Please, take this one," he said.

The other two men sat.

"Oh, no," said Stella. "Go ahead. She'll be back in a second."

Everett didn't sit, but neither did he insist.

"Stella Novak, please meet my friend Mark Rogers, who works at Allied Manufacturing with me."

Mark had fantastically orange hair, freckles, and mirrored sunglasses that looked like they'd come straight from a rotating rack at a gas station. He grinned at Stella and saluted. "Different departments," he said.

"Everett is not my boss, despite his best efforts to recruit me over the years. I only do free manual labor for my friends."

"He had better buy your lunch," said Stella. Hearing Everett refer to her by her full name—her married name, *their* name—had given her a twisty feeling she couldn't identify.

"Absolutely," Mark agreed easily. "Any good reason to get out of the office on a Friday."

Everett ignored the baiting. "And Jaime Mackenzie, who's in town from Michigan. He rode over on the ferry. For what, a week, Jaime?"

Jaime was thin, with slightly receding dark hair and half-moon purple smudges under his eyes. "Yep, about that. My brother and his wife are coming tomorrow."

"Do you work with Everett, too?" she asked.

"No, not now, although we worked together at the ca—"

"At summer camp after college," Everett interrupted. "We were camp counselors for the same bunch of poorly behaved children."

Stella had the feeling that was not what Jaime had been about to say. He gave Everett a flat glance.

"Yeah, we've known each other for a long time," Jaime said. "Since middle school. Boy, I could tell you stories about our young and dumb Ev. In fact, since we have the time, I will."

"That's really not necessary," said Everett.

Stella smiled at Jaime. "Oh, it absolutely is. Please, continue."

"He wasn't a total nitwit, as some of us were at that age," said Jaime with a chuckle, "but he was stubborn. You remember the darts?"

Stella looked at Everett, who frowned. "Yes," he said. "But that was simply because I—"

"We had cross-country meets on Saturday mornings in the fall," Jaime said, turning his attention to Stella. He leaned back in his chair. "This was the north suburbs of Milwaukee in the early two-thousands. Neither of us had the neurons to spare for contact sports, so we were often found wearing singlets and tiny shorts when the other dudes were wearing shoulder pads and helmets. We were not cool. Anyway, we were at—was it your basement or the Meyers' basement?"

Everett folded his arms. "Nathan Meyer's parents' house. With the pool table."

"Right. And, of relevance to our story, a dartboard. It was late on Friday, and some of us were a little drunk."

"Meaning you," said Everett.

"Although not as bad as Nate," Jaime acknowledged. "Everett wanted to leave because we had cross-country early the next morning. He was driving, but nobody else wanted to leave. There were about four of us who'd crammed into his hand-me-down Corolla to get to Nate's after school. They wanted to stay and play darts. Everett, because he is a stubborn asshole, plants himself in front of the dartboard to prevent us from starting another round, arms crossed. Yeah, much like he's doing right now."

Stella glanced at Everett, who let his arms fall to his sides. He was clearly indulging Jaime's enjoyment of the old story.

"Everett's blocking the dartboard. Nate, who was a real piece of work, I think he ended up in Columbus after his divorce. Or Cincinnati.

Anyway, after some shit-talking, he throws a dart at Everett. An actual dart with a metal tip."

Mark snorted a laugh.

"Ouch," said Stella. "Wait, did it *stick*?"

Everett rubbed a spot on his chest, as if remembering the wound. "Nope. Although I did get a little round bloodstain on my Weezer t-shirt, which I remember thinking was pretty badass. I wore that shirt all through college. It's probably still in a drawer."

"Then what?" asked Mark. "Everett gets the shit kicked out of him and misses cross country anyway?"

"Ha, no, I come to his rescue," said Jaime. "I am the hero of this story."

"That's true," said Everett.

"Nate thought his stunt was hilarious, and so did our other dumb friends. I heroically find suction-cup darts in the bin and convince Everett to take his shirt off. We spend ten minutes throwing darts at him as punishment for making us go home early." Jaime laughed. "And some of those, I recall, *did* stick to him, because he was sixteen and scrawny and totally hairless."

Everett laughed ruefully. "And I got everybody home by ten-thirty."

"But I was faster than you at the meet, even with a tinge of a hangover." Jaime lifted his drink in a mock toast. "It was a win-win."

Stella shook her head with a smile. It was easy to imagine a young Everett deflecting a dose of peer pressure, although not as easy to picture him spotted with plastic suction-cup marks. "Thank you," she said to

Jaime. "I hope I can call you the next time I need an embarrassing story about Everett."

"Please do." Jaime inclined his head. "It would be my honor. I have plenty."

The woman had not yet returned with the additional chair, and standing around while the other two waited was becoming awkward. Stella caught Everett's eye, then pointedly looked at his chair.

"Everett," she said. "Sit."

He angled the chair and sat.

Mark snorted. "He's never so obedient for me," he said.

Stella looked over her shoulder. No servers, and the patio was not busy. She circled around to stand before Everett. He raised his eyebrows. She turned her backside to him and delicately lowered herself to perch in his lap.

She couldn't see Everett's expression, but Jaime and Mark were both grinning. He was probably blushing. But his thighs were very warm, and Stella was quite content with her seating arrangement. She dangled her purse from the hook under the table.

"So, Stella," Mark said, "I wish I could say Everett has told us all about you, but the truth is he doesn't say much that's very interesting. How did you two meet?"

"Through family connections," she said. "We've known each other for years. I had a mortifying crush on him when I was a teenager."

Beneath her, Everett went very still. Maybe he hadn't expected honesty.

Mark chuckled. "Is that right? Well, at least Everett would have had no idea. He doesn't even see the women in our office who give him the look. I'm sure he wasn't aware of his future wife's embarrassing childhood crush."

"No," Everett rumbled.

His voice vibrated through her spine and ribcage. He had told his friends about their marriage after all.

"Thank goodness," Stella said. "He's very good at ignoring me when he wants to."

"That skill seems to have lapsed." He gripped the rounded curve of her hip.

She twisted to look at him. Every wiggle of her ass on his lap gave her evidence that he was affected by her, whether he liked her or not. Everett inhaled sharply. She squirmed back around to beam a bright smile at his friends.

"He made himself scarce for a decade," Stella said. "But we caught up again recently."

She tossed a grin over her shoulder toward him, but his expression was intense. Her smile faded. She vaguely heard Mark and Jaime discussing whether to order onion rings. Everett's gaze dropped to her mouth.

"You came here to torment me," he whispered.

"I came here for lunch."

"The result is the same," he said. He slid his hand up from her hip, past the edge of her coat, and under the loose hem of her sweater. His palm was warm against her lower back.

Stella allowed herself a liberty she had long desired, which was to thread her fingers into his dense hair. "Yeah?"

He raised his chin, cupped her breast under her sweater, and urged her closer. "Yes." His eyelids were heavy.

She could have kissed him. He wanted her to. His friends would have been surprised, amused. Stella resisted, although it required a monumental act of self-denial. She clenched her fingers in his hair and tugged his tempting mouth back away from her lips.

"You owe me," she said on a breath. He opened his eyes wide and looked up at her. "I have not forgotten the unexplained insult you dealt me."

"Ah." His warm hand fell away from her skin, and a draft of cool air permeated the knit weave before her coat resettled. "Yes. I do."

A staff member finally returned, breathless and apologetic, with the extra chair. Stella hopped up. She would not allow him to brush aside his bad behavior when she'd worked so hard on mitigating her own mistakes.

Before she could settle into her seat, however, Everett locked onto her wrist with a gentle but implacable strength.

"But I won't be built into one of your elaborate contradictions," he said quietly, his dark eyes steady. "To flirt and withhold, to tease and deny, everywhere, nowhere. Am I clear, my love?"

He echoed the mocking endearment she'd bestowed upon him on their wedding day. But coming from him, with his friends sitting nearby pretending that they weren't listening, it didn't sound like a joke.

"Sure," Stella said easily. She held his gaze. "Absolutely. Says the man who carves statues and promptly destroys them. *You* would never tease and withhold. *You* would never play such a silly game. Loud and clear, my love."

He frowned and released her wrist, and Stella sat down.

Jaime cleared his throat and leaned forward. "Are we heading to your studio after lunch to pack it up? The condo is basically done."

"No," said Everett quickly. "Thank you."

"Wait, we're packing up your studio?" Stella asked. "You're giving it up?"

"The rental space, yes," he said. "I noticed a shed in an open clearing on the south side of the house that I can use as a workshop."

Stella looked at him. He wanted to move his studio to their land. "Yes, of course," she said.

"It has power already," he said. "Although I'll have to have another water line installed from the well. Perhaps I should have spoken to you earlier about this plan."

"No, it's fine." He called her a mess of contradictions, but Everett never failed to startle her with his willingness to fully commit to their unusual arrangement. "I agree with Jaime, we should go clear out your rental space. When else will you have three muscular, gorgeous humans on hand to assist?"

"It's really not—"

Mark held up a hand to forestall him. "Oh, stop. You have to turn in the keys by what, next Friday evening? Stop trying to push us aside. We'll be done by the end of the afternoon."

But Everett wasn't ready to concede. He turned to Stella. "Didn't you mention a sofa? You wanted to go look at a sofa."

He sounded desperate. Stella smiled, leaned forward, and put her hand on his. "The less you want me there, the more determined I am to go there."

"That's what concerns me," he muttered.

Chapter 24

STUDIO NOVAK

After lunch, during which Stella tried to eat an enormous, delicious bratwurst while retaining her ladylike dignity, they walked together to Everett's nearby studio. It was on the second floor of a brick converted warehouse, alongside a wing of self-service storage units, a photography studio, and a dog-grooming business. Everett unlocked an unmarked door and led them inside. The space was open, with high ceilings, exposed beams, and a huge bank of steel-framed windows that offered a partial glimpse of the lake.

In the center of the room was a large worktable, covered with a fine, white powder but otherwise empty, and along the walls were two racks of boxes and equipment that Stella could not identify. The floor and every surface, in fact, was covered with the same powdery dust. Sunlight fell in hazy, diffuse puffs. She could understand why fastidious Everett would not undertake such an endeavor inside his home. It was too messy.

After a brief discussion, Mark and Jaime went to the racks and began hauling stuff from the shelves to the worktable. From next door came the doleful sound of a dog objecting to its bath. Everett fiddled with his phone and Spanish guitar music began playing on a speaker, which was also coated in white plaster grit.

But Stella's attention was captured by a low, round podium in a corner of the room. It held a large object nearly six feet high and covered entirely by a tent of coarse canvas. When she approached, she saw the podium was a rotating turntable, and a tray nearby held a neat lineup of two hammers and chisels with various shaped pointy ends. The piece was clearly a work-in-progress. She glanced over her shoulder at Everett, who was pulling the pieces of a disassembled packing crate from a shelf. He was distracted. She drew closer and reached for the fabric. Her fingertips brushed the cloth. She could glimpse what Everett's art looked like before he smashed it, as she'd promised Michaela she'd attempt to get a photo. Maybe it would offer insight into the workings of his mind. Maybe the sculptures were ugly, and destroying them was not an avant garde technique but rather done to disguise a bad outcome. Or if the sculpture was flawless, she could persuade him to put away his sledgehammers and save this one.

She clutched the covering in her fist. She could raise it an inch, crouch down, and peek under the statue's skirt.

But she did not. She released the cloth and stepped back. Everett had tried to dissuade her from coming to his studio, and he certainly didn't want her snooping around. He'd told her once that no one had seen his unbroken work. If she were to see it, it would only be satisfying at his invitation.

And certainly, the Stella of only a few weeks ago would have peeked without a second thought. No wonder Everett hadn't liked her very much.

There was a draft of cool, dry air, then Everett was there. He came so close behind her she felt the heat of his skin.

"I noticed," he said quietly, "that moment when you decided to behave yourself."

"It does happen occasionally." Her voice emerged hoarse. She promised herself it was from all the plaster dust. Not because the man behind her made her chest heavy and her heart pound.

"Do you want to see what's under that sheet?"

It was impossible to deny. His head was angled so he spoke beside her ear, and the intimacy made her throat ache. "Yes," she said. "Very much. If you want to show me."

Without making any sort of decision, she tilted her jaw to allow him better access to the sensitive side of her neck. He took it for the invitation it was. He dipped his head and skimmed his lips along the column of her throat.

"I do," he murmured against her skin. "But it's not done yet. Soon, I hope. I haven't shown the pieces at this stage to anyone, you know. It's a change for me. All of this is a monumental change. But it's something I have—have wanted. Do want. For a long time."

He must have felt her pulse thudding in her veins. Although she allowed him certain liberties along her neckline, she held firm against his persuasion.

"You can't flirt your way out of an apology," she said. "Remember that you don't even *like* me."

He moved his hands to her waist and snugged her tight against his body. Across the studio, his dutiful friends continued the real work while they dallied together. "I'm truly sorry I lectured you so callously about Allison."

"Not that. *That* I deserved. I meant..." It was still painful to recall, let alone speak aloud. "I meant what you said about me to Leon."

With a sigh, he tugged lightly at her hips. "Come over here."

She followed, but he didn't move far. He spun her around behind the covered statue so it blocked Mark and Jaime from view. Then he pinched a corner of the drop cloth and moved it upward—Stella held her breath and watched. But he wasn't revealing the sculpture, he was pinning the excess fabric against the shelf, enclosing them in a narrow, curtained space. He'd shed his overcoat, and the gray t-shirt underneath was old and threadbare. A shirt for physical labor. The cotton was so thin, she could make out every ridge and indentation of his shoulders and chest.

"Please allow me to apologize and explain," he said.

She nodded. He held her eyes with his dark brown gaze. There was a smudge of white above one eyebrow, and she did not reach up to smooth it away.

"I wasn't talking about you, but rather about myself. For a long time, I have felt that I did not deserve to—that I wasn't the right sort of man to marry. Um. That I shouldn't hold myself forth to any woman as a good decision she should make. When I said I would never approach you apart from the enticement of the estate, I meant the estate was an enticement *for you.* That you should not be lured by me, except I felt that offering to partner with you on your half of our unwieldy inheritance made me into a better bargain. A packaged deal that I could live with. Am I making any sense whatsoever?"

"Uh, no, Ev, you're not." She scrunched her nose. The instrumental guitar music began to grate on her nerves. The notes were all over the place. "I am going to repeat this back to you and hope you hear yourself more clearly. You consider Name Estate the reason you're a bargain? Like a...a buy-one-husband-get-one-mansion sort of situation?"

He frowned. "Well. Nobody *bought* anybody, obviously."

"*Clearly,*" she spat back, because nothing was clear. "Why? Why do you not deserve to marry whomever you want? Aside from being judgmental and aggravating, you must know you're also annoyingly beautiful. And you smell fantastic and have a steady job, which honestly, that trio of traits alone would make half the women in Chicago forgive you for your stranger habits, like making weird art and being...being *irksome.*"

Foremost, however, and causing the gritty sensation behind her eyes, was the awareness that if he considered himself a clearance-bin leftover in terms of husband material, Everett must also have felt that Stella herself was at the same level. Two bargain-shelf factory rejects paired up for fish husbandry and household chores. It felt worse than being chosen last for intramural softball—it felt like the team had gone home, and she'd gone into the trash bin. She should have considered this feeling before she'd proposed marriage to somebody who didn't like her. She squeezed her eyes shut to hold back the tears. Why had she demanded this terrible explanation? They could have continued their unexamined parallel lives without prodding at any of the complexities between them.

"Because I—because there is something I cannot offer, Stella. Even to you. I have been selfish to keep this secret from you, and I don't know how to ask you to forgive me. If you decide you want to move forward without...if you prefer to keep the house alone, I'll accede."

"Don't you dare try to preempt my decisions. Tell me."

Everett closed his eyes tightly and exhaled. Then Mark stuck his head and shoulders around the edge of their makeshift curtain and held up a broom head with no handle.

"Hey guys, what's happening back here?" Mark asked brightly. "Ev, do you know where I can find the—"

"Mark," said Stella, "go away."

Everett raised his hand, palm out. "Give us a moment, would you, please?"

"Uh," said Mark, and his complexion pinkened. "Sure."

After Mark withdrew, Stella looked at Everett and raised her eyebrows. *Well?*

Everett idly picked up the hammer from the tray of tools. He turned it around once, inspecting a minor ding on the head. It looked light and natural in his grip, and Stella constructed a mental image of him kneeling, focused, dust sticking to his perspiration. He squeezed the hammer's shaft until his knuckles whitened, then set it aside with a clatter. "I don't do this, either," he said.

"Make your friends do your work for you?"

"No—well, yes—what I meant was I don't talk about this part of my life," he said in a rush. "I don't show anybody the complete sculptures, and I don't really talk about this."

She shook her head. "No credit so far. I haven't seen any art that's not smashings, and you haven't actually told me anything."

"I am coming to the point. You are very demanding for someone who just called me irksome."

"Talk."

"I did work with Jaime as a fellow counselor at camp after I graduated college. That's true. It was in northern Michigan, and it was a great summer. What I failed to mention is that the kids were all dealing with various forms and stages of cancer."

She was startled. She hadn't known what to expect, but a pediatric cancer camp certainly wasn't it.

"Okay," she said.

"Jaime has had leukemia and a relapse of the same. You'll have to ask him directly if you'd like to know more. And I, ah, I had a scare with Hodgkin's lymphoma that year."

"What?" Stella grasped his forearm and squeezed, like he was about to teeter off a ledge. But the ledge was over ten years in the past. "Are you—what happened? How are you now?"

"I'm fine, yes. I apologize for the dramatic retelling. It was only a scare. The cancer turned out to be a false alarm. But the real problem is that before twenty-two-year-old young men are meant to undergo radiation, the standard practice is to collect and freeze semen so they can have biological children in the future, if they choose."

Everett pried her hand from his arm and put his hands in his pockets. He tilted his head up and contemplated the hidden top of the sculpture. "The clinic found no viable..." He winced. "Good lord, this is worse than I thought. I'm going to say it. No viable sperm, in three samples taken several weeks apart, due to a rare genetic defect in a membrane protein. I'm infertile, and I didn't tell you. I can never have children. My parents were devastated. And please don't say 'adopt' because I cannot imagine raising an innocent kid knowing I'd made them my less-preferred choice. It took me a year with a therapist to process the...to clarify my thoughts. But I knew all this, never told you, and I'm sorry."

She shook her head. *Infertile.* "But you don't have cancer."

"Correct. Neither now nor then."

"Okay." A heaviness lingered on her chest, but not so oppressive as it had been. "You should have told me."

"Yeah."

"You didn't tell me because you wanted the inheritance, and you were afraid I wouldn't agree to the deal if I knew you were infertile."

He hesitated. "It's not quite so—"

"But I did know."

He dropped his head and stared hard into her eyes. "*What?* From whom? And since when?"

"From an overheard conversation between my mom and Auntie Liz a long time ago. It must have been when you were first going through all this."

"Hmph."

"They spoke in hushed tones, made it all sound very mysterious, which of course only lured me in. I thought they were whispering because any conversation with the word *sperm* was automatically R-rated, but now I suspect it was out of concern for your privacy. Perhaps not *enough* concern."

"Or out of pity. Leon almost said something the night we first discussed inheriting the house. I suspect he feels bad for me."

She nodded, remembering. "Even if that's true, you are still the best possible person to caretake their estate. I wonder if Uncle Leon has the same genetic problem and never had it formally diagnosed."

"I wondered the same. You know I have neither siblings nor cousins, so I am the end of my particular branch of Novaks. A genetic dead end. After his death, Leon will leave nothing to denote his existence. Our house, nothing more."

"Hang on, hang on. It does offend me if you imply a lifetime of my beloved aunt's security and happiness and love is all *nothing.* To me, Leon will have left quite a mark, and to Elizabeth."

"I take your point, but security, happiness, love...these things are ephemeral, whereas creating a new generation—" He shook his head. "Life stretches out into the distant future.

"Ha," she scoffed. "Ask the last tyrannosaurus rex about how life finds a way."

"Stella, you're quoting movies about hatching babies from preserved DNA. You see that, right? I'm not really up for a conversation about cloning or...or sperm donors. That's not what I want. Is that what you would need to be happy with me? Or are you divorcing me after a week of marriage?"

She folded her lips between her teeth and considered before responding. He hadn't declared any passionate depth of feeling for her, but his explanation had the ring of a difficult truth. She believed he did not abhor her. He had given some evidence of at least tolerating her presence. Maybe he didn't even dislike her. It wasn't enough to make a person sob with relief, but for Stella's purposes, she had to consider this new information as a win over her previous assumptions.

"Maybe I should have told you that I knew," she said. "But it wasn't at the forefront of...it's not a big deal to me. You know my mom and I aren't especially close, and my dad's been mediocre at best. Parenting has never appealed to me. No, I don't need my own offspring."

He heaved a breath. "You don't care."

"No, I do care. I care because—" She puffed out her cheeks. *Screw it.* He'd finally been honest, and she could be, too. "Because I care about you, believe it or not. I don't think it's very cool that you felt you had to hide this detail about yourself, and you presented yourself as a valid husband only when packaged together with a valuable estate. But I understand the impulse to conceal what makes us different. I see it all the time in my work. And I definitely care about..." She waggled her eyebrows. "I happen to know, Ev, based most recently on sitting on your lap at lunch today, and a few other moments, that the hydraulics are all in perfect working order. Anything else I should know about in terms of sexual performance?"

His lips twitched. "I've received no complaints. And you don't need birth control."

She laughed. From elsewhere in the studio, she heard Jaime and Mark still packing, and the Spanish guitar music had switched to a new artist. She and Everett would have to get back to work. The sooner they were done, the sooner she could go home with him. "Noted. Perhaps I married you to save myself from taking a tiny pill every day."

He turned serious again. "But furthering a lineage is such a fundamental thing, an animal impulse. For a long time after I learned about my defect, I thought I was barely a man at all. What's the point of a male without the ability to propagate? I felt pointless, useless. Emasculated. It's difficult to admit."

"Do you still think that way?"

"No. As I said, after a year with a good therapist. Are you smothering those same ideas? The *I would rather be in a small house with a real man* thought, that sort of thing. Tell me now, I beg you, rather than months or years from now, when I have made you utterly miserable."

"No," she said. "And if I did feel that way, I would get the name of your fantastic therapist. You're a man like any other. No, far better than most. Irksome, handsome, troublesome. And mine, still."

He nodded once, slowly. "Yes. I had a serious girlfriend at school, and she...ah, she wanted kids, eventually, and she saw me much differently after receiving this new information. That was the end of that."

"I prefer receiving this news to learning your sperm was stolen and now you have two dozen biological offspring scattered around the country with your perfect face and no knowledge of their father."

"Happy to be of service in that regard."

"Or defective service, in this case."

"Are you going to make bad sperm jokes for a lifetime?"

"A month or two at the most. I'm actually glad to know you have a flaw." She grinned and lowered her voice as if imparting a secret. "I, too, have one or two defects, although mine are moral defects."

He huffed softly and straightened his shoulders, like a burden had been removed. "I am relieved. You are so beautiful, and so full of life and promise and a terrible, wonderful glow like you have absorbed time itself and brought the universe to a pinpoint moment. I hate to steal your future from you and keep you locked up out on the rocky, lonely shoreline with me. Although, to be clear, I would do exactly that."

Stella met his eyes. Everett looked at her with the steely intensity she expected from him, but instead of judgment or criticism she read longing. He'd been alone, too, until their wedding.

But he looked so serious. She couldn't soak up another of his compliments because she was too overwhelmed by him already.

"And our fish," she said.

"What?"

"Alone with you and our fish."

Everett broke into a wide, silly grin, then tipped his head back and laughed from his belly. He was spectacularly gorgeous. Stella giggled and reached up to loop her arms around his neck, leaning close against him.

"I think I finally understand your smashings," she said against the corner of his jaw. His hands roamed intriguingly down her hips and over her backside, and his cock thickened into a delicious pressure on her lower belly. "It's about your legacy, isn't it? You felt like a man who could create nothing for the future. No lineage stretching out over generations. So, after you make something, you destroy it."

Everett went very still. "Yes," he said. "That's it precisely. I don't know how I ever thought I could keep a secret from you, my keenly observant fortune-teller. Don't tell my gallery, please. They do seem to have a grand time trying to pin down my artistic motives."

"Will you make me an un-smashed sculpture someday?"

"My girl," he said, and she heard the smile in his voice. "My wife. What if you like it better in bits and shards?"

She stretched onto her toes and kissed him on the left corner of his mouth, then repeated with another kiss on the right, to learn the taste of his smile. Everett hadn't made a resounding declaration of eternal love, but maybe this trust and honesty and desire was the best they could hope for in their marriage. It was better than some people had endured. She would rather keep her one-sided feelings for him to herself than push him away by demanding something he could never give. Better to have a little of him than none of him.

"I'll take all your bits and shards, too," she said, then kissed him again.

Just when Stella thought he was about to break away from her, to run a hand over his hair and mutter something like *we should get to work*, Everett gathered her closer. With the strength of his hands under the curve of her ass, he urged her up onto her toes. She obeyed, and he groaned quietly, a rumble in his chest. Stella lost track of time in the giddy, dizzying rush of making out with her husband in a corner like they were students sneaking kisses beside lockers. When the guitar music fell briefly silent between tracks, she was startled but kept her arm around his neck, reluctant to let the world intrude.

Everett apparently felt the same. He leaned back and raised his eyebrows. "Follow me."

He led Stella out of the studio. In the building's fluorescent-lit hallway, Everett searched his pants pockets.

"Where are we going?" she asked.

He pulled out a set of keys and looked at them closely. "Not far." He walked no more than a dozen strides to the adjacent door. "The photographer who works here asked me to keep a spare key because she's often running late, and she didn't want clients to be left standing in the hall."

"Oh really? Is she cute?"

He turned the lock, then looked over and blinked at her. "I hadn't really thought about it. Remember that I thought I wasn't relationship material until two weeks ago, when somebody dangled you and an estate before my eyes. She has a friendly smile. Why?"

"Because that's the kind of thing I would tell the handsome man who worked beside me if I wanted to strike up a more personal acquaintance."

He held the door open, and Stella walked past him.

"I beg to differ," he said. "You're more likely to propose marriage, in my experience, than exchange a set of keys."

She laughed. "Fair. But your experience of me is limited."

They both looked around at a studio space like Everett's, with the same tall bank of steel-framed windows, but populated with a riotous mess of lighting equipment, backdrops, chairs and stools of various heights, and a low wooden dais. Most intriguing to Stella was a cushy, armless divan, upholstered in green fabric.

She turned around at the sound of the door's deadbolt sliding home. He wasn't looking at the lock, though. He was staring at her. He'd left the lights off, although there was enough low afternoon sun coming through the glass for her to read his intentions.

"That is exactly what I plan to remedy." His gaze settled on her heavily, and he ran a finger under the collar of his shirt. "Have you checked your email since last night?"

"No. Should I?" She watched the muscle in his arm. It was much more interesting than email. From next door, she heard that his friends had switched the music to bubblegum pop.

"I forwarded you a file from my doctor's office."

"About your poor, defective sperm? I believe you; I don't need to see—"

"No. Not that. It's my latest bloodwork panel for all the common sexually transmitted infections, and it's clear."

She held back a grin and sauntered toward him with an extra sway in her hips. That was about the most Everett form of foreplay she could imagine. "You're telling me you've been thinking about being with me since last night?"

He raised one arm and reached for her—not to cup her face, as she'd thought, but to grasp her ponytail. He tugged, and she tipped her head back. His eyes were dark and unfathomable. "I have thought of little else," he said softly, a promise. "The sound of your voice on the phone last night made me feel impulsive. I would have run to my car and driven to you if you'd said but one word. When you asked to come here today, to see me, there was no part of me that could have refused. So, yes, I sent you my STI bloodwork at midnight, because the only thing that made me feel calmer was the idea there would be not even a millimeter of latex between us."

Stella exhaled. His form of foreplay was startlingly effective on her. "Got it," she said, although it came out on a shaky breath. "I have mine in the health app on my phone, it's all negative, from a year ago but there hasn't been..." There had been no one for quite some time, and that scant handful of men all faded in her memory.

"Good," he said in a low rumble. He released her ponytail and worked the band free so her hair spilled across her shoulders. "We won't need those ever again. You and me, now."

"Yes," she said. The lifetime rigors of monogamy did not seem so rigorous when she applied the idea to Everett. She slid her hands under the hem of his shabby t-shirt and skimmed them up the warm, hard sides of his ribcage.

"You know I didn't marry you because you are beautiful," he said.

She stopped her hands in their motion, and her stomach clenched.

"But you are, and I won't pretend otherwise," he said.

Blood whooshed through her veins. "Oh. That's good, then?"

"That's terrifying. I confess that I could not have married you if I didn't want you so badly. Even as I talked about the house and the taxes, I was thinking about your silky skin and the taste of your sweet body. It's a flaw in me, but I cannot regret it. Yours is a stunning, tumultuous beauty, Stella," he said. "You are beautiful like a field of wildflowers."

She flexed her fingers and dug her nails into the dense flesh of his torso. He flinched. "And you," she said. "Are irksome and lucky I did not marry you for your delicate sense of tact. Take this off, please. Although it is now my favorite of your clothing. This shirt is practically lingerie on you."

He reached behind his head and pulled his shirt up and off. She'd known he was strong. She had not realized he was so pale, his skin looked nearly translucent, tinted only with the blueish tinge of the arteries beneath. The sun at some point had gilded his arms to the middle of his biceps and the back of his neck, but his stomach and chest looked...

vulnerable. In fact, she saw the pink crescent marks her fingernails had left along his sides. The coarse dark hair on his pectorals converged into a narrow band that led down the center of his stomach.

"Mm," she said.

He turned and pulled a crisp white backdrop from a folded pile of material, and Stella watched the stretch of muscle under his shoulders and across his ribs. He shook the sheet open with a crack. Then Everett crowded her backwards, his knees against her legs, his hands against her hips. He herded her across the room to the cushioned chaise and draped the fabric over the furniture. But when Stella hastened to lay herself out on it like a dessert on a platter, he stopped her. He turned and sat.

"I want you right here," he said, glancing down at his spread thighs. "Like you were at lunch today. But this time, I choose the ending."

"Yes." Stella braced one hand on his shoulder and slowly sank down to straddle his lap. He pushed his hands inside her sweater, his calluses rough against her waist, then slid the fabric up and over her head. Her hair was a mess. She wished she had worn something racier than the same pink underwear he'd already seen. There was a good chance she smelled faintly of the excellent sausage she'd had for lunch, and she regretted the soft curve of her belly over her waistband. But all those concerns fled when Everett unfastened her bra and tossed it away. He dipped his head to lick the tattoo that spread beneath her breasts, and Stella exhaled sharply. She clenched her fingers into his hair, and he rumbled a noise that could have been either a complaint or approval.

"It remains unclear to me," he muttered warmly against her skin, "how exactly I found myself in this position."

Stella laughed and dragged his mouth higher. "You're a very strange man, aren't you?" She rolled her hips. He squeezed her ass in response and tugged her jeans and high-cut bikini bottom down to the tops of her legs. "I thought you liked everything done precisely your way. Now I learn you don't know what you're doing at all."

"I've never been so muddled," he said, although his clever lips and hands seemed quite purposeful to her.

"You're doing fine," she said. It came out on a bit of a whimper as he kissed a hot trail up her throat.

Everett threaded an arm under her knees, then rose and quickly shifted her onto the chaise, pressing her back against the velvety cushion. The dainty scrap of her abandoned pink fabric dropped to the floor. "You called me strange," he said. "But if I have been so lately, it's you who made me that way."

"And it's me who enjoys you that way." She hooked a finger into the waist of his jeans and tugged. "Now, come here, husband."

He bared his teeth at her. "Say that again."

"Husband. Come here."

He obeyed, and Stella finally silenced her racing thoughts and let herself simply enjoy. She unfastened his pants to let his erection spring free, and the utter exuberance of his cock and the evidence of his raging desire for her made her feel free, too. She'd spent so long feeling trapped in her life, and then she'd manage to trap herself into marriage, yet perhaps the marriage might loosen her constraints, after all.

"Stella, I promise," he whispered, "that I will try not to fuck this up."

It was a perfect repetition of her awkward wedding vow, and she giggled as she let one knee fall to the side, then trailed her hand slowly up the inside of her own leg. Everett watched her like a hawk, his eyes dark.

"Ah, but fucking me," she murmured, and she dipped her fingertip into the wet center of her vaginal folds, "is exactly what I need you to do."

He uttered something in a growl she couldn't decipher. He lowered his mouth to her left nipple, and she arched her back at the bolt of connection from her breast to her clit. He soothed the insistent throb there with the heel of his hand, and she ground herself shamelessly against him.

"Stella, Stella," he rumbled, as he slid one finger into her hot center, "I don't want to wait another—"

"Yes," she agreed. She reached between them and centered the tip of his cock against her opening. He pressed himself home on a groan, and she canted her hips up to meet him to the hilt. "Yes."

Everett seemed lost to words. She squeezed him closer as he began to glide slowly within her, then with a more insistent rhythm. The side wall of the studio was largely mirrored, and she saw a perfect reflection of them moving together, of her mess of wild hair and the ivory expanse of his skin. But the normally rigid, upright line of his spine was curved. He bent toward her, with his arms wrapped around her, embracing her tightly. He looked...protective.

He turned the work of his mouth to her other breast, and Stella buried her nose in his hair to catch the addictive scent of him. He pulled her thigh a little higher, and the slight motion changed the angle of their entwined limbs to catch such a perfect friction that she...she was loosed from herself. She was free from any thought, free from stopping herself before emitting a feminine moan, untethered from her brain and lost to a rush of pleasure. She writhed and gasped.

"My good girl," Everett whispered. With a final hard pump, his cock hardened another impossible fraction, filling her terribly, and he came inside her.

She stroked his sweaty back, her lips on his shoulder. Nothing they had done together felt like the first time, perhaps because she'd been ready for him since their interrupted dalliance at home, or perhaps because she'd always been ready for him. He straightened up and examined her face. Stella didn't like to think of herself as easy to read, but Everett found enough in her expression to make him raise her hand and kiss her knuckles.

She turned and looked at them in the mirror, the image of satiated lovers. His face was relaxed and flushed with a masculine, youthful vigor. Her own face, however, looked pleased and yet strangely wistful.

Chapter 25

COLLECT CALL

Stella heard her phone's repetitive buzzing, somewhere in the pants she'd dropped on the floor, but the noise wasn't enough to pull her away from where she'd curled against Everett's side. It wasn't even interesting enough for her to open her eyes. Nobody called her other than robots selling extended warranties.

Then Everett's phone sent an alert, too, a single chime. He groaned.

"Leave it," she mumbled into the crook of his arm.

"Jaime and Mark are probably looking for us," he said drowsily.

"They'll survive for five more minutes." She needed more time to soak in enough contentment to last her for the rest of her marriage, if necessary.

But then somebody called his phone. He gently shifted her aside and fished for his crumpled jeans below the divan. He shook them until the device fell out into his hand.

"Leon," he said.

Stella rolled over and looked at him, eyebrows raised in a question, but Everett stood and took the call. He pinched the phone between his ear and shoulder and awkwardly hop-stepped into his briefs and pants.

"You called the *hotline?*" He strode across the room and carded his fingers through his messy hair.

"What hotline?" Stella asked.

Everett did not respond. He frowned as he listened intently to whatever Leon was saying.

"Right, but we're the property owners," he said after another minute. "No, I know. But for this year—"

Stella got dressed. Everett resumed listening and frowning. He glanced at his wristwatch.

"All right," he said. "Not all right, obviously. Very damned inconvenient. Let me speak to Stella and call you back in half an hour. You stay put. No, I insist, Leon. Do you understand? Good."

He ended the call and slid the phone into his front pocket. Stella balled up his shirt and tossed it at him.

"What's happening?" she demanded.

He squeezed his eyes shut briefly, then donned his shirt. "Leon," he said, "called the Wisconsin DNR hotline and reported himself."

"*What?*" Stella suppressed a flush of resentment. She had agreed to safeguard Leon's house and legacy, not to protect him from his own stupid decisions.

"Yes. That was the day after I'd called and told him we received that threatening letter."

Which Everett had done because Stella had left him without anybody else in his corner. She winced.

"Well, shit," she said.

"It gets worse. Apparently, somebody in Wisconsin coordinated with a counterpart in Florida, and Sunshine State law enforcement arrived at their condo today."

"*No.* That's ridiculous. Over these damned fish? I cannot believe it."

"I wouldn't believe it either, except Leon sounded so rattled. The officers showed them some paperwork, and by *paperwork* please understand that I mean *arrest warrant.* Everything has been faxed back up here for review, but in the meantime..." He looked at his watch again. "The Florida cops haven't gotten the all-clear yet, and they're saying if they don't hear back from the Wisconsin DNR folks by five o'clock eastern, we could be looking at a weekend jail stay."

Stella wanted to punch someone. She settled for pacing in circles around a dressmaker's dummy. "They're going to keep a seventy-plus year-old man with a heart condition in jail over the weekend due to a bureaucratic hang-up?"

"Stella—"

"And why are they *faxing* anything? They might as well throw paper airplanes! I'll call the Wisconsin—"

"Stella, listen. It's not Leon who's locked up. Elizabeth decided he wasn't up for the stress, and he says she insisted. Your aunt is in jail in Florida."

Chapter 26

IN MURKY DEPTHS

Stella crammed her feet into her boots. "This is fine," she said. "This is fine. Elizabeth is in jail in Florida, and I'm here in Milwaukee having brain-melting sex with my husband, and I need to get to the DNR office in Madison before—what time is it now?" Then another horrible thought intruded. "Oh, no, does my mother know about this?"

"Three-fifteen, and no," said Everett without looking up from his phone.

"Good. Do not tell my mother, or she'll find a way to make everything ten times worse. I'm going to the DNR office—"

"You won't have to drive to Madison," he said. "There's one here in the city. You need to be there before four o'clock."

"Great, yes. Send that address to my phone, please. And you're obviously going to..." She had no idea. "Sorry, what are you doing?"

He looked up, frowning. "I'm obviously going to fly to Orlando, drive to Vero Beach, then help arrange your aunt's bail," he said. "She'll have to appear before a judge. Avoid the bondsman, if Leon hasn't managed that already. I'll take her home. I'm going to help them find and hire a lawyer, and I'm going to make sure Leon is fed, watered, and taking his medication."

Stella blinked. She stepped forward, put her hands on either side of his face, and pulled him down for an emphatic kiss, brief but heartfelt.

Of course, white-knight Everett would gallop to the rescue. "Yes," she said. "Thank you."

He held her gaze. "Stella," he said. "Listen. This is important. You need to make sure the Wisconsin DNR has cleared their paperwork with Florida, all right? Elizabeth will need to go before a judge to set her bail. If Wisconsin is dragging their heels, the Florida court isn't required to hold a first appearance until Monday. Do you want me to ask Mark to go with you?"

"We can't leave her behind bars over the weekend!" Stella said. "She needs her weighted duvet and oolong every morning. She is made for silk scarves and caviar, so jail is not the place for Elizabeth. No, I can handle this."

He looked grim. "Good. Make sure the diligent wardens here aren't the cause of an unnecessary delay."

Stella took a deep breath and nodded. This was exactly why they'd taken possession of Name Estate. All she needed to do was prove to him she could be trustworthy and helpful, too. She left him sunk deep into booking a flight on his phone and hurried out of the building. Her car was parked a block away, and she was nearly there when she heard her name.

"Stella! Stella, wait," someone called.

She turned. Mark jogged toward her while attempting to work his arms into his coat. "Heard you have an errand. Want me to come with you as backup?"

She glanced at the time. "Oh, no. Thank you, though. I wouldn't trouble you."

"No trouble. I'm sick of moving boxes."

"It's a private family matter," she said, then hesitated before providing a smidgen more truth. "I'm proving a point about my competence and reliability, so I need to do it by myself. Can't have a sidekick along sharing credit for victory." She smiled to ease any sting.

"Got it, I'll leave you to it." Mark waved a hand to show he wasn't offended by her dismissal. Stella turned away, but Mark caught her elbow. She looked at him with raised eyebrows. "I haven't seen him like this before, you know."

She didn't need to ask who he meant by *him*. "He's not handling the news about Elizabeth's problems well?"

"Elizabeth who?" Mark blinked. "No, about *you*. I haven't seen him like this over anyone. Until today."

The Department of Natural Resources's Milwaukee office was an uninspiring stucco building tucked beside an interstate off-ramp. Stella arrived twenty minutes before closing. Hardy, battered weeds clung to the cracks around the foundation, and dusty miniblinds shaded the windows. She pressed the doorbell to gain admittance.

The receptionist at the front desk eyed Stella skeptically.

"Hello," said Stella. She tried to convey authority, dignity, and cheerful good humor in a one-word greeting.

"Violations can be reported on the hotline," said the man behind the desk, apparently not impressed by her authority or dignity. "Or there's an online form." He tapped a sign displaying a phone number and a website.

"No, thank you," she said. "I'm here regarding an open violation. Sturgeon regulations. It's against the Novak property, Name Estate, on the lake shore past Racine—"

"You said Novak?" The man pushed back his chair and stood. "Oh. I'll be right back."

Stella waited, her patience held firmly intact.

When the receptionist returned, several minutes later, he was accompanied by Officer Diettrich.

Stella glared at the front-desk man for this betrayal. He returned her gaze placidly, either unaware of or uninterested in her previous unpleasant interaction with the agent.

"Mrs. Novak," said Diettrich. "I'm not at all surprised to see you."

He drew out her married name enough to make it insulting, and the remains of her patience thinned. "Officer," she said. "I understand that my seventy-something-year-old aunt was arrested in Florida. Over a violation on *my* property. I would like for you to please contact your colleagues down south and have Elizabeth Novak brought before the judge at once so she can be released."

He waved a thin manila folder held between two fingers. "And *I* would like to close my case file for the regulatory violations on your property, so I guess we all want nice things today, don't we?"

"Elizabeth doesn't factor into it. I own the land. Please, she's frail, even if she won't admit it, and my uncle has health problems. You need to deal with me directly."

"The last inspection was done when the property was owned—" Diettrich opened his file and consulted the top page. "By Leon and Elizabeth Novak, and that was over ten years ago. Is that you? Do I have a case of mistaken identity? Elizabeth?" He squinted, hunched, and peered at her. "I thought Elizabeth was the one cooling her heels. No? Bought the place in nineteen-seventy-seven? Boy, you've held up nicely."

His sarcasm grated.

"I'm telling you, I own it now. Our lawyer filed the deed with the county."

"Doesn't matter." He closed the file and rocked back on his heels. "We don't do inspections until spawning season. There is no new violation under your name until you miss an inspection. In the meantime, the old violation stands. Got it? You haven't personally violated anything yet. I can't arrest you, as much as I might enjoy that." He smirked.

"But it's my property." Stella was mortified that her voice shook with her increasing desperation.

"You want to do it now, while there's no sturgeon?"

"Don't they have, like..." she waved a hand vaguely. "Radio-frequency tags? To ping their locations?"

He snorted. "They're fish, ma'am, not leopards. They're not wearing tracking collars."

"I read about scientists in Michigan who had tags and antennae to locate the fish."

"Great, she did five minutes of googling and now she's an expert. No, I repeat, the sturgeon along your spawning run are not traced. Listen, if I round up three or four of my guys, and we spend a couple days sitting out at Name Estate, all to find no sturgeon, you're going to have big problems. Remember that felony I mentioned? You really do *not* want me counting fish and arriving at a grand total of zero. And I don't want to waste my time in the cold. Come back in a month, six weeks maybe, then we'll talk. Get you on the calendar."

"My aunt—"

Diettrich's soft pink mouth twisted in distaste. "She's facing the consequences of her actions."

"At least get her out of there today." She was begging, and she didn't care. "Don't let her sit in some awful Florida jail over the weekend for no reason. Are they waiting on you to file charges?"

The officer glanced at his watch. "Well, I might have something in my inbox with the name Novak on it, but I've been busy up here with you. They're probably all packing up now." He offered a false smile. "Can't expect to flout the rules for years and years then demand instant service, can you?"

"Please," she said.

His raised lips approximated nothing like a real smile. Stella looked at the heavy stapler atop the receptionist's desk and wondered if she could murder him with it.

"Ma'am," he said. "You obviously don't know much about jurisdictions. Let me tell you, there's no motivating out-of-state folks along your personal schedule—"

"But *you* did! You called some bro friend in Florida and motivated him right along to my elderly relatives' retirement complex!"

"Did you have any information relevant to the existing Novak violations, ma'am?" he asked. "Because if not, I'd best be getting a response sent back to my bro friend...I mean my colleague down south." Then he pointedly lifted his wrist and checked his watch. "Ope, would you look at that. Couple of minutes past quitting time. Happy weekend."

Stella fumbled for her phone to check the time, and he wasn't lying. "No, please," she whispered. This was the one thing Everett had asked her to do. "There has to be something we can do today."

"Sure there is."

She glanced up sharply.

Diettrich handed her his business card. "We can carefully consider our options for the future. Call me when you're ready to talk about bringing your property back into compliance with state regulations."

Stella, defeated, took the card from him. She couldn't think carefully about any options when all she could imagine was Elizabeth sitting on a metal cot. The receptionist locked the door after she departed.

She drove in silence back to Name Estate, but she wasn't ready to go back into the house. Nor was she in the mood for the enormous indifference of Lake Michigan. Instead, she parked halfway up the lane and got out of the car. She followed the mulched trail into the woods toward the sturgeon pond. The smell was the same as the last time she'd taken the walk, of wet, composting leaves, but she did not have the same eerie feeling that someone was watching her from among the trees. That had been Officer Diettrich, and she knew he wasn't there. She was totally alone.

Upon reaching the clearing, Stella stopped a few yards away. She sat on a damp old bench and contemplated the pond. Although it had become such a source of hassle, it was still peaceful, if not exactly beautiful. She remembered clearly the feeling of cold mud oozing into her shoes.

Was Elizabeth cold in jail? Not in Florida, surely. Surely, they were required by law to feed detainees reasonably nutritious food and provide proper heating and air conditioning. If Diettrich had offered her the option to switch places with her aunt, she would have taken it in a second. But he hadn't. Everett had given her one responsibility—to make sure the Wisconsin DNR didn't delay Elizabeth's court appearance. And she had failed him, failed Elizabeth. Poor Leon was probably beside himself with stress.

She considered the depth and breadth of her personal deficiencies for a while longer, like rubbing at a torn cuticle. She grew cold and hungry, but when she imagined Elizabeth suffering, she decided it wasn't yet time to go into the warm, welcoming, lovely mansion that she had been gifted. She could wait on the damp bench.

The shade under the trees was deepening to true darkness when her phone buzzed, and Stella straightened with a jolt. She'd been sunk into her morose reverie for so long that her joints felt stiff. The screen showed Everett's name.

"Hey," she said softly.

"Stella," he said. The background noise was that of an airport. "Is it done?"

He sounded brusque, distracted. Stella closed her eyes. She still felt squashed by the defeat she had taken at the DNR office. It would have been nice to absorb some kindness from Everett, but he clearly wasn't in the same mood.

"No," she said. "It's not."

"What?" he barked. "Why?"

"The officer is still sitting on paperwork for Elizabeth's charges. I don't think Florida law enforcement will be able to put her in front of a judge today."

"I thought we agreed you were going to handle it."

"We did, Ev, and I *tried*." She gritted her teeth and waited as a canned security announcement cut through the line. "It's not like asking for a receipt at the post office. The DNR wardens are not in the business of doing me favors."

"My flight leaves in half an hour. What the hell am I going down there for if her case isn't moving forward?"

"As you said, to hire a lawyer and arrange her bail."

"Yes, on Monday morning, if we're lucky. Two and a half days from now. Are we on the same page about this? You sound so resigned. I hope you told them we own the property now. If Mark had been there, he might have...never mind. You don't want your aunt stuck in jail, do you?"

She was stung by the accusation. "No, of course not. And yes, I told them. Mark couldn't have accomplished anything different, I promise you. Why are you making this my fault?"

"If I thought you couldn't handle the DNR, I would have gone there—" He cut himself off abruptly. "Good lord. I sound like...I *am*...the worst sort of inconsiderate asshole. What is wrong with me? Why on earth do you give me even a moment of your time? I'm so sorry."

"Hmph," she said.

"I take it back, and I'm sure you did everything humanly possible. Look, I'm about to board, but I will beg your forgiveness more later. Did they give you something to work with? Any hint of a solution to this mess?"

"Sort of. We need to get a fresh violation of our own that supersedes the old one, but that's not feasible until spawning season."

He sighed audibly. "Preventing a situation like this was why we married, Stella. Wasn't it? Tell me you didn't marry me for the pretty house."

I married you because I wanted to let myself fall in love with you.

She couldn't say it, especially while he was so frustrated with her.

"I know," she said. "I'm sorry."

"We were supposed to take over the running of Name Estate for Leon and Elizabeth. None of this was meant to land on their shoulders."

And now it was all on him, alone, she heard him imply. Because she had failed to uphold her end. She wasn't the partner he needed.

"I said I was sorry."

"Fine. I'll call you once I assess the situation in Vero Beach."

He ended the call. Stella stared at the blank face of her phone. It felt like Everett had hung up on her. She wanted to chuck her phone into the pond. She stood and paced along the sloped embankment.

Wasn't Everett right, though? She deserved the admonishments. He could have been a lot meaner, and she would have deserved that, too. He ought to have yelled at her. Nobody ever expected very much good from Stella Woodward, and when Everett dared to extend a little more trust, he was disappointed.

She was angry with herself and made more furious by the tears in her eyes. She was selfish and unreliable. As much as she wanted to protect Elizabeth, she wanted even more to protect herself from Everett's sharp judgment. Which was ridiculous. He had never vowed to dole out his approval. She was the one who had let down her end of the bargain.

She had cobbled up a career of nonsense bullshit, and she'd scraped together a marriage based on an honorable man's sense of obligation. Nobody should trust her ever again.

But...but Everett did trust her. Even her clients came back time and again. It was Stella who never bought into her own baloney.

However, Everett had not earned *her* trust. Beginning with when she'd overheard him speaking to Leon, and his impenetrable demeanor, then confusing mixed signals she'd received from him, now he was brusque and disapproving. She couldn't trust him because he was far too capable of hurting her.

Her mind was a morass of conflicting impulses. *The mess of contradictions you contain, as Everett had once said, must be difficult.*

It was very fucking difficult.

She staggered on one leg and pulled off a shoe, then reversed herself and removed the other. Her bare feet sank into the cold, weedy mud. Without conscious decision, she crept down the bank and into the pond. It was where she'd gone the morning after she'd proposed to Everett, the place where Diettrich had startled her. The sturgeon were the source of the estate's phenomenal caviar and many of its current problems.

Stella wiggled her toes. She let herself feel a little smaller as the earth absorbed part of her. Then she roused the intuition she used in her work but had always discounted, the murmuring insight that was the background noise of her mind.

The mud was chilly but nice, almost like a foot spa treatment. She exhaled slowly and imagined her breath seeping into her feet. She felt everything around her.

It was embarrassingly easy, when she allowed herself to think and feel, and her conclusion, when it eased to the forefront of her mind, was fully formed. She did have skills and insights. The wanderings of her brain were no less correct for being illogical.

She wasn't alone in the pond. The winter had been too warm. She wasn't alone. She'd seen nothing and heard nothing, but she felt them. Ancient, gross, whiskery swimmers.

There was only one thing to do about it. Still standing ankle-deep in cold pond water, she pulled out her phone and the business card Diettrich had handed her. She called him, half expecting he wouldn't answer on a Friday evening, but he picked up on the first ring.

"Mrs. Novak," he said, again drawing out her name like an insult.

"Officer," she said briskly. "Am I correct that you assume my Uncle Leon has avoided the inspection because the Name Estate sturgeon population has been fished to extinction?"

"Some folks might think that," he said. "I, however, would never assume, ma'am. I am tasked with investigating. Making sure the rules are followed. Everybody playing fair. The only thing I know for sure right now is that he's evaded the required population count. Only a few reasons why a person might do that."

"Here's what we're going to do, Officer Diettrich." The plan was still coming together as she voiced it. It was hardly a plan at all, more of a desperate wild hunch. Failing to protect Elizabeth and disappointing Everett was intolerable. She had to do something. "Are you listening? You're going to have Elizabeth Novak sprung from jail tonight. In the next hour. Don't make excuses about—listen." She cut off his sputtered objections about the impossibility of her request. "Hey. No. Get her out tonight. You clearly have somebody down there who owes you a favor, so cut the bullshit. We're not leaving my elderly aunt in jail overnight. And in return, I'm telling you to come out here and count my sturgeon. First thing in the morning. Bring your guys, bring your nets or whatever."

"It's too early," Diettrich said. "That'd be downright dumb. They won't be back until spring."

"Fuck you and fuck *dumb*. Come here and find out."

Heavy breathing over a long pause. "You had better be right about this, Mrs. Novak," the man said finally.

"I know."

Chapter 27

NOT A VECHERINKA

Stella emerged from the pond, muddy and shivering, and rinsed herself off at the utility sink in the garage. The big house was quiet, drowsy, but her sense of momentum kept her in motion. She flicked on the lights and the kettle in the kitchen. The thermostat woke up and triggered the furnace. Then she texted Michaela and requested her presence as backup for the weekend. Stella didn't know when Everett would return, and she didn't like the idea of DNR wardens crawling over the property under only a single pair of watchful eyes. Michaela agreed on the conditions that she could bring her husband and children and that the kids could ride their scooters up and down the long driveway, to which Stella readily assented.

Her next call was to a local family-style Italian restaurant, where a vexed-sounding young woman took her order for a tray of lasagna, shrimp alfredo, an unreasonable number of garlic bread sticks, plus a large salad, all to be delivered late the next afternoon. She had Michaela's family plus a whole team of DNR folks to feed, after all. Elizabeth would not have wanted Name Estate to be known for bad hospitality, and Stella needed the wardens cheerful and lenient.

Then, feeling as reckless as a bicyclist hurtling downhill, from the open tab on her phone she purchased the sofa she'd been eyeing, although she and Everett had not had a chance to visit the store in person. Life was too short to worry about the precise color of the upholstery. She paid an extra hundred dollars for next-day delivery.

When an unknown number called the house's landline from an unfamiliar area code, she picked it up, thinking it might have been Florida law enforcement or the jail. But instead, the caller was Jaime Mackenzie, sounding uncertain.

"We couldn't reach Everett on his cell," he explained. "Is he there with you? The studio is all packed."

Stella winced. She and Everett had abandoned his friends with rather a lot of work to do. "No, he's not here. Um, do you want to drop that stuff off here at the house? Or I could...I could come meet you in the city and pick it up. Somehow."

"No, no, it's all loaded in a borrowed trailer. But it's after six now, and I need to shower before meeting my brother and sister-in-law for dinner. Mark is heading home, too. Could we swing by later tomorrow afternoon?"

A rising hilarity caught in Stella's throat. It was shaping up to be a busy day. She turned off the kettle because tea was not going to be nearly strong enough. "Sure, why not? In fact, stay for dinner. We're having Italian food delivered, and there will be fresh caviar." *I hope.*

"That's very kind, but I have my brother with me all weekend."

"Bring him, too, and his wife. And tell Mark. I seem to be hosting a party." Everett would probably disapprove. She longed for him anyway, for the way his gaze moved around the room looking for problems to solve.

"Are you sure?"

"Of course. It's the least I can do after all your work in the studio today."

"All right, thanks. We'll be there."

Stella vacuumed the floors and scrubbed the powder room. The kitchen was clean enough, and the guest bedrooms were ready for Michaela's family. Then she ventured downstairs in search of Leon's stash of wine bottles. She needed to grab an assortment for her guests, but she also wanted a drink.

The wine wasn't kept in the lower level, however. It was stored in the subbasement, a smaller, cellar-like area completely cut into the rocky cliffside. Stella had only been there once as a child, and only because she was nosey. She remembered it as chilly and damp.

The unassuming cellar door was around the corner from the laundry room, built against an interior wall and always kept closed. Stella freed the hook-and-eye latch and opened the panel to release a wash of stale air. She turned on the lights, which were newer LED bulbs dangling from bare sockets. The stairs were narrow, steep, and unpainted.

From the three-tier wooden wine rack at the base of the steps she pulled three dusty bottles and wedged them under her arms. Everything was quiet. But the same intuition she had trusted outside began to fail her. She felt the same *not alone, not alone* vibration she'd experienced while standing in the pond. It was impossible, so she was wrong. Of course she was the solitary occupant of the cellar. Her husband and family were in Florida.

Stella stood motionless, listening to the faint whoosh in the air ducts and the hum of the overhead bulbs. It could mean she'd been wrong earlier, too. Maybe what she'd interpreted as *not alone* was actually *you'll always be alone.*

Or, more likely, her so-called intuition was and always had been pure bullshit, as she had explained to her clients.

"Everett?" she called out irrationally. He was in Florida. She was so desperate for his voice in return that she could almost hear the exasperation. *Stella, what are you doing? You're alone, you're alone.*

But the instinct would not be ignored. *Not alone, not alone.* She smothered a flash of irritation with Leon and Elizabeth for saddling her with the place and with Everett for leaving her behind. The only choice was to manage as best she could. That's what she agreed to do, and it's what Everett expected. She sighed and set the bottles upright on the last step. Then she walked around the back of the staircase, deeper into the cellar.

The space wasn't nearly as large as the footprint of the full structure. Stella refused to shiver, cower, creep on tiptoes. It was her house, after all, and she was truly alone. She walked past a wire shelving unit stocked with a sealed five-pound bag of flour, canned soups, cleaning supplies, replacement furnace filters, Christmas ornaments, and a box of tangled power cables and extension cords.

On the next shelf were six cut-glass jars of black caviar, gleaming like a handful of gems on the otherwise empty rack. *So few.* In Stella's imagination, the caviar at Name Estate was endless. She could too easily imagine Officer Diettrich pointing at the low inventory as evidence the sturgeon were all gone. But there were several more jars in the kitchen for her to serve from, so he would have no reason to visit the cellar anyway.

A ventilation fan whirred as she proceeded deeper. The cement floor gave way to bare, rough rock. Stella's phone had no signal, but she switched on the flashlight. The ceiling was lower, only a foot above her head, and it too was bare rock.

Finally, in the furthest reach of the cavernous cellar, she came onto a pool of water collected in a depression in the rock. Stella stared. Was there a leak, a burst pipe? It was too large to be a puddle of condensation. The rugged stone looked natural, not shaped by hand. It wasn't intended as a charming feature of the house. The water's surface was utterly still. She could see no source for it. A rivulet ran down the wall on a mildewy green track and silently joined the larger body.

Stella crouched and wetted one fingertip. The small pool didn't smell offensive, perhaps due to the noisy efforts of the exhaust fan behind her, but it also didn't seem healthy. Wouldn't standing water contribute a lot of unnecessary humidity to the house? Leon should have mentioned it—but then again, there were a lot of things she wished Leon had done differently, such as adhering to state regulations.

She stood, swiped her palms against her thighs, and resolved to tell Everett what she'd found. He might have known they had a grotto, or he might be willing to...to drain it, or otherwise clean it up somehow. She wasn't sure she wanted a grotto.

A glint caught the periphery of her vision, and she pivoted. It was an orange...something. She crept closer and inhaled sharply. The thing was an orange earring. Under the lip of the water, atop a jagged spit of rock, was her missing bauble earring. She'd lost it weeks ago in the pond outside.

She bent and retrieved it, shaking droplets of moisture from the little orange beads. Then she pocketed it.

It wasn't possible that Officer Diettrich had found her earring, or that he had been in the cellar. He had never been inside the house. Stella forced the unsettling idea away as nonsensical, paranoid, and she retreated quickly.

Back upstairs, in the relative civilization of the finished lower level, she carefully relatched the cellar door. She kept the swirl of her own mind at arm's length, straining to keep herself from overreacting or jumping to silly conclusions. Then her phone chimed with a new voicemail. It hadn't vibrated when she was underground. Stella was embarrassed to see her hands shaking as she fumbled to play the message. *Everett. Everett.*

Instead, it was Officer Diettrich. His message was brief, but he said everything Stella needed to hear.

It's done, he said. *Elizabeth Novak will be released. My contact down there is putting everything in motion. Expect me and my team tomorrow morning by ten o'clock.*

Chapter 28

PRE-DAWN PROBLEMS

Stella awoke to the alarm she had set for a horrid pre-dawn hour. She spent a moment flat on her back, confused, staring at the ceiling, before she remembered where she was. In her bed, in her room, in her house. The bed was new, a king-size monstrosity that appealed to her sense of grandeur, yet she was slivered along one edge of it like she was getting a refund for the unused portion. But the plush rug underfoot was nice. She had secretly daydreamed that the large room on the mezzanine level would become a private retreat for her and Everett and furnished it accordingly. Based on their previous phone conversation, however, he might not be interested. Neither the room nor the bed was proportioned for a single person. Stella had to hope they still had a chance at a real marriage. After the vecherinka—*not a vecherinka*, she corrected herself scrupulously. After the inspection and the dinner that evening, she would know much more about Name Estate's legal troubles, and therefore her marriage. All she had to do was keep the conservation wardens busy and happy and pray there were at least a few fish in the pond.

In the meantime, however, she made the effort to fend off her emotional turmoil. Like a rambunctious toddler covered in ketchup, she continued to hold herself at a distance lest things become very messy. And it worked. She felt slightly numb, but at least she didn't feel everything else.

She wandered downstairs wearing only underwear and a thick cardigan belted around her waist. Some of her clothes were still in suitcases from the move, and she needed to run a pile of others through the washing machine. Her immediate priority was coffee. The main floor, however, was sweltering hot, and the furnace was running.

"Ugh," Stella muttered to herself. She must have messed up the thermostat. She brewed coffee, then played with the thermostat's programming until it had a reasonable schedule. Would Everett disagree with her about domestic matters like their brand of coffee or the ideal indoor temperature? It seemed like the sort of thing he wouldn't deign to notice, much less comment on.

But, she reminded herself, she was not preoccupied with Everett's thoughts and feelings. He would never concern himself with hers, although it didn't matter. She was gliding through what would surely be a long day, like a graceful swan paddling on the surface of a calm river.

Once she had a cup of coffee properly dosed with cream and sugar, she was too hot to sit around drinking it. She carried her mug out the patio door. Nobody would see her lack of pants, and the weather felt more like May than mid-March. Stella pulled her sweater a little closer, then sipped from her steaming mug. On her phone she found a missed late-night call from Everett and a message, which she played.

Stella, he said. He sounded tired. *She's home. Elizabeth is home and resting. She's fine, and they're meeting with a lawyer on Monday.* But Stella... He paused, and she heard traffic in the background. *The people who released her made it sound like no charges will be filed, and they weren't in uniform. I think they came in after hours specifically to release her. They raised their eyebrows at me like I knew something, but I don't. I wish you had been there to interpret the odd looks I was receiving. It was all a little too under-the-table wink-nudge for me. Leon didn't notice anything off, but he was focused on Elizabeth, of course. Why do I feel as if I exchanged Elizabeth for an illegal payoff? Anyway, I'm rambling. We'll speak about this later. I have a flight soon, so I'll be home in the morning.*

Stella listened to it twice. It was timestamped three forty-five. Then she turned around, and Everett was there, standing in the open doorway. She exhaled slowly to fight the lurch in her heartrate. He dropped his bag on the floor and came outside.

Without a word, he came right up to her and wrapped his arms around her. He exhaled a huge breath that ruffled through her hair.

"It's very hot inside the house," he whispered.

"You're back." She strained against his hold. "And you haven't slept. And you're angry with me."

"You're not wearing any pants," Everett said, releasing her. "I have so much to say to you, but the only thought in my head right now is that you're not wearing pants."

She turned away. His roaming hands moved down her sides and over her hips. He would soon find out she wasn't wearing anything under her cardigan, either. Stella stared at the lake while Everett pressed close behind her. Her husband wanted her. She wanted him, too, but she was a swan. And she wasn't sure that sex with Everett was going to resolve any of their problems, which were mainly that she was useless, and he didn't entirely like her, and that their rare fish needed to make an on-demand appearance.

"I am a graceful swan," she whispered to herself.

"What?"

His warm hands felt so good pressed against her stomach.

"Nothing," she said.

He twisted her hair and pushed the bundled strands over one shoulder, then leaned in and nuzzled the side of her neck. "I'm so tired I can scarcely think," he said. "I cannot resist you. I hated being away, even though I knew it was necessary. Stella, Stella," he said on a groan. "I'm sorry I was such an asshole on the phone. I was tired and worried, but that's no reason to vent my frustrations on my only partner in this odd endeavor. I would do nothing to damage your opinion of me, and I only hope for the chance to earn your favor."

Graceful swan, she reminded herself. He didn't *like* her; he was just a red-blooded man.

"Do you want a cup of coffee?" she asked.

But her body betrayed her better intentions. Something undeniable in the warmth of his mouth, the smell of his skin, urged her to press her hips back.

"I don't want coffee," he said. "I want to remove your sweater."

Stella craned her head to one side to give him better access to her throat. The harsh words he'd said the night before were still replaying in her mind. He didn't yet know about the deal she had made with Diettrich. He didn't yet know about the DNR agents who were due to arrive soon, about the party she'd planned for the evening.

She hated herself for a moment. How could she be so remiss in gratitude? His apology was sincere. His life had been upended, too. Hadn't she gotten basically everything she had ever wanted? Everett married her, Everett wanted her. The beautiful house was theirs. Elizabeth and Leon were safe and far away. But it wasn't enough. Could she still enjoy what she did have?

"You are stunning." Everett leaned in to kiss her, but Stella ducked.

It wasn't enough.

Everett widened his eyes when he realized she was declining his advances. He looked faintly nauseated.

The traitorous sunrise was spectacular, of course, with a flowering of bright colors that slowly shaded to morning pastels. It was too beautiful. Tears prickled her eyes.

"Stella, are you all right?" he asked, a crease appearing between his eyebrows. "You seem to be...elsewhere."

"I'm right here with you." She smiled, hoping it didn't waver.

"That's not what I meant."

She considered how brusque he'd been. *Are we on the same page about this?* The hard-clipped bite to his words was still ringing in her ears. Maybe he'd been rightfully annoyed, and maybe she was incompetent and annoying to work with. And he'd flown overnight to come home. But he'd been abrasive with her, and she hadn't forgotten, despite his apology.

"You always do the right thing," she said after a moment. "You don't always *say* the right things."

He puffed out his cheeks. "Better that than the reverse."

"See? That's a very Everett thing to say."

"Because it's the wrong thing?"

Stella laughed ruefully. She couldn't ask him to be an entirely different man. The evident concern and confusion on his face was what changed her mood toward him more than his words. "I forgive you, Ev. Let's go inside."

"No, wait. I'm not a card reader. I mean—is there anything you want to..." He captured her hand and flattened it over his heart. "Sorry. I always wanted what Leon and Elizabeth have. That type of love, full communication, and commitment. It seemed impossible."

"You settled for me, instead."

"No. I see you as the sort of woman who deserves a real family, which as you know, isn't something I can provide. But when you said you didn't care about...that, about my genetic infertility, it made me wonder if I could have a complete life with you. Honesty, passion, everything. But I don't think I need to convince you that I'm worth the risk. You need to convince yourself that *you* are."

"Uh-huh," she said. "I just forgave you for being a jerk, so maybe don't tee up your next asshole remark right away."

"I'm not. You're right, though, that I haven't said all the nicest things. You deserve this good luck we've fallen into and so much more. I've been thinking that I would like to talk, really talk, to you about our future together."

Listening to him saying the right things was unnerving, and Stella didn't know exactly what to do with his sincere kindness. She diverted instead.

"Yes," she said. "Me, too. In our immediate future, for example, Officer Diettrich and several others from the DNR are going to be here."

He released her hand and blinked. "Pardon me?"

"Which part didn't you hear?"

"I heard you, but I didn't understand you. When are they coming?"

"A few hours. I bargained for Elizabeth's release. Name Estate is having its required annual inspection today." Stella watched him buttoning his cuffs as carefully as if he were donning armor for a battle. She probably needed her pants for the day ahead. And a bra. "If we pass, it's over. The old violations are closed. If we fail, if the fish are missing..." She shrugged. "Then I'm on the hook. No pun intended. It's written up as a failure of the current homeowner, not the previous one. Elizabeth and Leon are safe either way."

He looked at her with slow-dawning horror. "Stella, it's *March*. The fish aren't here yet. They put Elizabeth in *jail* over this mess. These people are deadly serious about their protected wildlife. You can't have signed up for the inspection today. Please tell me I've misunderstood."

"Nope. I think it's going to be fine."

"You think it's going to be fine."

"Oh, and your friends Mark and Jaime are coming by later to drop off the stuff from your studio. I asked them to stay for dinner. Jaime is bringing someone; I forget whom. Was it his brother and sister-in-law? Or sister and brother-in-law. I'm leaving to pick up Michaela, Henry, Kira, and Jackson from the train station in Racine in about...Do you have the time?"

He glanced at his wristwatch. "A few minutes before seven. So, we're having a vecherinka here? Tonight? Are the DNR officers attending?"

She squinted at him. "I can't tell if that was sarcasm."

"No, I would genuinely like to know."

"It's not a vecherinka. I will certainly provide food and beverages, if the officers are hungry. They probably won't drink our booze. And I wasn't planning to share the caviar with them. There are only a few jars left in the fridge and six down in the cellar." She snapped her fingers. "That was the other thing. The cellar—did you know we have a grotto? It's weird."

Everett planted one hand on his hip and used the other to rub his forehead. "All right. I'm going to make sure we have food for—"

"I ordered Italian."

"Fine. Then I am going to take a shower."

"Perfect."

"And, ah, which bedroom and bathroom are ours at this point? Or am I...?"

She glanced away. It should not have been a complex question, yet even the simplest logistics between them were fraught. "The mezzanine. I told Michaela she could use both downstairs rooms. I hope that's not a problem."

"We have several problems, but Michaela is not one of them." He raised one hand and ticked off points on his fingers. "First, I would like to think of a way to lure a school of large, prehistoric fish to their traditional spawning grounds. That is a problem. Second, I would like to keep my wife out of jail. That is a problem. Third, I need to find a place to store all the supplies from my studio. That's not truly a problem, it's a chore. Fourth, I didn't know we had a grotto, and I am choosing to ignore any insinuation of its existence. Fifth, I need a shower."

Stella nodded. "And sixth, I was hoping you could repair that broken section of the boundary wall today. You know, the segment out by the state road?"

He sighed. "Yes."

"Hey." Stella took pity and clasped his forearm. "We're going to be fine. All right? Trust me. I have a feeling about the sturgeon."

"Why?" he asked sharply. "The kind of feeling based on facts? Did you see something?"

"Not exactly." Stella felt the tendons flex in his arm, and she released him. "Anyway, what did you want to talk about?"

Everett twisted his lips. "Some other time. Let's get through today."

Chapter 29

THE NAME OF NAME ESTATE

Stella drove Everett's car to the train station because it was both larger and cleaner than hers. The station itself, a newer, charmless building with a tacky faux turret, was well inland of the lake shore. But the train was on time, and Stella's sense of relief upon hugging Michaela made the drive worthwhile.

Michaela perceived immediately that Stella's serene exterior was not quite right.

"What is it?" Michaela whispered and gripped Stella's elbows. Behind her, Henry helped Jackson with an Iron Man suitcase while Kira ran in dizzying circles around a car seat that held a quantity of crushed cereal.

"I don't know," said Stella. "I'm all upside down, Mickey. Auntie Liz was in jail, then Everett was mad; I had to do something. So, now we're having a caviar inspection party tonight. I'm not sure that was the right response."

Michaela raised her expressive brows. "Wait, Auntie Liz is in *jail*?"

"Not anymore. I made a deal with the DNR."

"Okay, so you're upset because you're worried about the fish."

"No, of course not. I'm upset because I like my husband more than he likes me. Now you see why I needed you."

"Yeah." Michaela turned to her children. "Let's get moving. Auntie Stella has a super long driveway now, you guys."

Michaela loaded the kids into the back seat as Stella hugged Henry in greeting. Michaela's husband was calm and steady, a trim Chinese American man with fantastic biceps and a warm smile. He wore scholarly tortoiseshell eyeglasses, and he would talk about CrossFit if she engaged him in conversation for more than a few minutes. He adored Michaela, so Stella liked him just fine.

With Henry and the kids in the back, Stella drove and told Michaela about the DNR survey, the typical late-spring spawning window, and Everett's friends who would be arriving later.

"Have you asked Leon and Elizabeth why they didn't bother keeping up with the state regs?" Michaela asked.

"We've been trying to keep them out of it. Or we were, until Elizabeth was arrested. It's supposed to be my problem now. *Our* problem. The only thing that Leon said is that the vecherinka, the caviar-harvesting party, turned into a hassle and that we shouldn't continue the tradition."

"But that's the party we're having tonight."

"It's not a vecherinka. I don't even know if there are any sturgeon to be caught."

"You'd better hope so, or you'll be swapping DIY jail makeup tips with your aunt."

Stella huffed a dry laugh. "Thanks, Mick."

They drove in silence, which was actually a near-continual stream of chatter from Kira. She talked about preschool, about dinosaurs, about a friend whose name was either Lark or Lauren K., about the many merits of a YouTube cartoon she had watched, and about how to know when you need to pee.

Stella slowed at the gate to Name Estate and punched in the code. As the barrier swung open and she eased through, Kira piped up again.

"Nah-mey," Kira pronounced. "Like the fish."

Stella glanced in the rear-view mirror and saw the little girl reading the estate's name wrought in iron.

"That's *name*, pumpkin," said Henry. "As in, your *name* is Kira."

"I *know*, Dad," said Kira with withering disdain. "I said nah-mey like the fish. Because we are learning Potawatomi with Miss Caldwell." She pronounced Potawatomi very carefully, a word learned through practice. "Like pnéshi for bird, gigyago for girl. Name for fish."

Michaela turned in her seat. "Are you sure, baby?"

"Yes. Miss Caldwell told me." Kira clearly considered her teacher the final word on the subject.

Michaela twisted back and looked at Stella, who shrugged. "Yet another fact I didn't know about my home. I'm sure she's right, and it was named for the sturgeon who pass through here, and we've been pronouncing it wrong. Name," she said, testing out the Potawatomi word. "For the fish."

"Good job!" said Kira.

Stella brought the vehicle to an abrupt halt near the top of the driveway. She could go no further because the pavement was crawling with men wearing black pants and khaki uniform shirts. They all had nametags and badges, and they were unloading gear from several pickup trucks.

"The DNR has arrived in their glory," she muttered. She turned off the car. "You guys make yourselves at home, all right? The front door is open. I'll be in soon to put out some sandwiches for lunch. But right now, I need to speak with my husband."

Everett was planted in the middle of the drive, arms crossed, expression thunderous. Stella approached him cautiously. Kira ran past them, hooting like an owl, and disappeared into the house.

"Michaela is here," said Stella. "Um. Obviously. With Henry and the kids."

"Yes," he said.

"Well? How's it going so far?"

"They arrived no more than ten minutes ago." Everett narrowed his eyes at a woman carrying a long spear with a wicked, barbed point. "It's fine except I don't like it. I don't like the intrusion. And I like that person least of all. In our brief interaction, I found him to be oafish and self-important."

He ducked his chin in the direction of Officer Diettrich, who was near the tree line, speaking into a handheld radio.

"Listen to you, exercising your powers of insight," Stella said.

One of the other wardens turned his head sharply in their direction, and Stella suspected they were being overheard. Everett must have noticed as well, for he closed the gap between them, then looped one arm around her neck. He tugged her forward in something an observer might categorize as a hug, but Stella could not relax into him. He spoke into her ear.

"We don't know what they're going to find," he said quietly. "I'll keep an eye on things here. Why don't you get back in the car and take a drive to—"

"*No.*" Stella stepped back forcefully. "No. I'm the one who made the deal. I'm the one who has a feeling about the damned fish. I will stay. If you want to go, then go."

"You offend me," he said with a scowl, "by implying I would abandon you here alone. I would never."

"Because you don't trust me to handle the agents."

Everett tilted his head. "It's you who remains wary of me, Stella."

Stella flinched. She was stunned to silence by the accuracy of his remark. She, of course, knew he was right, but she hadn't realized he *knew* that truth. Considering that and the sarcastic remark she had made about his intuition around Diettrich, Stella was compelled to arrive at an uncomfortable conclusion. She had underestimated Everett's capability to read and understand people. He was often stiff and formal, but not because he couldn't relate.

"If I am," she said quietly, "it is in my own defense."

"We haven't had a chance to—"

"Mrs. Novak!"

They both turned in the direction of the shout. Officer Diettrich beckoned her. Stella started to walk away, but Everett caught her elbow.

"I'll be out repairing the boundary wall," he said. "Text me, or send Michaela or Henry to fetch me, if these men trouble you."

She offered him a slight smile. "There is only one man who troubles me, and he troubled me so much I married him."

Then she turned and went to find out what Officer Diettrich needed so urgently.

Chapter 30

FISHING

"We're running a power cord from the house," Diettrich said, pointing at a spool of heavy-duty orange line, "to plug in big lights down by the pond."

"All right," said Stella. "You need my permission? You have it."

"Make sure nobody pulls it at the outlet, all right? Or flips the breaker. You have lawn-care guys out here today on riding mowers?"

She shook her head. "Run the cord. What have you found so far?"

"Nothing."

He strode along the path toward the pond, shoving branches out of the way and uncoiling the orange line, and Stella followed. Standing along the weedy bank she counted six wardens, all staring into the water. Two of them had nets, two held hefty fishing rods, one wielded the spear Stella had seen earlier, and one wielded a clipboard.

It would have been funny, watching them all stare blankly into the murky water, except Stella wasn't in the mood. Diettrich plugged in a work light on a tall tripod, and the shadows receded.

"What if," she asked, "the fish are out there but decided not to come *here*? Say they found a bigger pond, a better food source."

"That's not how they work. You really bought this place without knowing a damn thing, huh? They come back time after time. Those lake sturgeon have probably been coming to this spot for a thousand years. The oldest living members of this school were swimming here to spawn long before the house was built."

Name, Stella thought. The original inhabitants of the area would have known. She considered the Novak family, turning the land over to the next generation. But she and Everett were the end of it.

"What do you do when you find one?" she asked. She refused to say *if* you find one.

"Catch it, weigh it, measure the length," he said. "Determine the sex and estimate the age, if possible. Have you caught your one-fish limit for the season?"

"No."

"Then we sell you a tag, and you can harvest it."

"Meaning kill it."

"Correct. The males some people have preserved and mounted, or if it's a female carrying eggs, you get your bounty of roe."

She pursed her lips. "I like to eat caviar more than I like to think about killing a fish and slitting open its belly."

"Because you're a city girl," Diettrich said bluntly. He put his fingertips beneath his chin and fluttered his eyelids, a mockery of a feminine pose. "Rather go shoe shopping than ponder little things like life and death. But don't worry, I can kill the ugly old fish for you and pass along the roe."

Stella's dislike intensified. That little bit of scorn irritated her more than was rational. She needed to get away from him. "Fine. If there's nothing else...?"

"Nope."

She smiled tightly and turned away, leaving the wardens to their fishing.

Inside the house, she served grilled-cheese sandwiches and apple slices to Michaela's kids. After lunch, she and Henry convinced Michaela to take the afternoon off. Stella and Henry walked with Kira and Jackson down to the beach to play with buckets and shovels. Henry let them take their shoes off and wade into the water. It was freezing, and Jackson screeched with delight. Stella checked her phone every fifteen minutes, hoping for some sort of fish alert from Diettrich, but she received nothing.

Later, while the children napped, she found herself at loose ends. She wandered the house, idly dusting all the flat surfaces. Atop the fireplace mantel, a large, framed photo of herself and Everett outside the courthouse in their wedding clothes had appeared. *Michaela*. The couple in the image were smiling broadly, hands clasped, young and beautiful. Stella straightened the frame. Then she sat down with a book but found herself staring into her phone. The afternoon dragged relentlessly without any news of the sturgeon.

After an hour or two, she couldn't tolerate further waiting. She pulled on boots and a hooded sweatshirt and returned to the pond.

The DNR wardens were still on duty, standing around with fishing gear, looking at the pond. Stella sat on the same mildewed bench she'd used the day before. Diettrich marked her arrival with only a brief glance and a grunt. In the distance, she heard the hollow, scraping, clunking sounds of heavy stones moving. Everett was not far, restacking the tumbled-down wall. The thought was comforting, even if she wasn't in harmony with him.

The surface of the water was still. Stella stared as intently as the officers were focused on it, hoping to see...what?

"We'll be able to see them?" she asked.

"You think we're standing around here looking at our feet all day?" Diettrich scoffed. "Yeah, we'll be able to see them. The water is shallow. But I can't say if *you* will. You have no idea what you're looking for."

"I guess this is why we taxpayers pay you experts the big bucks, huh?" she snapped back.

"Mrs. Novak, the pay in this public service job is terrible, whereas you live in a mansion."

Stella pressed her lips together instead of instigating an argument. She sat on the bench and looked for sturgeon. She saw nothing, not even a ripple.

Around four o'clock a diesel rumble caught her attention, and she stood and hurried back along the path toward the driveway. It was the delivery truck with the new couch she'd ordered, and she spent half an hour supervising the movers who unloaded the piece, a sleek, modern sectional in deep blue, and positioned it before the fireplace. On her return route to the pond, she saw Everett emerging from the woods to meet Mark and Jaime as they parked a rental truck. Everett raised his hand to Stella in a brief acknowledgment, but he did not stop. The three men extended the ramp and maneuvered down a two-wheeled dolly bearing a large statue covered by a white sheet.

"Anything?" she asked the group of agents, resuming her position on the bench.

"Yeah," said Diettrich.

"*What?*" She hadn't expected good news and quickly stood. "Where?"

He pointed at the bank near where another officer stood wearing hip waders, holding a dripping net. "Right there. Look."

Stella looked. On the ground, flattened in the long grass, was a lake sturgeon. It was at least four feet long, narrow, a muted greenish-gray color, and it had wiry tendrils around its mouth. It looked like a prehistoric serpent.

It was also clearly very dead and had been so for quite some time. Pieces of flesh were missing, exposing delicate bones, and the tail fin was ripped to shreds.

"Ugh," said Stella.

The other officer, not Diettrich, grinned and brandished his net on its extendable pole. "Scooped it right off the bottom. Damned thing's probably been there since last season. Water's cold enough, not a lot of other fish to nibble its guts in this creek system."

"Did Leon Novak catch this male, kill it, and toss it back?" Diettrich demanded.

"I...I have no idea," Stella said. "How did it die?"

"Hard to say. Looks like its mouth was damaged, which could have been from a hook." Diettrich nudged the dead fish with the toe of his boot. Then he squatted and with a bare hand, raised the head. "You can see the torn patch of skin where there would have been a barbel, and they need those for searching out food. Here, look."

Stella wanted to gag. She detected the undeniable stench of rotted fish. "No, thank you."

Diettrich stood up in a violent motion. His face turned a mottled red. "Afraid to get your hands dirty, lady? You think I'm the bad guy here, coming in to force you to follow the law, but you've got this land with this priceless resource that you know nothing about. You assume the worst of me while standing ten feet away from the dirty work. You want to eat caviar with a little pearl spoon and never touch a dead fish. To be quite honest, ma'am, I don't think you deserve these incredible creatures."

"They're not mine," Stella said softly. Her professional skills kicked into gear, and she read his face and his words more carefully. He was truly upset. "They're wild animals, and they're protected by law. That's why you're here, right?"

The other agents made themselves visibly busy, making notations and fiddling with equipment. Stella understood they didn't want to be involved with Diettrich's outburst. Everett had disappeared with the statue and had yet to return.

"I am here because—" He scrunched up his face and made ridiculous pouty lips. "I am here, as we both know, because you're falling on your sword to protect your old auntie from the rigors of a locked room in Florida. Wouldn't want her to miss her weekly appointment at the salon."

Then, to Stella's consternation, Diettrich made the silly twinkly-fingers-under-chin motion he'd done earlier. The mockery that had so annoyed her.

And she remembered, with a jarring sensation, that she'd heard about that quirk. From Allison, her client with the terrible husband. But Allison lived in Chicago. Hadn't she said her husband had started a new job? Stella wished she had paid better attention to the woman's many complaints. The terrible husband had effectively moved out... Where had he surfaced?

"Officer Diettrich," she said, "may I ask your first name?"

He eyed her. "You filing a complaint?"

"Is it Lawrence?"

The slight flicker of his eyes was enough to confirm. She didn't want him to know her connection to Allison. She continued hurriedly. "I think one of the neighbors mentioned seeing you in the area. That's all."

Diettrich relaxed. "Oh, Marvin?"

"Uh, yeah." It didn't matter, as long as she kept Allison's name out of it. She needed to get away from him, needed to think. Why was Allison's husband assigned to the Name Estate case? It felt too strange for mere coincidence. "Must have been. Anyway, I need to go set out the food for dinner. I ordered enough pasta to feed a crowd, so I hope your team is hungry."

She didn't wait for a response from him before she left.

Chapter 31

SURRENDER

Stella found Michaela in the kitchen, revived by her nap and wearing an outfit of snug pants cut like men's breeches in a finely woven windowpane pattern, buttoned at the knees, with a wine-red vest and yellow silk scarf tying her hair back from her face. She looked fantastic and was smiling broadly, whereas Stella, in comparison, felt about as fantastic as a long-dead sturgeon.

"Mickey, I need to talk to you about—"

"You won't guess who's here!" Michaela exclaimed, and she flung her arms toward the living room. Stella obediently looked.

She blinked and looked again. In the next room was a tall, tousle-haired man and a woman she recognized— "Annie Evans?" she blurted. "What on earth?"

She and Michaela and Annie had been friends in college, several degrees closer than acquaintances although never best friends. Annie was close with a separate group of women, and she always seemed to have important things to do. Stella and Michaela were usually watching movies and drinking cheap wine.

Annie looked pleased. "Stella! I could hardly believe it when Mickey answered the—Wait, you're—Jaime said this place belonged to an old friend from his cancer support program, so you're...?" She trailed off, having finished none of her thoughts.

"I live here with my husband, Everett." Stella engulfed Annie in a tight hug, pleased and relieved to see her. Back in college, Annie had a reputation for efficiency and thoroughness. Stella detected a more relaxed set to Annie's neck and shoulders, however, in comparison to her memories, which were of Annie battling final exams like the professors had personally wronged her. "You're Jaime's sister-in-law?"

"Yes! I had no idea you were married."

"It's very recent. You are, too?"

Annie nodded and touched the arm of the man beside her. "My husband, Carter Mackenzie."

Carter stepped forward with a charming, dimpled smile, and Stella shook his hand. "The rugby player, right?" she asked, smiling.

"Ah, no," said Annie quickly. "That was my ex."

"Oh, god, I'm so sorry," Stella exclaimed. "I didn't realize."

"No problem," said Carter. "We were married recently, too."

Annie leaned against him. "Carter and I met in Scotland—"

"No, we first met long before that," Carter said. "Even if she doesn't remember. We got together in a dark, damp forest in Scotland."

"There were these little critters that we were trying to spy on but... no, never mind. Anyway, it's kind of a great story," Annie said. "I'll have to tell you about it sometime. I hope you don't mind the extra guests. When Jaime said he had a caviar party to attend at a mansion, we couldn't resist."

"I'm honestly glad you're here," said Stella, "although I swear it's not a party. Annie, you won't be surprised to learn this not-a-party is not going exactly to plan. Well, truly there isn't a plan. Mickey, can we find a—"

"Food, yes, I'm on it." Michaela turned away.

"I can help," said Annie.

"No," Stella said hastily, and Michaela spun back. "I mean, yes, food is a good idea, but I want to talk to both of you separately." She turned to Carter. "You look both decorative and useful. And I mean that as a compliment. Will you please recruit your brother to help you find the covered aluminum trays in the fridge and put them all in the oven?"

Carter, unoffended, laughed easily. "Sure. I'll even turn on the oven."

"Excellent, thank you. Annie, I like him."

"Me, too." Annie playfully tweaked her husband's chin, and Carter kissed her forehead before walking away to rummage in the fridge.

"Things are mostly under control, I swear." Stella beckoned Michaela and Annie. "But...let's go into the other room."

"Why am I not reassured?" Michaela murmured as she collected a bottle of chilled wine and three glasses.

They gathered in the living room, where Stella's freshly delivered couch occupied the center of the rug. Stella seated herself and attempted to pretend as if she'd sat there before. Her life would seem even more of a shambles if her friends knew she'd spent big money on a big couch, unseen and untested. But the new furniture looked marvelous and modern, and it was comfy. Michaela poured the wine.

"Everett and I inherited this place from my aunt and uncle," she explained for Annie's benefit. "They got themselves into trouble with the state's Department of Natural Resources for one or two sturgeon-related violations, so I'm trying to have all that cleared up by passing a renewed inspection. The problem," she said, then held up one finger as she swallowed a sip of her drink, "is that the DNR officer is also the spouse—or ex-spouse, separated, somewhere in that liminal marital space, nothing familiar to me, of course—of one of my clients."

"Client?" Annie asked. "You're not still doing..." She glanced at Michaela, who made a gesture Stella didn't catch. "Oh. So you *are* still doing the fortune-telling tricks."

Annie's opinion of that career path was evident.

"Yeah," said Stella. "I'm getting out of the work, I swear. But a couple of weeks ago, I might have convinced this particular client to end her marriage. Which, in my defense, was a terrible union, and he's a terrible guy. Now he's outside inspecting my fishpond."

"Right," said Annie slowly. "You're suggesting the officer may act unethically? Because he wants to write a bunch of violations to punish you for advising his wife?"

"Maybe." Stella hesitated. "I know he trespassed on our land at least once."

"That cop could poison your caviar," said Michaela. "It makes me nervous. He could say you obstructed his investigation or that you were aggressive or violent."

"Yes, and it could be simpler than that," Stella said. "All he has to do is not find any sturgeon. It's a bit early in the season for them to have arrived here on their travels through the interconnected waterways. I asked him to come now to spring Auntie Liz from jail."

"How early?" asked Michaela.

"Wait," said Annie, her eyes widening. "Your Auntie Liz was in *jail*? Over sturgeon?"

"Not anymore. And this is about a month early for traditional spawning season. Six weeks, maybe."

Michaela puffed air through her lips.

"But it's been so warm this winter," Stella continued, "and something about the pond made me so confident..." She groaned. Whatever fleeting impression she had intuited the previous afternoon was gone. Why had she allowed herself to feel anything about fish? She had no connection to them, and she knew almost nothing about their movements. "I don't know."

"What does Everett think?" asked Michaela.

"I haven't mentioned my connection to Diettrich's wife. I don't know what he thinks about the damned fish. Things between us are..." She lifted her hand and tilted it back and forth. She couldn't admit in front of Annie that he probably regretted marrying her at all. "He disapproves of how I handled what happened with Elizabeth."

"Too bad," said Michaela bluntly. "Is he outside? Text him."

Annie laid a hand on Stella's shoulder. "Hey, I haven't met Everett yet, but anybody should want to hear what you think, Stella. Your instincts are great. I was often envious of your perfect track record in judging new people during college. I don't have that skill."

Stella thought back to introducing herself to Michaela in left field and slipping instantly into a lifelong friendship. Then she considered, inevitably, her first memories of Everett when she was nine and he was kind and wonderful.

Annie apparently considered her at least somewhat judgmental, which was what she'd often accused Everett of being, at least to herself. She had to interpret the subtle variations of humanity for her work, and she had to be good at it, but she didn't like to consider herself excessively critical of others.

"Oh, maybe not perfect," Stella said weakly.

"It's true," said Michaela. "Don't argue."

"I didn't even really notice my husband the first time I met him," said Annie. "I couldn't tell you about the moment we met, yet now he sits at the center of my heart and the front of all my thoughts. But you have the skill to read people. If you think Diettrich is sketchy, then I think you're right."

"Uh, thanks," said Stella. "You both think I should tell Everett all of this," she said.

"Like, five minutes ago," said Michaela.

"Yep," said Annie.

She extracted her phone and texted him.

Can we talk?

He was probably back out in the woods, so he might not receive the message right away. She shoved the phone back into her pocket, then lifted her head and looked at her two friends in turn. "Let's go check on Carter and Jaime with the—"

Her phone vibrated, startling her. She had the device in her palm without thinking.

Perhaps not now, Everett had written. **I am on the terrace.**

But Michaela had already learned that. "Stella," she said, "you need to see this."

Stella's stomach tightened at the odd, strained note in Michaela's voice. She followed her line of sight out the nearby window and out onto the terrace, where twilight receded to the west of the house.

A whole crowd of people seemed to have materialized, but Stella only saw Everett. He stood alongside Diettrich, who presented him with a clipboard and pen. Everett raised the pen like he was about to sign the page, and Stella had a terrible feeling. Worse even than when Elizabeth was jailed.

"No," she said softly. Then, louder, "no!" But he couldn't hear her from inside. Everett signed. Stella dashed through the kitchen and out the glass doors.

"Stop," she said. "What is that? What are you doing?"

Dietrich took the clipboard with a satisfied smile. "It's done. You really should have told me, Mrs. Novak. Your husband has very properly confessed to poaching and killing dozens, if not hundreds, of protected, endangered lake sturgeon. This concludes our inspection. I expect he will be charged with state and federal crimes."

Chapter 32

TOO MANY VISITORS

Stella's dismay must have shown on her face. Everett surged toward her, stopped, then reached for her hand and guided her away from the group. They moved to an alcove at the corner of the terrace.

She stared at him, a dozen questions circling in her mind like a school of sharks.

"Why are there so many people here?" was the first to emerge, although not the most important. Everett tugged at the neck of his t-shirt, which was darkened by sweat despite the cool breeze.

"You invited most of them," he said. "The others are members of Diettrich's team, in addition to Marvin and the other fellow."

"I can't recall his name," said Stella. "The other one."

"Nor can I." He focused on her intently. "Stella, listen, I had to give a statement to Diettrich. They've been searching for hours, and there are no fish. That man has your name on everything. All his paperwork. Stella Novak, Stella Novak, Stella Novak. His case file looks like the inside of my skull sounds. I could not watch idly while he assigned crimes to you. So, I confessed."

"But you didn't kill any fish."

"No, of course not."

She felt more keenly the aching distance between them.

"Because you don't think I can handle it," she murmured. "The consequences. *Any* sort of consequences."

"No, because you shouldn't need to. None of this is your mistake."

"Neither is it yours. But you were so angry with me yesterday when I failed to persuade Diettrich that I—"

"*What?*" He loomed closer and set heavy hands on her shoulders, and she fell silent. She could not see the crowd beyond the shield of his torso. "Angry? With you? You're more wrong than you have any—Please, let's walk down to the beach where we can have some privacy."

"I need to remind you," Diettrich chimed in from across the terrace, "that I will be taking you back to the office tonight for processing. No long walks on the beach."

"Officer," snapped Everett, "with all due respect, which I expect is very little indeed, I will walk where I want with my wife until the moment I am handcuffed."

Diettrich subsided, palms raised in surrender. Stella followed Everett toward the stairs that led to the shore. She paused beside Michaela.

"Get a hold of the judge," she whispered. "The woman who married us. You know."

Michaela nodded, and Stella continued.

In the darkness of the staircase, Everett took her hand. They walked together down to the beach. Stella stumbled slightly at the transition from the pathway into sand.

"I'm unsure of how to say any of this," he said, looking not at her but at the endless expanse of the water.

The whooshing ambient noise of wind and waves drowned her thoughts in one gulp. He'd been trying to speak to her all day, and she wouldn't let him waste another moment. "Say it anyway," she said.

"I wasn't angry with you when we spoke on the phone yesterday. I'm not now, either. I was furious with myself, Stella, for asking the impossible of you and leaving you alone. I'm sorry. I told myself I wouldn't do it again, and I hope you can forgive me."

She squeezed her eyes closed. "That was very nicely said but for the wrong thing, Ev. You can leave me to deal with things. I am capable, and I hope you can trust me to manage difficult tasks, whether it's our elderly relatives, our house, our finances...this is our life now. I can do hard things."

"I know you can, I was only trying to—"

"Let me finish. You were angry with yourself, and you vented it in my direction. You can let me in, you know, to the strange machinations of your clockwork mind. Tell me when you're frustrated. Don't snap your jaws at me out of irritation with yourself."

He exhaled shakily. "God, you're right. I did, didn't I? I am a beast, and I'm so sorry. No wonder your reception has been so frosty. When you turned away from me this morning, I realized that I—I can't promise I'll never do it again, because never is a very long time, but I can absolutely promise I'll try. If you'll give me the opportunity."

She had wanted him for such a long time. Even when she first proposed, some part of Stella had wanted to be with Everett, even under external pressure and unusual pretenses.

Which made her a fool twice over, because she no longer wanted more of what they'd established—more hesitancy, more caution, more circling each other at a safe distance. She remembered her initial position regarding him. *Making a bad impression was better than striving for his good opinion.* What if she'd been right about that, after all?

"I don't know, Ev," she said. "Do we really need two cracks at mediocre? Two chances at..." She gestured between them. "Making things kinda-sorta okay? I don't know."

"It's my fault," he said. "For most of my adult life, I assumed my future would be me, alone. Now I have failed to readjust with any semblance of grace to a new reality that includes you. Of course it includes you. Stella, please."

He sounded sincere, almost desperate, but she already knew all that. He hadn't said anything different.

Instead of shouting *say something real!*, she shifted the subject. "It's just that these damned fish are stressing me out. I need to tell you that Diettrich is married to Allison."

"Allison?"

"My client. The stalkery one with the terrible husband."

He shook his head, and a section of dark brown hair fell across his brow. He looked in dire need of a trim, a shave, and a nap. "So, the terrible husband—"

"—Is Diettrich, yes."

Stella quickly filled him in on the unexpected connection while Everett listened intently. She gave him a moment to absorb his surprise.

"I think Diettrich is out for me," she concluded. "Because he blames me for influencing Allison against him. You might have foiled his attempt to hassle me by confessing, but I still think he didn't look very hard for those fish. He wasn't motivated to find them. I want to take a shot at convincing him to look harder. All right? Before I let you fall on your sword."

Everett inclined his chin and slid his hand down her arm to intertwine their fingers. "It can't hurt. Don't sign any false confessions like a fool. Let's get back to our very large crowd of guests."

"It's too many, isn't it?"

"Far too many."

Chapter 33

UNREAD CARDS

The terrace had not grown any less crowded in the previous few minutes, but at least Carter and Jaime had managed to heat up the pasta and set out the trays beside disposable plates and plastic cutlery. Her Midwestern ancestors would have been glad she was serving food to some of her least favorite people.

Stella gave them both a brief smile, then turned her attention to her neighbor.

"Marvin." She wracked her brain for the name of his houseguest. "I wasn't expecting you and your friend...Sergey!" She was so surprised at recalling the man's name, she sounded absurdly thrilled to greet him.

"Didn't invite us," said Marvin in his blunt fashion. "Leon always invited me. Been attending this vecherinka since nineteen ninety-nine."

"It's not a vecherinka."

Marvin eyed her flatly.

"And you're here now, anyway," she added.

Sergey stepped forward and kissed her on both cheeks. "Stella. How lovely to see you again. I heard it's not a vecherinka," he said with a twinkle, "because you have not yet harvested a fish. No fish, no fresh roe, very standard American party." He tutted. "I was told this this would be different."

"It's true we haven't caught a fish." Stella looked squarely at Officer Diettrich, who was listening. "I suspect the officer here hasn't really tried to catch one. What if he's not giving us his very best?" She beamed a winning smile. "What if we all starve from an utter lack of caviar?"

Diettrich scowled.

Marvin raised a hand. "Everybody wants to find the fish."

"On the contrary, I believe he would rather arrest me and have done with it," said Everett.

"You? No," said Diettrich. "You're an asshole, but I don't think you killed any fish. I called my buddy in Florida. Vero Beach, Florida. Might be easier for me to go back to my original plan and take in the old lady for her crimes."

"No," said Stella on a gasp. "Take Everett, not Elizabeth. Everett at least can defend himself in prison."

"I appreciate your vote of confidence," he murmured. "Let's not put it to the test."

"Then where are the damned fish?" Diettrich shouted. "She said they were here, that they were early."

"Did you, my dear?" Sergey asked. "You have seen then?"

"I felt...something," she admitted. "I was so certain, but now it's gone. Maybe it was allergies."

Sergey suddenly brightened. "The cards. Mrs. Novak, consult the cards regarding the fish."

"Oh, no. That won't work. I don't think my cards are, um..." Stella fluttered her fingertips in a faux-mystical flicker. "My cards are not aligned to cold-blooded creatures."

"Then lay the cards for yourself. Ask yourself what you know, what you don't know, what you've seen and haven't seen, and what you don't know you haven't seen."

"Can't hurt," Marvin said.

"There's nothing to see." Stella directed at Michaela a silent plea for reinforcement. "Really."

"Yeah, no, Stella's cards are pure horseshit," said Michaela. "Right, Annie?"

"Mm-hm," Annie said, her lips tightly folded.

"Yes, thank you! Officer Diettrich will need to look a bit harder before making threats about arrests. Fish better. That's all I'm asking. No falsified supernatural intervention required."

Michaela stepped forward. "But I wasn't finished. Stella, *you* are not horseshit." She clasped Stella's hand. "I think you should consult your cards, not because the cards mean anything, but because your strange mind makes interesting connections all the time. Let yourself think."

Stella squeezed Michaela's hand and let it drop. Then she looked at Everett.

Everett lowered his chin. "There is something in you," he said slowly, "I don't understand, but I do respect. Your mind works in squiggles, my love."

The mockery was absent from the endearment. She inhaled and shifted her gaze back to Sergey. "Fetch the cards. Find a small wooden chest in the coffee table drawer."

He passed his wineglass to Marvin, then hurried inside.

Diettrich shifted his weight from side to side. "Novak already signed the paperwork—"

"You," said Stella, "will please be silent and wait." Then she smiled sweetly. "For science, you understand, and the good of the species. In deference to the importance of the ongoing scientific research you so strongly champion. Thank you."

When Sergey returned with the box in his hand, Stella hesitated. She didn't like to touch the cards in case it imbued them with any aura of authenticity. But a circle of faces watched her expectantly.

She wanted them all to be gone. She wanted the correct number of fish in her pond. She wanted Elizabeth to be entirely unbothered. She wanted to seize Everett by the jaw and force him to explain himself, to make *sense*. She needed to drink wine in peace, preferably with a nice tray of caviar and Takis Fuego beside her, and she wanted to watch the sun rise over Lake Michigan.

It seemed to her that all those simple pleasures were out of reach unless she could figure out what the hell had happened to the sturgeon.

So, she accepted the cards. Nobody knew what it meant except Michaela, who inhaled audibly and murmured something to Henry. Stella ran her hands over the old, smooth wooden lid, then flicked open the brass catch with her thumbnail. She removed the cards, which felt cool in her hands.

Then, with a swift and careless swipe, she pushed the top card off the deck and onto the ground. It fluttered and drifted. She did not glance down. She watched the people, as always.

Diettrich, first. He was easy. In his face and posture, she found annoyance and impatience. He thought she and Everett were city snobs.

She pushed another card and looked at Michaela, who was faintly amused and sipping her rosé. Stella smiled at her. Standing beside Michaela, poor Henry's brow was furrowed in confusion.

She threw another card on the ground. Annie and Carter, leaning shoulder-to-shoulder, young and beautiful and in love. Stella despised them a little. Carter was eating from a plate mounded with rotini, which Stella appreciated because she didn't want too many leftovers, and Annie stole a noodle from the edge of his dish. Carter jabbed at her with his fork, and Stella decided she didn't hate them, after all.

Another card, then she refocused on Marvin and Sergey. Marvin, she found to be nearly impenetrable in his brash obtuseness, although she suspected he had suppressed a romantic interest in his handsome European houseguest. Sergey, as she had told him before, was self-consciously urbane and harboring old parental resentments. He watched the card fall to the concrete, then angled his head to better assess which image appeared on its face, as if it mattered.

The only others in the group were Diettrich's people, who interested her very little...and, of course, Everett, who interested her most of all. She pinched the next card between her first two fingers and tossed it. It twirled down slowly, like a maple seed pod. Everett didn't watch the card. His eyes were on her. His expression was guarded, his eyes half-lidded, his mouth hard. He had his arms folded across his chest and his feet planted squarely. As usual, he was so lovely and painful to her that she couldn't see the truth of him. She was overwhelmed by what she felt for him.

She wished fervently for Elizabeth and Leon. Partly to yell at them and compel them to explain what exactly they had done and *why*, and partly because she missed them. The house held so much of Elizabeth's airy, loose spiritualism and Leon's fundamental, bedrock love of the land. Even the concrete terrace under their feet and its solid walls had been repaired with cement mixed with sand and gravel taken from the beach only fifty yards away.

Sergey knelt to retrieve her dropped cards, startling Stella from her reverie. She closed the box and set it atop the terrace wall, turning away from the group. With a fingertip, she traced the path of a patch that Leon had applied sometime in the previous year or two. He cared so much for the place that it was hard to believe he would have harvested all the sturgeon. The only entity he cared for more than Name Estate was Elizabeth. Stella dug her thumbnail into a small fissure in the wall and flicked out a piece of concrete. She intended to ask Everett about his repairs on the boundary wall, once things got back to normal. *If* things ever got back to normal. Not that she was particularly worried about strangers accessing the property. Leon loved to change the gate code, after all. What had Everett once related in passing? That Elizabeth laughed off the idea of poaching sturgeon from Name Estate.

Stella glanced down and spotted a fallen card that Sergey had missed. She bent and picked it up—a yellow dog with wide eyes, an orange spiked collar, and bared teeth, snarling. It meant nothing. But that wasn't exactly what she had said.

"Everett." She pitched her voice so only he could hear her, and he watched her mouth to catch the words. "What did Elizabeth say about poaching from Name Estate?"

"I don't recall," he murmured.

"Yes, you do. Your mind doesn't let go of anything." She held his gaze. "Zero-five-zero-eight."

"Oh, yes. That was when I changed the code to your birthday." A radiant flush appeared on his cheekbones. "She said nobody was staging a land invasion."

Stella nodded. Something about that struck her as odd. She looked at the dog with its orange collar, the color of a traffic safety cone, and thought of her orange earring. The earring that had fallen loose outside and turned up in the cellar.

"Officer Diettrich," she said suddenly, a weird quiver in her stomach, "you haven't been to our cellar, have you?"

He'd been present the moment she'd fallen into the pond, the moment she assumed she'd lost the bauble.

"As in a wine cellar?" he said. "No. I haven't been past the kitchen and the hall bathroom. Why?"

She turned and examined his face. He was telling the truth. He hadn't picked up her earring at the pond and dropped it in the cellar.

Yet it had arrived there somehow. Maybe it had been snagged in a hem of her clothing, or maybe the biweekly cleaning crew had dropped it.

Stella knew, in the cobwebby corners of her mind, that wasn't the case. The pond, the grotto. They were connected, probably underground. Her jewelry had...drifted. No land invasion necessary.

"Stella?" Everett asked.

She turned her head in his direction but kept her gaze on his shirtfront. "Will you..." she began, an ill-formed thought with no coherent end.

"Yes," he said, and he held out his hand.

She took it. The familiar strength and rough artist's calluses there provided the confidence she needed to follow her odd instinct to its strange conclusion. She stretched onto her tiptoes and whispered into his ear, aware of the others watching eagerly. "Will you come into my grotto?" she asked.

Everett repressed a smile, his mouth twitching. "As you like. Friends, please excuse us."

"Where are you going?" Diettrich demanded.

"To check on supplies," said Stella, which was true enough, although she did not mention *supplies of sturgeon.* "It won't take more than a moment or two. Would you like to hold our passports as collateral? I swear we won't flee the country."

"That won't be necessary," said Diettrich.

"Good." Stella tugged Everett by the hand, urging him toward the door to the house.

"Because we'll be coming with you," Diettrich added.

Stella spun and scowled at the officer, who had his six-pack of lackeys lined up behind him. "This is still my private property—"

He wafted Everett's signed papers in her face. "Do you want this done or not?"

She tilted her head back and stared up at the sky, which had deepened from navy to nearly black. The heavens offered her no consolation. "Yes. Fine. Follow me. It's dark and dank, and I hope you don't like it."

"We're coming too," said Michaela.

"Sure. Why not?" said Stella. "Bring the wine."

Chapter 34

THE GROTTO

Annie had an open bottle in her hand and a fresh one tucked under her arm. Every single one of the guests filed downstairs behind Stella and Everett. Henry shushed Mark, saying the Yang-Jones children were sleeping behind one of the closed doors. Sergey elbowed his way to the front of the line. He looked around at the comfortable lower level, with its pair of bedroom suites and the coffee bar, and said, "Dark and dank? Perhaps I do not know the meaning of that latter word."

"Not here," said Stella. "One more level down."

She opened the cellar door, flipped on the lights, and walked carefully down the narrow stairs.

"Ah," said Sergey at the base of the stairs, looking around at the bare walls and damp floor. He sniffed. "Yes. This is my understanding of dank."

"How kind, thank you. So glad you could make it to our party."

"Sorry."

"To be clear, I am allowed to mock the beloved mansion that I own but do not deserve. *You* are not allowed."

"Yes, I have understood that point."

Stella passed the nearly empty shelf of jarred caviar and led Everett to the very back, where the ceiling was low, the overhead lights did not extend, and the water pooled.

"The grotto," she said.

He assessed it, arms folded. "I might have said overgrown puddle."

"I suspect the sturgeon pass through here."

"But how? They're enormous, and I see no connection to the stream outside.

She shrugged. The whims and travel strategems of the creatures did not concern her. "Will you go along with me on this or not?"

"As usual, I certainly don't have a better idea." He slid his arm around to encircle her waist, and she leaned her temple against the rounded bulk of his shoulder. "And because I believe in your instincts, Stella. You're right about people so often that it's a bit terrifying, and I saw your face when you made the connection outside. You're right about this. I know you are."

Somehow his confident affirmation worried her more than a half-hearted assent would have. Now, if she was wrong, not only would she be dumping him with the legal consequences, she'd also be disappointing him. Both were as unpalatable as the water in the murky, shallow pool. She peered into it. There was no movement.

"Here," she called over her shoulder. "Diettrich. Have your people bring their fishing gear."

"This." Diettrich ambled over, leaned in, and scoffed. "This?"

"Yes," she said with a confidence she didn't feel. "They have to be here."

"Yes," Everett echoed firmly.

Diettrich actually did it. He marshaled his officers, sending two of them to fetch their gear, and assigning two more to don hip waders and enter the pool. Marvin and Sergey stood nearby, watching avidly. Stella and Everett retreated to the base of the stairs. Their friends waited, and Annie passed Stella a glass of wine.

"This could be awhile," said Stella. "They were outside all day."

"And we're standing in your cellar based on something you divined from the cards you don't believe in," said Michaela. She leaned back against the moist wall, then straightened rapidly with a moue of disgust.

"Could be worse. We could be standing here without drinks," said Mark, who was pouring Leon's expensive wine into Jaime's plastic cup.

"I was once at a party in a place almost like this in Brooklyn," said Carter. "Except there was music, and a lot more people doing drugs. I left early."

Everett nudged her. He mouthed silently, *You are right about this. You know what you know.*

But Stella, reading his lips, understood something very different. Not about the fish, nor the house, nor their elderly relatives. She saw the softening around his eyes when he looked at her. Despite the strange circumstances and their terrible party, he was thinking only of reassuring her. Everett was thinking of how she must be feeling, and he'd said exactly the right thing.

I am right about us. The conclusion arrived fully formed, and her doubts receded. It was not a bolt of lightning but a roll of slow, vibratory thunder that shuddered through her ribcage. She felt it with more certainty than anything she'd felt about the damned fish.

He loves me. He loves me. She laughed aloud, and she could hardly wait to inform him.

You love me, she mouthed in reply, but Everett had turned away. She looked. There was some commotion at the water's edge. The DNR officers were clustered together, hunched over. She heard splashing and urgent commands. Then, with a great heave, Diettrich together with another man hoisted a net from the water, and it held a fish.

A lake sturgeon. They laid the writhing, suffocating fish on the stone floor.

"Got one," said Diettrich, grinning in macabre satisfaction.

Stella and Everett hurried over to inspect. The fish was a mottled gray-brown, with the species' characteristic whiskery barbels in front of its gaping mouth. It was at least four feet from nose to tail. One of the DNR officers hooked the net to a hanging dial.

"Thirty-eight point one kilos," she announced. "Not too big, not too old. A male."

Marvin had been watching with interest, but he was clearly disappointed at that news. "Need that caviar."

"I don't care about caviar." Stella clasped Everett's hand and leaned against him in relief. "The school is here! They're not all dead, and surely that male is not the only one. This proves our property is not in violation. Correct?"

"We're still conducting research on the—ope!" Diettrich shouted. "Got another one. Damn, this pool is thick with them. They're swimming in through an underground passage. This pond was here long before the house."

"Name," Stella whispered, in the Potawatomi pronunciation. Someone had always known the sturgeon were here. Elizabeth and Leon had surely known.

"Female, sir," said the officer kneeling over the latest catch. "Forty-seven point six kilos."

"Harvest," barked Marvin. "Probably thirty pounds of roe in there."

"That's my call," said Everett sharply. "Not yours."

"You want it or not?" asked Diettrich. "You each get one fish. Tags are twenty bucks."

Everett glanced at Stella, who nodded.

"Do it," he said.

Diettrich signaled one of his men with a large bowie knife. He clubbed the fish's skull with the hilt, and the creature, still tangled in the net, went still. Stella gasped and pressed her face into Everett's chest.

"Watch," Everett murmured into her hair. "This is part of living in this place."

Stella forced herself to observe. The man hung the fish from a convenient hook in the rafters, and she wondered how many fish had been gutted from that exact spot. There was a drain in the floor, too, and her cellar began to resemble the killing floor of a slaughterhouse. He inserted the knife into the fish's belly near the tail and dragged it all the way up to the gills. Inside was an intact egg sac, and he slid it out into a bucket that Diettrich held ready. There was some blood, some yellow fat, and a huge volume of the small, black pearls that people had lusted after for centuries. The bulging, slippery mass was gross and yet mesmerizing.

Marvin stepped up. "Know what to do now?" he asked.

Stella shuddered. Everett looked wary.

"Mesh sieve," Marvin said. "Separate the eggs from any other guts and junk. Then canning salt. There on the shelf. Not too much. Twenty minutes, then jar 'em. Got your jars? Good. Can tell you how to pasteurize, too. Not tricky. Not tricky at all."

Stella swallowed hard and nodded. If she wanted to continue eating caviar off a chilled stone platter with a pearl spoon, she had best learn the way the product was made.

Another fish was pulled from the pool, measured, killed, and slit open. Another batch of roe. Stella searched among the clutter of items on the shelf and found a fine wire screen, a clean bucket, and Elizabeth's canning salt. She rolled up her sleeves and washed her hands. Within moments, she was kneeling on the ground, sunk past her wrists in thousands and thousands of dollars' worth of slimy raw fish eggs.

If the caviar were for sale, of course. Which it was not. The law stated the product was solely for personal use. She and Everett would host more parties, give jars away as gifts, and enjoy the luxurious taste alone together. She glanced over at him. He was hoisting another huge sturgeon on the hanging scale so Diettrich could record its weight. She must have watched for too long, or too intensely, because he looked over and caught her staring. But she didn't drop her eyes. She held his glance. *He loves me.* She needed to get all the extra people out of her house so she could inform her husband that he loved her. He might be shocked to hear it, but she was confident that she could make him understand. Everett had been correct to insist she follow her intuition.

One of the DNR wardens netted another fish and hauled it from the pool. The mood had turned boisterous, with Annie pouring wine liberally, and Mark and Jaime sneaking bites of caviar straight from the bucket. Even Diettrich was smiling. She'd been so paranoid about the man, about his connection to Allison. But he looked happy to see his job done properly. He had a flashlight in one hand and a clipboard in the other. He was a professional, after all, and surely the Name Estate data would be good for science. Of course he was pleased.

Henry and Michaela had removed their shoes and were wading directly into the grotto.

"Mickey, don't you terrify my fish," Stella called out with a laugh. "I need at least a few to return next year."

"This water is cold!" Michaela shouted. "My God, Stella, there are *so* many. I can see them. And if anyone is traumatizing the wildlife, it's the men with the weapons."

She was right. The DNR officer beside her with the wicked spear heaved his implement with a quick lunge. He grunted and levered the butt of the spear over his knee to secure yet another fish.

"Not so near the humans," Everett snapped. "In fact, are you quite finished here? Why are you spearing fish when we've already culled our allotment?"

Another sturgeon hit the floor with a wet flop. Someone quickly had it strung up on a hook, then Diettrich's lackey was there with a knife to slit its belly. More roe slid into the bucket.

"Lotta fish," Marvin said.

"Too many," Diettrich grunted. He made a mark on his checklist before passing a rag to the officer beside him, who had blood running down her arms to her elbows, even as her colleague prepared another sturgeon for gutting. "This population is listed at two- to three-dozen members. I've seen at least that many in the past ten minutes."

Stella rose slowly. Her neck and spine tightened, like she was about to take a punch. "Too many?" she repeated. As she moved away from her ad hoc roe-processing station, Sergey moved in to take over.

"Population should be maintained," said Diettrich. "Overgrowth is bad for the species, the waterways, other fish. The whole balance."

"That's not what we were told," she said. "You said you suspected Leon of killing all the sturgeon. Clearly that's not the case. I think we're done here. You have your data, so it's time for you and your team to pack it up."

Diettrich turned away.

"Forty-nine kilos even," said the warden with the latest dead fish. "Big girl."

Diettrich made a note, then nodded. "Harvest."

The officer with the knife stepped in. More fish guts fell to the floor with a terrible splat, and red blood mixed with water ran toward the floor drain.

Everett appeared beside Stella, his posture correct. "My wife has asked you to leave."

His voice split the room like a cracked whip. Near the stairs in the civilized half of the cavernous space, Mark, Jaime, and Carter left off their joking conversation. Annie went still. In the grotto, Michaela took Henry's hand.

"Well, see, now, that's not possible," Diettrich said in an affected drawl. He lowered his clipboard and looked straight at Everett, contrary to how he had ignored Stella's prior remark. "This is overpopulation, you see. These fish require culling." He smiled.

Stella repressed a chill. She looked at Michaela and jerked her chin toward Annie. *Take her upstairs.* She wanted both of her friends clear of the unpleasant discord brewing, but she also knew Michaela wouldn't abandon her without a good reason. Michaela, thankfully, nodded in understanding. She tugged Henry by the hand, and they both collected their shoes as they left. Mark, Jaime, and Carter remained.

The cellar grew quieter.

"No, thank you," said Everett calmly.

The wardens were still catching sturgeon at the rate of one every couple of minutes. The males they weighed, measured, and released. But the females...

The knife-holder raised the blade for the next slaughter.

"Stop," Stella said. "That's enough."

"Ma'am, I already explained the overpopulation to you," said Diettrich, his tone dripping with contempt.

"And we said no," said Everett. "This is happening inside our house."

"If a regular harvest had happened every year as intended, you wouldn't be in this position," the officer said. "I suspect the Novaks—the old Novaks—hadn't taken more than one fish in quite some time. Years, maybe. And now you're seeing the consequences."

"Hang on," Stella said. "Marvin attended the vecherinka. Isn't that right, Marvin? Didn't you tell me Leon and Elizabeth were regularly hosting their caviar soiree?"

"Yep. I saw…" He exchanged a look with Sergey. "Caviar. Every year. Already jarred, of course. None of this gutting."

Another sturgeon was pulled from the water.

"Female." The man with the knife hesitated and looked to Diettrich.

"Do it," said Diettrich.

"For the love of—*no*, I said no!" Stella shouted. It wasn't necessarily for a love of the fish, but rather for the responsibility she had to her family and to the estate, the land. Something was wrong about all of this. She couldn't claim any knowledge of overpopulation, but this wholesale slaughter of an ancient protected species wasn't right.

And when the officer ignored her and followed his boss's command instead, Everett raised his arm and caught the man by the wrist. The blade glinted, stopped midair.

"That's enough," he said, and his three friends coalesced behind him in a solid wall of unrelenting muscle.

Stella did not relish the idea of a slimy fight developing in her house, even a subterranean brawl. They weren't armed, were they? Surely conservation officers didn't carry guns, at least not inside private residences. But they had plenty of bloody knives on hand. She thought frantically, searching for any way to change the outcome of a scenario she had never envisioned. *Too many fish.* She had been so worried about a complete absence of sturgeon.

Diettrich was divorcing Allison. But Diettrich hadn't mentioned his spouse or any antipathy toward Stella for her role in advising Allison. Was he truly following the rules by killing dozens of sturgeon?

Even as she considered it, another fish was hauled from the pool and hit the floor, in defiance of Stella's shouting and Everett's harsh command.

Then Everett moved. He lunged forward in one long stride and seized the spear, ripping it from the officer's grasp. Stella had rarely seen him angry, and certainly never physically violent, although she knew intimately the hard musculature of his body. The DNR agent was astonished, mouth agape, looking like nothing so much as an air-drowned fish. Jaime and Carter, working with the deep familiarity of brothers, together took the befouled bowie knife before forcing that officer to his knees. The woman, sensing the change in leadership in the room, laid aside her net. Mark took the spear from Everett, and Everett turned his attention to Diettrich.

"This is the last time I'll say it. You're finished here," said Everett. "We both know the excuse of 'overpopulation' is flimsy at best and criminal at worst. You cannot possibly have any further purpose."

Diettrich glanced down at Sergey, who crouched beside the five-gallon bucket nearly brimming with pearlescent black roe. "Plenty of purpose. We aren't done. There are so many fish crammed into this little submerged pond, I'm doing them a favor."

"Take the roe." Everett shot a glance at Stella, who nodded in confirmation. She'd much rather have this standoff ended and save the lives of their sturgeon for fresh caviar next year. "As a gesture of our cooperation with your efforts to bring Name Estate back into line with all the regulations. Yes? Plenty of caviar to be made from that."

"Plenty more caviar still swimming around in there." Diettrich reached out and grasped the spear, but Mark resisted, his hand tightening on the haft. "This is state equipment."

"Shall I call the DNR headquarters?" Everett said in a stinging tone. "The deputy secretary? They should know that you're declining to leave. Surely your office can read to me where the law states that sturgeon should be slaughtered en masse by the warden who finds them. Your attempts at resource management have baffled me, so I would appreciate an official explanation."

"You won't find anyone at nearly midnight on a Saturday," said Diettrich. "Your wife is the one who was so desperate to have this inspection done. She asked us to come today. She asked to inspect this grotto." He flipped his clipboard back to the topmost page, then turned it around and waved it at Stella and Everett. "And please don't forget why you signed this paperwork. If you fail to comply, Mr. Novak, I might lose a few key pages from my file. I could choose to refocus my efforts on Mrs. Novak."

"Fine. Then take me in," said Everett. "Take that bucket, too, if that's what you came here for. But you're not killing this school of fish, and I won't have that threat continually hanging over Stella's head. None of this has to do with her."

"No, don't say that," Stella said vehemently. "These problems are *our* problems. We made vows to each other and to our aunt and uncle. I don't want these sturgeon killed, and I certainly won't let you take all the troubles in our world onto your shoulders. I won't."

CAVIAR MARRIAGE

"There's nothing else," Everett said. "He'll be back next year with more spears, nets, and demands."

Stella grimaced. There was truth to Everett's concerns, and she had an inkling of suspicion about what Leon must have faced. But why was Diettrich there at all? Elizabeth and Leon had managed to evade the DNR. Diettrich, that first day at the pond, hadn't even known that Elizabeth and Leon had departed.

Diettrich moved warily toward Everett, one palm raised in front of himself, as if approaching a cornered dog. He wanted to control Everett. He held a pair of silver handcuffs.

Stella glanced back at Jaime Mackenzie, then Mark and Carter. If it came to a fight, it would be the five of them against seven DNR officers, although Stella was nearly useless in a brawl. She had never thrown a punch. If she was angry as a child, which she often was, she lashed out verbally using cruel observations as ammunition. But she'd still back Everett against those odds. He was strong, angry, and he was in his own house. Neither of them, however, needed an assault charge added to their list of legal problems.

"You can't," she said desperately, although she had no real reason why they shouldn't do as they pleased. "Take the caviar you've already harvested. Isn't it enough? There must be twenty pounds there. Who could possibly need more than that?"

Then, oddly, Diettrich looked to Sergey. As if in search of an answer to her rhetorical question. *Who could possibly need that much caviar?*

She stared at Sergey, too, in astonishment. A fresh, reformed understanding began to unfold in her mind. What did Sergey know? And why did Diettrich care?

"Stella," Everett murmured. "You're making the face again. You're making connections."

"Yes," she whispered. "I'm right about this."

"If you think so," he said with a nod, "then I believe you are, too."

Stella patted his cheek, heedless of the sticky film of roe goop drying on her palm. "You're sweet. But it really doesn't matter what you think. *I* know I'm right."

Michaela reappeared at the base of the stairs in time to overhear. "Finally," she muttered.

Everett smiled.

Chapter 35

THE CONNECTION

Marvin. Stella stared at him. The connection was Marvin. He had known when Elizabeth and Leon departed for Florida. Marvin knew about the vecherinka, had attended every year, so Sergey knew, too. And Allison had met them both. Stella remembered the brief moment she had glimpsed Allison and Sergey with their heads together. Was that all the time he needed to learn about Diettrich? Based on that expectant look between them, Stella sensed that they were working together.

Because it was an inside job. A theft. If Sergey spoke with Allison, then he knew that Diettrich had a motive against Stella. Diettrich probably hadn't needed much convincing. She'd counseled the man's wife, after all, to leave her bad marriage. Marvin knew that Elizabeth and Leon were gone. Those two pieces were all it had taken to put Diettrich's sham investigation into motion.

And Diettrich could notch a win either way—with illegal caviar money or with a significant, legitimate case to present to his superiors.

She didn't know what Sergey would do with a hundred thousand dollars' worth of fresh caviar. Sell it, she expected, perhaps to overseas contacts. But Diettrich she did know, although not directly. She'd listened to Allison's stories and complaints for so long.

"Officer," she said calmly. "Can I speak to you for a moment? I believe we may yet have relevant information to exchange."

He dropped his hand and stopped menacing Everett, and Stella breathed out carefully. She led him upstairs, away from the growing smell of fish guts.

"I'm going to have to charge the Wisconsin DNR for a heavy-duty detox cleaning," she said conversationally. "Like one of those crews that comes in after a crime."

He scoffed. "You can sure try. What information do you have? I'm not looking for more excuses."

"No, no excuses." She opened the patio door and gestured for him to precede her onto the terrace, where the abandoned food was rapidly cooling. "I admit Leon and Elizabeth should have been much more diligent about fulfilling their state requirements. But here's what I think you should know, Officer—Lawrence. May I call you Lawrence?"

"Officer Diettrich is fine."

"Larry?"

He frowned. Stella smiled.

"Larry. I think Leon and Elizabeth kept well clear of the local office. Maybe they were paying off someone, or maybe they had an honest friend in the building. Someone who wasn't interested in invading the house every year to tick a checkbox on a trivial report. Maybe they meant to call us in the spring and provide instructions or advice. Maybe I forced all this to happen."

"I don't know what you're talking about. *I* forced this to happen because the inspection is required by law."

"But now? Wouldn't Sergey have waited a few weeks?" She enjoyed his effort to mask a spark of surprise, like he'd swallowed a bite too large for his esophagus. He hadn't known that she knew. "He's your client, yes? He wanted you to find the fish, whereas you kept threatening me about the consequences of *no* fish. He doesn't give a shit about Everett in handcuffs. But Marvin knows Leon, and he knows Leon would never murder a bunch of protected sturgeon. And so, Sergey made you an offer. I think I forced this to happen when I pissed off both Sergey and Allison that night. The night of my wedding."

"You don't know what you're talking about."

"Then what?" She peered closely at him. "At the pond that day, you really didn't know anything about me. You were just there doing your job. Newly hired, flipping through case files for a way to make your mark."

He shifted his weight.

"Marvin called you after he knew Leon was gone. You still weren't particularly interested in the case. You left a letter taped to our mailbox, right? You remained clean. But Marvin called again—or was it Sergey? No, Marvin. But Sergey was the one who understood your connection to Allison, and Allison to me, which is what motivated you to really come after us. Didn't take long to drift to the dark side, did it? You've been paid for. You're dirtier than my cellar drain. How much did you get?"

"I don't have to stand here and listen to this nonsense—"

That bluster was enough. Stella knew she was right. "You want to threaten me instead? I know that you hate me because your wife trusted me." He made the ridiculous choking face again, and his expression was hectic. *Good.*

However, she had to venture past what she knew and far into what she could only assume. She remembered what Allison told her, and more importantly, what Allison hadn't revealed.

"You think I didn't know?" she said with a lashing tone. Let him become a little afraid. "Don't you remember what I have done for money? Don't you wonder what else I have seen? I'm tired of your threats, and you're bothering my husband. So, I am going to counterbalance your threat of fines, legal charges, endless inspections, and jail for me, my husband, or my sweet old relatives. Then we'll be even, and this will be over. I am going to tell you *once*," she said. "I am only going to say it once because you're so filthy it makes my mouth taste bad to say it: Allison told me everything."

"Allison doesn't have jack shit to complain—"

"She had plenty." She felt only a bit guilty for spilling Allison's confidences. "I know about Raquel. Very pretty lady who looks nothing like you. How much are those men paying you for their time flirting with Raquel? Does Raquel have a grandma who needs expensive car repairs? What are you going to do when they want to buy Raquel a plane ticket for a romantic rendezvous?"

He folded his arms. "You're some damned woo-woo fortune teller. You have zero real evidence. You think anybody is going to believe you picked up this info from the stars? Who cares what you think? Even if you testified, it would be superstitious nonsense. No court would even—"

"The courts like people like me," she said.

"What, people with fake carnival tricks?"

"No, registered therapists," she said calmly. It was a qualification she hadn't claimed in years, one that she'd been thinking lately of reclaiming. "I went to school, you know. I'm licensed in Illinois. All my clients sign an intake form. It turns out that fake cartomancy pays better than real, careful assistance. But there's a surprising overlap in the skill set. And judges love my credentials. Very profesh."

Keeping up with the continuing education requirements finally felt worthwhile.

Diettrich growled something that sounded unflattering. He reached for Stella's wrist and grabbed her viciously. "You sneaky, witchy, freaky little *bitch*—"

"No." Suddenly Everett was there behind Diettrich, who whirled around and released Stella. "No, we're not doing any of that, thank you."

Polite, starchy, handsome. Everett was somehow even still entirely clean, whereas Stella couldn't get the iron smell of blood from her nose. With an implacable hold on Diettrich's shoulder, he stared the man down.

"You doubt her?" Everett said in a dangerous whisper. "You don't think she knows about you? I have seen her read a stranger's misdeeds from across the room. She could ask three questions and tell you the name of your middle-school crush. She knows why you're...such an unpleasant man."

"His father wouldn't buy him a puppy," Stella said, only half joking.

"If Stella says she holds your secrets, then I wouldn't test her," Everett continued in his relentless way. "If I couldn't have her for a wife, I certainly wouldn't want her for an enemy. It's too late for you, of course, given the state of my cellar, but it's not too late for you to give this up and leave now."

Diettrich opened his mouth, but there was a commotion inside, then everyone else spilled outside in a rush of warm air.

"He cannot leave yet," said Sergey. "I already paid him for a hundred pounds of fresh lake sturgeon caviar, and only fifty has been collected."

"Not my problem," said Everett. "He can go spearfishing in Lake Winnebago next month with everybody else."

Michaela held up her phone. "Hang on, new info. My close personal friend, the Honorable Madeline Ramseyer, has graciously commented on a hypothetical fact pattern I posed to her. Transporting the caviar out of state, or out of the country, would be a federal crime, and thus not in her jurisdiction. But she doesn't recommend it."

Stella took one glance at Michaela and knew her friend had invented all of that, but it sounded plausible. Sergey glared at Diettrich accusingly, and Diettrich turned pale.

"Jesus Christ, you people aren't worth all this trouble." He flicked an angry hand at his officers. "You two, get the gear. We're packing up."

"One more thing," said Everett. "I suggest we might avoid this sort of unpleasant waste of resources in the future if you notate in your findings that the sturgeon at Name Estate are only accessible from inside the house, and we homeowners can assist you by filing an annual count of our own. With photos or whatever data is required. It's all your idea, of course, and we're willing and eager to assist. The time savings, et cetera."

"That's brilliant," said Stella. "My love, you're clever."

"Thank you. Think of all the real science that can be done with our data."

"Now, all of you, go," she said. "It's entirely too crowded at my mansion."

"I will be taking the fresh caviar from the harvest today," Sergey announced. "My customers are waiting."

"Sergey, you weary me, darling." It was Annie Evans—Annie Mackenzie—who spoke up, much to Stella's amusement. She sounded posh and entitled, and Stella wondered where her warm friend had acquired such a skill. Somehow even *darling* had a condescending ring. "Judge Ramseyer was clear. Go and bother Officer Diettrich about this problem elsewhere. You really ought to learn when you're not wanted at a private event. And the U.S. legal system is really such a hassle about these things, honestly. And for what, a hundred fucking grand? That's dregs. Couldn't a resourceful person such as yourself pinpoint a better return on investment? Think of the vast time needed to unspool and respool this little opportunity. Unless you haven't much else to do, I suppose."

It was gloriously rude.

"Too many noses," said Marvin. "Not worth it, Serg. I still have to live in this county."

Sergey grumbled but for a miracle, he slunk away. He and Marvin followed Diettrich down the exterior steps and disappeared around the side of the house. After some clatter and fumbling, the herd of wardens went with them.

Stella's shoulders slumped. They were gone. She was exhausted and desperate to be alone with Everett. She gave Michaela a pleading look. Michaela nodded, clapped her hands, and began urging the others inside.

A wave of gratitude rushed over Stella. Michaela always knew. On impulse, Stella pulled her into a tight hug. "Thank you," she whispered.

"You owe me at least a pound of caviar," said Michaela.

Stella laughed. "Done."

Annie was behind Michaela, smiling, and Stella returned her affectionate look. She'd have to find a way to send pounds and pounds of fresh caviar to all her friends as an apology for her terrible party.

Finally, when they were alone, she faced her husband. "Everett," she began. She wanted to bury her face in his hair; she wanted to make him decide to love her. But when she locked eyes with him, she realized he was angry. He was *furious*. His nostrils were flared, his jaw clenched. He was holding on to his temper by a thread. "What...um. How are you?"

He relaxed his tightened lips only enough to speak. "You pointed to Marvin, and you're right. Of course you're right. But *Leon*." He shook his head slowly. "My God, Leon. The absolute *bullshit* he left for you is unthinkable. I may never forgive him. Leon is the one who—I must speak to him."

Stella's immediate reaction was relief that his anger wasn't directed at her. She'd never seen that expression on his face. He had his phone out, and a video call to Leon's mobile was connecting.

She wrapped a restraining hand around Everett's forearm. "His heart," she said. "He loves you, you know. Go easy on him."

"Bullshit," he repeated in a growl.

Leon answered. "Hello, my boy, caught me climbing into bed. How're things—"

"You bastard," Everett interrupted. "You knew. Tell me exactly what you knew before I find myself on another plane to fucking Florida."

There was a short pause. Stella flattened herself against Everett's flank for a better view of Leon's face on the screen. He looked tanned and uncomfortable.

"Ah," Leon said. "This is about the sturgeon."

"Yes, it's about the damned fish," Everett snapped. "Keep talking."

"Now, listen..."

Leon trailed off, and Stella had the impression he had nothing planned to say beyond that.

"Hi, Leon," she interjected. "We had a bit of an event here."

Elizabeth's head popped up behind Leon's shoulder. "Is that Stella? Hello, sweetie. How are you?"

"Fine. How was jail?"

"Oh, terrible. I'll tell you about it sometime. But I had my book club ladies enthralled this afternoon, I'll tell you that much. Even Bari shut up for once." Elizabeth looked faintly pleased by her short ordeal. "I heard you were the one who made a phone call to the authorities on my behalf."

"Yeah," said Stella. "I lied and said you were harmless."

Leon sighed and angled the camera away from his wife. "The DNR giving you more trouble?"

"Yes," Everett said.

"Damn. Now, listen," he repeated, "I hoped you'd have at least a month or two of peace. I extracted a promise from Keith that he wasn't going to call right away. He always starts calling me around this time of year, but I told him to at least give you a minute. Newlyweds and all that.

And after Lizzie was picked up and suddenly released, I figured Keith had straightened things out for us."

"He hasn't called," said Everett. "I don't know who the hell that is."

"Keith? Officer Baybrook?" Leon raised his eyebrows. "If the DNR was on the line, then you do. Of course you do. He's not retiring until this summer."

"I'm telling you I don't know anything about him or why I should care about his retirement."

"Well, I'll be damned. Then who phoned you?"

"Nobody *called*, Leon. They showed up. First Marvin and his interesting friend Sergey—"

"Hold on, now. Sergey Golubev was there? At the house?"

Everett exchanged a glance with Stella. "Yes. You know him?"

Leon visibly paled. "You shouldn't have let him in. I'm sorry, kids. Really, I am. This is not at all what I—I had to protect your aunt, Stella. I hope you see."

"Tell me everything," Everett said flatly.

"The, uh, first time I had a conversation with Marvin about the caviar," said Leon on a heavy sigh, "was shortly after we moved in. We were sitting out by the fire with a few beers, shootin' the shit, and I mentioned one thing or another, and he got the understanding that we had a fortune in sturgeon swimming through here every spring. You went to the cellar?"

"Yes."

"Then you know. They don't stay, of course, but they do pass through. I stuck a little underwater camera down there once. The opening is about five or six feet down, no more than a few feet across. Every year, from a stream through a deep corner of the pond to the house to the lake, and back again. Marvin got himself a fish that year. Sergey first came...I don't recall. Maybe a decade ago. He really leaned on me, you know. God, it was annoying. I played him off that year. He got a fish. Legal. The next year, however, it got worse, and I reported him to the DNR. Got Keith Baybrook involved. He intervened with Sergey. Just a conversation, of course. And so Baybrook got a couple of fish for helping me out. I'm an idiot, I suppose, because I really thought that would be the end of it. Maybe Elizabeth would say *optimist* instead of *idiot.*"

"Or possibly both," Stella said.

Leon rubbed his unruly eyebrows. "Baybrook was supposed to get a fish every year in exchange for being my shield and skipping our inspections. He's a bit underhanded but he's by far the best in that office. I wouldn't have minded doing the inspection—I only harvested two females per year, one each for me and Elizabeth, which is what the law says, although I never bought tags. But inviting wardens into the cellar would have been asking for trouble, and Baybrook couldn't guarantee who would be assigned. I thought no inspection was the simplest thing. But Marvin knew enough because of my big mouth, and I started finding boot prints and cigarette butts around the pond. Which is pointless, of course, because the tunnel entrance is deep. Not gonna catch a thing. Rumors started up that the fish were dying off. And me, optimistic idiot, I even thought that might help. But Jesus Christ, Everett, some people are dogged. You get it, right?"

"No."

"Marvin wanted a cut, Keith had a brother-in-law who got my phone number, my goddamned HVAC guy. Christine's useless ex-husband. Sorry, Stella, no offense to your father. It got to the point where I tried to keep my head down all year round. Felt like a moron sneaking around corners in my own local hardware store in case some fool was waiting to smile and pretend like he was my buddy and beg. The place I loved the most in the world had become such a burden. I tried to make—the annual vecherinki became a way to give away caviar legally, but no one was ever satisfied. The only thing I could do was keep it off Elizabeth's shoulders. She didn't know. She still doesn't know. Especially with my health issues, I can't burden her with beggars and thieves after I'm gone. Can you imagine Elizabeth taking those rude phone calls? No. I wanted it to go to you, Everett, because I knew you could handle it. You don't give a shit about people, never have, and so I knew it wouldn't get under your skin. But Elizabeth wanted Stella to have an inheritance, too, and..." He shrugged. "You know the rest. You two both got it."

Everett had been listening intently, and Stella felt the tension all along the line of his arm and shoulder. "I don't give a shit about people?" he echoed. "*I* don't give a—"

"I meant the importuning bastards would get nowhere with you."

"No, they won't. But you left a mess behind when you left, Leon, and you acted like you were doing us this magnanimous favor."

The volume of his voice did not rise. If anything, Everett grew even quieter, but the intensity of his tone rose to a commanding, clipped admonishment. Stella watched Leon pucker his lips and squirm onscreen. She remained quiet. It was not her place to criticize Leon, and Everett was doing a fair job of it. She guessed that Elizabeth knew quite a bit more than nothing. Part of her was waiting for the moment when

Everett would explain that Stella had made everything worse through her awkward connection to Diettrich's wife, but he didn't seem eager to spread the blame to her.

"You're a competent man—" Leon began.

"I'm not talking about me. You left a mess for Stella. We had a warden lurking uninvited around the property, Leon. We had agents inside the house making demands. We had blood and fish guts up to our ankles in the basement. One of them *grabbed* Stella's *arm*. They weren't asking, they were demanding, and they were threatening both you and the two of us with legal repercussions."

"I said I was sorry for the hassle. I couldn't have Elizabeth—"

"Yes, so you've already said." And the volume of Everett's voice finally rose to something approaching a yell. "But you were protecting *your* wife at the expense of *mine*. You put this on Stella. That cannot happen again. Never again, Leon. Am I making myself clear? You should have told us both. She married me without knowing the full picture, and now I must convince her to stay married to me without the peaceful, easy situation she was promised."

Stella was startled. He was worried about the effect on her? He was concerned about convincing her to stay?

Everett didn't glance over at her. "If I lose her over this—"

"You won't. You aren't," she murmured.

Everett fell silent.

"I am truly sorry, Stella," said Leon. "I'm sorry I didn't put a stop to all this a decade ago when it first started."

"Thank you," she said softly. "It's fine, really. We handled it."

Leon's expression lightened. "I'm sure you did. I knew you would. Both of you. My Elizabeth always knew about you two, you know. She's smarter than this old optimistic idiot. She's got a touch of what you've got, I think. She knew you two were better together than apart."

Everett snorted and shook his head. "Goodbye, Leon. Take care of yourself. And call me if you remember any other illegal dealings we should know about."

He ended the call, craned his neck to stare up at the night sky, then turned to Stella.

Chapter 36

UNSMASHED

Stella reached for his hand before he could speak. "I have something to tell you," she said. "Something I only learned recently, and I hope you'll be pleased to hear this."

His jaw was shadowed by a very long days' worth of stubble. He hadn't slept since he'd been to Florida the day before, and he looked weary. "What is it? Not about our relatives or the damned sturgeon, I hope. I don't want to think about them again for another year."

"No, better. Or worse. It's about us." She patted his cheek. "I'm just going to say it. I need to tell you that you love me."

His eyes widened. "Don't you mean...you love me?"

"No—yes—I meant exactly what I said. You love me. You have been kind, considerate, and noble. You have thought of me and worried about me and put your hands all over me. You danced with me in the kitchen and made me a namesake milkshake. You protected me and yelled at your uncle on my behalf. You called me late just to talk, and you flew home overnight to be with me. You complimented me when I didn't deserve it and scolded me when I did, and I suspect you're often thinking of me. I see you looking at me when you aren't speaking to me. I noticed when you—"

"Stop, stop, I beg you," he said with a laugh. "I know. Oh lord, I know. I'm not completely unattuned to my own emotions. You're right, you're right. I love you quite unexpectedly, and I will continue to love you in a way that terrifies me completely. You are the piece of life that I needed, a happiness that snuck in like fog from the lake, and the future I can only strive to earn. Now that I have you, I want to do everything for you. If you'll let me. Could I be so fortunate that the exact woman I needed found me and opened my eyes?"

"Well, yes." She was overwhelmed, battling a satin edge of tears in her eyes. "You're welcome. I love you, too, and I have loved you for a long time. I think I might have loved you when I proposed to you."

"That reminds me." He reached into his pocket and pulled out a small black box.

A ring box.

Everett knelt, opened the lid, and turned his face up to hers. The moonlight on his perfect face illuminated the imperfect lines of tiredness, of worry, of age and stress, and Stella loved his face better for seeing him so clearly.

"Stella Woodward Novak," he said, "will you do me the honor of being my wife?"

She laughed. "Everett, you beautiful, strange man. I *am* your wife."

"I know, but you got to propose the first time. I wanted to do it myself this time. In perpetuity, in truth, with no inheritance or caviar or family obligations between us. Just us. I want to marry you because of who you are, Stella, who you see inside me, and who I am with you. I've known for a while now, but I needed the time for my brain to catch up with my heart."

"You haven't known for long. I only figured you out earlier today."

"I have so," he said, indignant. "Come with me. It's not finished yet, but you'll see."

He squeezed her hand and tugged, and she willingly followed him. He led her not into the house but down to the beach. No indication of dawn shone on the eastern horizon, yet Stella saw everything clearly. She saw herself walking side-by-side with Everett down the path and onto the sand. It was so easy.

Set back several yards from the shoreline was the sheet-draped statue from Everett's studio. It glowed faintly in the night like an apparition.

"How did this—"

"The guys wheeled it down for me earlier. I might not leave it here forever, but I didn't want you to run into it and get curious."

"I *am* curious."

He grinned at her, boyish and pleased with himself. "Close your eyes."

She did. She heard the fabric covering being whipped away, then Everett's body was pressed behind hers. She shivered at the warm point of connection between them.

"Open," he said.

Stella looked at a white marble statue of a life-sized woman, graceful and serene with windblown hair. The figure was posed on an unfinished rocky base with a slightly bent knee, one hand behind her hip, the other raised to her temple. From the legs down she was only roughly hewn, a sketched suggestion of a form. "Oh, it's lovely. I thought you never showed your work to anyone before it was smashed?"

"Look closer."

She stepped around to the statue's front, then squinted up into the woman's face. She gasped. It was her face. The statue was of her.

"This is me."

"Yes."

"But you must have started creating this—"

"Weeks ago, yes. I couldn't get the image of you out of my mind. Defiant, hopeful, a little wild. I knew I had to put my hands to work." His hands at the moment were ranging along her ribcage and stomach, and his lips were close to her neck. "I spent a lot of time carefully envisioning every inch of your beautiful form, my love. This is my memory of the morning after we agreed to marry, when you stood on that rock right over there," and he lifted Stella's arm and used her forefinger to point at the flat stone where she had perched, "and tried to convince me to back out of marrying you. I wouldn't have done it, of course, because I think some part of me knew you were right about us. You couldn't have talked me out of this in a hundred years, and I find you very persuasive. I didn't think I would ever find somebody who could take me as I am, with my lack of a charming demeanor and no chance of a family, until the absolute miracle of you."

She exhaled slowly. Her nerves were singing, and her blood was thumping like it was looking for an escape from her veins. "I'm flattered, really. But *we* are a family. *We* are your chance at a family. And your work is smashings. Are you going to smash me up and sell me?"

"This one is not for sale. It's marble, and it's not for smashing."

"Will it be difficult for you not to destroy it with a hammer?"

He paused. "I thought it might be, at first. Everything I've ever sculpted has been reduced to dust and tiny bits. But with your face looking back at me, there's no way I could do anything to harm this piece. Artistically, it's terrifying. But in my heart, it's...right. It's right. I've created something I intend to keep, and I don't mean the statue. This marriage could not have been bought or sold with the lure of any inheritance on offer. We started from an unusual place, and we found ourselves in an even stranger one tonight. But I wouldn't face the strangeness of life with anyone but you. Will you now please answer my question? Marry me in truth, marry me for love, marry me forever."

"Yes," she said through tears. "Of course. I was already married to you in my heart, and it's a relief to say it aloud." She turned to the vast indifference of the lake. "Yes!" she screamed. The water and the wind absorbed her voice and made it indistinguishable from the early-morning stillness. "He is mine!"

"I am hers, and she is mine!" Everett screamed promptly, and then they were laughing, and then they were kissing, and much later, the sun was rising over the water.

the end

Acknowledgments

My sincere thanks and appreciation go to trusted first readers Sarah Perchikoff and Haley Warrington, and I appreciate the early query critique from Carey Blankenship-Kramer. Thank you to Michael Braun, Dana Breunig, and the team at Ten16 Press. I also want to acknowledge input from several intelligent humans on a previously shelved manuscript, since I firmly believe unpublished works help in developing the books that do eventually see the light of day. I therefore extend my thanks to Rosie Russell, Michael Bullerman, Molly Filler, John Potter, Kiri Blakeley, and Lalaine Byrd.

Thank you for the love and support from my main squad, the NYC book club, and my beloved mom and family.

Brian...you already know. I'll tell you again.

www.ingramcontent.com/pod-product-compliance
Lightning Source LLC
Chambersburg PA
CBHW072025020726
47501CB00006B/1963